ISOTOPIA

A Novel

Jeff Greenberg

ISOTOPIA

ISBN-13: 978-1717138293
ISBN-10: 1717138292

Cover Design by Betti Gefecht
bettigefechtdesign.blogspot.com

Images: ©andreiuc88 ©kaninstudio – stock.adobe.com

This is a work of fiction. All events, places, and characters herein
are products of the author's fertile imagination.

For Jeffrey, who died with far too much music inside him.

PREFACE

This story belongs to Jeffrey, but he wrote it to share with the world. My goal was to bring Jeffrey's story from the obscurity of his laptop into the light of day, staying as true to his voice and intentions as possible. Fortunately, just a few weeks before he died, Jeffrey and I had the opportunity to spend many hours together, specifically reviewing my notes on his most recent draft and brainstorming ideas for the ending. His manuscript was nearly finished before I touched a single word.

Over the course of the four years he worked on *Isotopia*, Jeffrey spent many hours crafting complex characters—pondering names, learning their strengths, flaws, and desires, defining the external power structure that directs their interactions and dialogue, working out character arcs and constructing the plot. Jeffrey designed the rich architecture of the forest, the marketplace, and the battlegrounds that comprise the world of Isotopia, whose setting in both time and place is intentionally ambiguous and universal. Without formal training in writing, he sought out critical feedback and worked hard to learn and improve as he did whenever he became passionate about something, whether it was DDR or music composition or computational neuroscience.

Jeffrey's choice of title and his story notes reveal a yearning to heal a broken world and create a true Isotopia, a society where all people have an equal ("iso-") chance to contribute freely and meaningfully. The heroes of Isotopia are not without their challenges, nor can any individual solve the problems alone. I believe this story filled many important roles for Jeffrey: a poignant ode to the mentors, coaches, and teachers who nurtured his mind, body, and soul; a sandbox where he could try his own hand at writing the character-driven stories he so loved on TV; a place to reflect on his own contribution to society; a fantasy neuroscience lab, where he could bend the laws of physics and biology; a safe distance from which to grapple with his own demons; and a long, banter-filled conversation with friends.

As to the nitty-gritty of who wrote what, the majority of my edits were fairly straightforward: formatting, punctuation, or minor style points Jeffrey had agreed to during our conversations. (His three pages of notes from our last meeting include many exclamation points and shouty caps to himself.) Out of the 760 comments I'd left on his last draft, he bristled at only one "suggestion," a character's name he was reluctant to change; I didn't touch it. I did, however, remove almost half of his uses of the word "fuck" (leaving a mere 99). In addition to the occasionally coarse language, the story contains at least PG-13-level violence. I didn't sugarcoat his action scenes, even where they made me queasy. The last few chapters required substantial sections of original writing on my part, only because Jeffrey hadn't fully fleshed out the details of his newly discovered ending. I'd like to believe he would be very pleased with the outcome.

Jeffrey is all over these pages if you know where to look; those are the passages that both tortured and sustained me during these last seven months. You might find yourself, too, in a gentle bit of wisdom from Ol' Koop or a snarky comeback from Patch. Jeffrey had a way of incorporating the best of everyone in his life.

Obviously, I wish with all my heart Jeffrey could have been here himself to finish this story (and many, many others). Having been thrust inside this tragic void, the act of putting the finishing touches on Jeffrey's story has truly been a privilege and a gift. I hope you'll enjoy Jeffrey's *Isotopia*.

Beth (Jeff's Mom)
Weston, Massachusetts
April, 2018

Ben Zoma says:

Who is wise?

The one who learns from every person.

- Pirkei Avot 4:1

ISOTOPIA

THE HUNTERS / PATCH

Allix Maris leapt effortlessly over a protruding jumbo-root, maintaining his graceful hover through the thorny crimson woodlands like it was his own red heaven. "Here!" he bellowed with a war cry that echoed backward through his whirlwind of stones and dust.

The rompogg marked for death let out a desperate squeal as it scurried from the veteran hunter. The creature was small and agile, probably only a couple months old but still a catch that would rake in at least twenty isocoins.

"Quick!" Maris shouted again, too focused on his prey to notice that only one of his students was keeping up with his frantic pace.

Patch, youthful and daring, never fell behind his fearless leader. He darted through the trees with such precision that clan myth deemed him a son to the rompoggs themselves, and Patch certainly never went out of his way to deny the rumors. A few turns back, the remaining pair of squadmates brought up the rear. *If those hyperventilating, stampeding clowns make any more noise, even the deaf poggs will split.* Patch shifted his focus from Zap and Arlo back to Maris, who skidded to a stop and reached for his jade, steel hunting bow. *Ah, here we go… dinnertime.*

As the squad cornered their prize, all sound evaporated from the clearing like suns beneath the daunting abyss of the night sky. No feeling matched the intimacy of a shared silence between a killer and his beast, when the hunter locks eyes with the hunted and one soul prepares to snatch another. For an instant, Patch surrendered his eyelids to

1

the pull of nature's blissful tides, teetering on the fragile edge of existence.

"*Patch!*" Maris whisper-shouted, hurling the hunter back into the land of the living. "*You're up.*"

Patch noticed the clumsy panting of Zap and Arlo as his senses returned. He smirked; what was a quality hunt without a proper audience? He raised the heat rifle slung across his back and narrowed his predatory vision through the shiny metallic sight. Without a moment's hesitation, he pulled the trigger, blasting a glowing red pellet through the air. The pellet itself was almost too miniscule to be seen, but the pin-sized hole just above the rompogg's glossy green eye was undeniable. A faint sizzle emanated from the corpse.

The heat rifle and its special ammunition were the result of a recent collaboration between Hunter Clan Representative Trey Bowman and the brightest minds of the Scientist Clan. Designed for maximum hunting efficiency, the pellets packed a surgically precise punch with enough stopping power to neutralize even the largest beasts in Isotopia. But the feature that set this weapon apart from Bowman's past inventions was its heat-resistant metal barrel. Inside the chamber of the weapon, the pellets were heated to approximately three hundred degrees— enough to flash cook Patch's last catch of the day. Within seconds, the scrambling baby pogg was instantly reduced to a delicious, high-protein meal, ready for delivery to the city's merchants.

An overwhelming sense of pride swept over Patch as he towered over the corpse. It was a beautiful shot that could have been executed only by the clan's top marksmen. There was no blood.

Before Patch sank too far into his own glory, Maris motioned him to his side. Patch huffed quietly. Maris' bullshit lectures were always the same. It was way more fun to eavesdrop on the youngsters.

"What did Patch fuck up *this* time?" whispered Zap to

Arlo.

Haven't these morons figured out yet that these trees amplify voices at least five-fold? Patch, attempting to appear invested in his mentor's pep talk, resisted the urge to roll his eyes.

"That shot certainly didn't seem like any sort of fuck up to me," replied Arlo.

"It's got to be something, man. Maris is the last person in Isotopia who would pull a pupil aside just to give a compliment or chat about the weather. He's never wasted a word in his life—when Maris speaks, you can bet your ass it's about something important."

There was a pause before Arlo responded. "You've heard the rumors about him, right? About Patch? They've spread through the clan—Maris must've found out."

"Rumors?" asked Zap. "What rumors?"

Patch's eavesdropping shifted from self-indulgent delight to anxious curiosity, making it progressively harder to feign interest in whatever words Maris was yammering. *What rumors indeed?*

Arlo's answer confirmed Patch's growing sense of alarm. "You haven't heard about the juice?"

"Wait. Nectar? *Patch?*" Zap slapped his hand over his mouth to squelch his surprise, but he'd never been sly.

All the confidence and pride over Patch's fresh kill dissipated, leaving no trace of the triumphant grin he'd worn only seconds before.

"Word is that ever since the healers first mixed and marked it, Patch is more careful to carry a jar of that stuff on him than his own rifle," said Arlo.

"But Patch is the best." *That's more like it.* "I mean— besides Maris, obviously. Are you telling me our star sharpshooter, the man who passed the clan's entrance trials younger than any hunter in history, is a reckhead?"

"I'm just telling you what I heard," replied Arlo. "That's the word 'round the roots."

"Bullshit is what it is. The guy could never do the things he does if he was a junkie. I don't buy it for a second."

Patch had never been more appreciative of Zap's obliviousness. *Hopefully that's the end of that.* He disengaged from the conversation of his foolish disciples, realizing Maris was winding down his speech.

"Are we on the same page here?" asked Maris.

"Um, yes," stammered Patch. "Of course."

"Good. Now go discuss the technicals with your squadmates. I'll be over in a minute."

As swiftly as life had departed the dead pogg at his feet, Patch's confidence came rushing back. Despite the scolding from his boss or gossip about his extracurricular activities, Patch was still a prince of the forest, and he would never let that reputation crack.

"I hope you ladies learned something from that," he remarked to Zap and Arlo. "Free tip for both of you: keep your attention focused on your elders, and maybe one day you'll be able to hunt like them." The two novices exchanged a quick glance, then turned at Maris' question.

"Zap. Arlo. What's your assessment of Patch's execution?" Maris' directness admittedly made it challenging to think on the spot, but Patch didn't really expect any genius insights from his peers.

Zap opened his mouth first, as usual. "Perfect, sir." Patch beamed at his squadmate's assessment.

"And is that what you think as well, Arlo?" asked Maris. "Perfect?"

Arlo hesitated, then spoke. "Clean shot, no blood. I agree with Zap, sir."

Patch's grin spread further until Maris responded. "Then you two mustn't have heeded my instructions." He pivoted toward Patch. "Or should I say you three?" The trainees, including Patch, shrank and shifted their glances to their feet. "Perfection is what we strive for, and it is surely something a hunter can achieve, not just the best hunters—almost any hunter can achieve perfection on occasion—but it requires a moment of maximum unity among the hunter, his squad, the environment, and the prey. It requires the hunter to hear and see everything, not just what is in his own head."

Maris focused his gleaming blue eyes on Patch. "I told you to strike through the pogg's pupil. Accuracy is a low-level benchmark for a good hunter, not the quality that sets them apart, and you, Patch, with your raw skill, clearly possess it. What you don't have yet is the ability to listen. But you will learn that just as thoroughly as you have learned to kill. Won't you, Patch?"

"Yes sir," Patch replied, and then rolled his eyes for only Zap and Arlo to witness.

Maris forged ahead of his three trainees, scanning the trees and shrubs for signs of other potential targets, giving Patch the opportunity to save face.

"Maris is a warrior and was once a great clan leader. But he's also getting older and refuses to see beyond his immediate surroundings in the forest. The citizens of Isotopia—the healers, the scientists, shit, even the Panel of Representatives—they all just want more. More food, more clothes, fiercer weapons. They don't give a shit about perfection and unity with the forest and all that hippie bullshit. As hunters, the way we give the people what they want is by being fast and fierce. We rule this forest, and we have the power to slaughter and roast every creature in here in the blink of an eye. If we stop to analyze every single kill, we will never keep up with Isotopia's unquenchable appetite." Suddenly gripped by the same sternness that had overcome Maris just moments before, Patch looked deeply into the eyes of Zap, then Arlo. "Don't ever forget what it means to be one of us." Patch paused and softened. "Now, go murder some poggs. I'll be right behind you."

Zap and Arlo turned to each other, shrugged, and then headed off to catch up to Maris. Patch reached into his pocket and disappeared.

THE HEALERS / PAN LINNER

The sun switched places with the rising moon, shifting the colors of the sky from a bright green to dark lavender. Echoing cries of the waking owlers filled the northern forest. Near the main entrance to the city, a small group of healers was camped out, plucking leaves from nearby shrubs and mashing them together in their mixing bowls. The youngest of the healers glanced up from her task to see a group of hunters approaching on the trail. They were clearly coming back from a productive day's work, she thought, seeing that each man had a rompogg or mini-tissilisk slung across his chest.

"Patch! Lovely night, isn't it?"

Patch's face lit up with recognition. "It's as if the moon has come to tuck us into our beds and sing us a lullaby," her old friend joked.

Pan Linner had spent her many years as a Youth bending the codes of Isotopia with Patch. As adults, the two liked to keep the good times rolling, occasionally indulging in recreational experiments involving Pan's latest herbal mixtures—Nectar being their current concoction of choice. Life was never boring when Pan passed the time with Patch.

"Well, anyway..." said Patch after a quick catch-up and awkward pause, "I gotta head home and get some rest." He tugged on the rope holding his impressive haul. "Promised 'ol Koop I'd bring these to him first thing in the morning." The two friends smiled at each other wider than either of them meant to, and Patch headed toward the city gates.

A soft chuckle drew Pan's attention to the Head Healer, who sat beside her with a playful smile on his kind face. "You're allowed to like 'im you know. I know you ladies all think he's so handsome."

Pan blushed and denied it, but she also got over it quickly. She loved the sweet old guru and never minded his gentle teasing. "Very funny, Maxx," she replied with a bright grin. "You can make fun of me when you find yourself a nice hunter or one of the cute merchant women. Just please promise me you won't mess around with any of those grimy scientists—even in their older years, they still know how to talk smack and stir drama."

"I'll take your word for it," responded Maxx easily. "I just don't get what you young people see in those scientists that throws you all for such a nasty-mannered spin."

Pan sighed, knowing that no matter how many times she explained it, Maxx couldn't agree with her point of view. "They mock us, make us look like we don't matter because they can tackle any problem we stumble aimlessly around the forests to solve."

"But, my dear, we *don't* stumble around aimlessly. We help people. We understand the leaves and berries of the forest better than anyone. We provide cures to illnesses no one else even understands. You know that, of course."

"The problem is *they* don't know that." The conversation followed this general arc whenever it resurfaced. Pan still felt her insides hollow out every time.

"Who doesn't know that, Panny?"

"Oh, Maxx. Everyone," said Pan, unable to prevent the trembling in her voice. "The scientists are smart, and Isotopia knows it, so Isotopia listens to them. And they tell Isotopia things about us that put down the great work you and I do here together every day."

Maxx patted his student's hand. "I'm sorry that such a thing itches at your soul, but you shouldn't let it. Just remember that everyone has his or her place in this world, and you have found yours, just as I have found mine. We were meant to heal the world, because oftentimes it seems that everyone else is trying to poison it."

Pan looked up from her current leaf mixture and giggled. "You had your daily dose recently, didn't you?"

"Oh, my dear—you have no idea!" Maxx's eyes opened wide, exposing pupils the size of bog berries. "The plants themselves are telling me which ones are destined to mix together. I strongly suggest you take this opportunity to learn from your guru!"

Pan giggled again. Maxx Spike was renowned throughout Isotopia for his healing and mixing talents but was also notorious for his lack of sync with reality. Despite that fact, Pan had discovered fairly early on that her clan head worked more efficiently when guided by the mystic pull of their various psychoactive herbal mixtures. There was an undeniable touch of magic in the way Maxx's brain connected the dots of the universe, and for better or worse, hallucinatory concoctions hastened his success. His madness always had a method even if Pan didn't always understand it at the outset.

Pan decided, as she always did at this point in the conversation, to resist the dark pull of the ancient clan rivalry. The mutual disdain between healers and scientists was the only topic that challenged her loving nature, and the shadow it cast on her soul frightened her. It was moments like these she felt so blessed to have such an optimistic leader, and for both their sakes, she mustered up the strength to lighten the mood.

"We have a connection with this forest unlike anyone in Isotopia—even the hunters. One day it won't matter what anyone says about us—our work will speak for itself."

Maxx smiled gently, and both promptly returned to their work.

THE MERCHANTS / KOOP

The next day, the city resumed its usual bright green morning tint from the rising sun. Many said that Isotopia seemed to re-blossom into the same jumbo plant each day. The city contained everything that any decent city in its place and time would be expected to have, yet it was also small and homey. Clans tended to live together in separate communities, residing in cozy huts built by individual families. However, during the height of daily craziness when every merchant in Isotopia had their shops up and running, it wasn't uncommon to see a chaotic blend of the entire population milling about the square—from Panel representatives to clan leaders to loud, joyous Youth... and even the occasional Forgotten.

Whether they needed something specific or not, everyone walked the main streets of the city during Merchant Hour. Koop Whimsy, Isotopia's oldest and wisest merchant, knew everyone there was to know and didn't even need to look up from his stand to sense Patch approaching with his daily haul. Koop had known the lad ever since Patch passed his entrance exams for the hunting clan and could pick him out of the lively crowd by his unhurried, confident gait.

"How's my favorite all-star hunter doing this morning? You got some good stuff for me?" asked Koop, still focused on setting up his stand for the day.

"For Koop Whimsy, only the best." Patch untied his strap and slapped a fat rompogg across the counter.

"That's what I like to hear! Let's see what you—"

Koop's chipper mood was spoiled when he looked up and spotted the lack of color in Patch's cheeks.

"What?" asked Patch.

The old man sighed. "Son, you know I'm the last person to judge, but as someone who's been down that road, I can't just sit here and keep my mouth shut."

"What are you talking about?"

Koop leaned forward and softened his voice. "You know what I'm talking about. Those dopey eyes tell the whole story. Trust me, I know what it can cost you."

Koop knew exactly when Patch caught his drift; the young hunter fell silent and the jovial flash in his eyes vanished.

"I wasn't always the man you now know, Patch. I wrestled many a demon when I was your age, and my world was a morbid place. I never had a death wish; I never thought I'd struggle like I did, but that's how it works. It sneaks up on you, and by the time you realize it, it's too late. I just don't want those demons to infect you too, Patch. You're a good kid with a bright future. Unfortunately, futures have a funny way of ruining themselves."

Patch's expression didn't move an inch, but after Koop finished his speech, Patch's mouth contorted into a smile that his eyes didn't quite match. "Whatever you think is going on... isn't. So please, old man, don't you worry about me."

Koop was deciding whether he would bother saying anything else on the matter to stubborn young Patch when a passing officer stopped by the stand.

"Mornin', Koop."

"*Ayy*, Jimmy Lask! How are the streets of Isotopia treating the IES today?" Although Jimmy Lask had only five years under his belt, the detective showed promise without acting completely full of himself—unlike the cocky hunter standing next to him.

"Same shit, different day," Lask replied. "Mostly calm

except for a reckhead or two who needs to be put in his place." At that moment, Lask noticed Patch, who sheepishly averted his gaze.

Koop liked Lask; he paid attention to his surroundings and chatted with everyone, regardless of clan or age, and had the mental capacity to store the name of every Isotopian he encountered. The two men's shared knowledge about the city always allowed for interesting conversations. Though Koop indulged in discussing the everyday ruckus and drama he witnessed purely for entertainment purposes, he was happy to help the detective on numerous occasions in the past when Lask had needed information.

Patch fidgeted with his Isodex while Lask and Koop chatted, seizing on the first pause in their conversation to make his exit. "Well, Koop, I'm going to head back out to the forest. Maris is waiting, and those poggs aren't going to cook themselves." He smiled awkwardly at the detective and waved to Koop. "You both live grand today."

"You too, boy," Koop responded. "And please, just think about what I said." He watched Patch walk off toward the main gates and shifted his gaze back to Lask.

"Who's the kid?" inquired the detective. "Don't think I've seen him before."

"A man as well-traveled as you has never before crossed paths with the up-and-coming hunter, Patch?"

"Patch? Is that his real name?"

Koop realized he actually wasn't sure and shrugged. "That's the name he gives when asked. Probably figures it'll help him stand out more once he becomes the most famous hunter to walk through the city gates."

Lask raised his brows. "That good, huh?"

Koop laughed. "The boy seems to have talent. Quite full of himself but not too different from most young men in Isotopia. Overall, he's a good kid, and he's got the determination to go places if he wants to."

"Well, let me know if he ever becomes a not-so-good

kid," joked Lask. "Usually those young hunters get into trouble, thinking they're as invincible as the IES." The detective paused to look down at his new generation Isodex, and his expression shifted from jolly to curious. "Hmm."

"Interesting news?" asked Koop.

"Potentially," said Lask, looking back at him. "In your years watching the city streets, have you ever come across a man named William Krakken?"

Koop shuddered. "You know those people who are at always at war with the world even when the world isn't at war with them?"

Lask leaned in. "I think I know what you mean."

"Years back," Koop continued, "that boy would show up on the streets now and again with gangs of Forgotten."

"Running with a tough crowd, then?"

"A few robberies, perhaps," said Koop, straining his mind for details. "It's always hard to tell who's actually doing what when a gang decides to strike. Thing about Krakken, though—he always seemed especially dangerous."

Lask looked distraught. "How so? He hurt someone?"

"Worse, actually," said Koop. "He got elected."

THE FORGOTTEN / LEVOL

As Merchant hour drew to a close, Levol decided to strap up and go for a stroll. The city always seemed like a dark place, so he found it fitting to restrict his roaming to the night.

Stumbling upon an empty street corner, Levol stopped to refuel via a quick boost of reck leaf, which he crushed up and injected into his arm. Not having much use for conventional society, Levol cared little about the herbs and medicinal concoctions of the healing clan, but he sure as shit knew how to synthesize reck leaf. Everyone did—even the Youth could mix the formula if someone had ill enough intent to teach them.

The first rush coursed through his veins, and he closed his eyes as the blissful transformation of his consciousness took place. He felt strong and alive; he felt like he could do anything. Then, just as quickly, an urge for violence overtook him. His eyes snapped back open.

In place of the peaceful, winding down of a city day, Levol saw targets—walls to vandalize, merchant stands to rob, lingering Youth to terrorize. With widened eyes and all five senses firing vivid, rapid messages to his brain, Levol identified the perfect target: a pathetic-looking man with a scraggly beard down to his knees, huddled between piles of garbage—a makeshift bed for the night.

"Beautiful night, isn't it?" Levol called out as he walked toward him.

The man slowly turned to face him and, in a frail voice, responded, "I guess so. Not so different from any other night."

Levol was amused. "How so, old man? I like to think of every day as a new adventure. It's what keeps me going."

"People come and go. Children, clan members, merchants... all scurrying about to constantly improve themselves." He sighed heavily. "But here I stay, day in and day out, and nothing improves. In fact, nothing even really gets worse. Time just keeps moving, and I just keep sitting here, and no one even knows."

Levol moved closer, putting on a sympathetic face. "I know, friend. I know what it's like to be forgotten, lost in the shuffle, confined to a life in the darkness." Levol's excitement level rose as he neared the end of his speech. He glanced around to check that they were the only two remaining occupants of the street. "What if we could make those self-important fucks notice us, if only for a second? What if we could make Isotopia turn their heads and think about all those they've abandoned? Now, wouldn't that be nice?"

The man looked skeptical but interested. "What did you have in mind?"

Levol reached inside his torn rompogg-hide jacket and pulled out a small knife. "Do you know what a martyr is, old man? It's someone who dies for a cause. For example, if a poor pathetic forgotten member of society were to be found in the middle of the city with his insides spilling out onto the streets, he could get people to notice us. That man would be a martyr. In fact, he would be a fucking hero."

Levol recognized pure terror in the man he was now towering over. "Please," pleaded the man, scrambling to crawl away, "I don't want to be no martyr. I just want to keep sitting here and going about my business."

"Well, that's depressing," replied Levol, close enough now to smell the man's sour breath. Adrenaline coursed through Levol, merging with the rush of his reck leaf peak.

"You have such low expectations for yourself, but I see big things for you. You are going to be famous, my friend, and the whole city will finally know you!" Levol cackled as he raised his knife. "Yes, yes, I think we should go ahead with this ingenious plan. The rest of the Forgotten will thank you for your service. Now close your eyes."

The man used his last breath to beg for his life, but it was too late. Levol sliced through the man's neck, spilling blood onto the pavement. He grinned as he watched the last signs of pathetic life leave the old man and stood over him for another minute to take in the beautiful sight of the flowing fountain of blood. It spread outward and seeped into the grout between the tiles, creating an intricate and mesmerizing masterpiece. A rare feeling of peace came over Levol.

Levol sheathed his weapon and strode down the empty street. On his right, he passed the tallest building in Isotopia, the house of the Panel. The top floor was lit; some super important meeting must be taking place. He rolled his eyes and continued on his way, eager to see what else the night might bring.

THE PANEL OF REPRESENTATIVES

Bogue Issler, Chairperson: Good evening, ladies and gentlemen of the Panel. Please, take your seats. First, I would like to take this opportunity to formally welcome our new IES Rep, William Krakken, to the Panel. I know you have all gotten to know him in the past couple months while he was working to obtain your votes, but please take a minute to give him a warm welcome. As I mentioned when I nominated him for this position, William is an old friend of mine, and I am very pleased to have him at our table as we work together to keep Isotopia a safe and productive place. He is an extremely valuable asset, and I am looking forward to integrating him into our inner circles. William, would you like to address the group?

William Krakken, IES Rep: Thank you, Madam Chairperson, and greetings, fellow members of the Panel. I am honored and excited to take on my new role. As most of you know, I have spent a great deal of time training in both combat and enforcement tactics, and I believe I have the perfect skill set to protect Isotopia and all her inhabitants from any threats that may arise whether from within or outside the city walls. I plan to throw myself fully into this role, and I am eager to work with all of you as we make sure our city continues to thrive.

Issler: Thank you, William. Now, let's move on. What do you have for us, Ivy?

Ivy Tikki, Merchant Rep: Business is running as usual—

our stands have been fully stocked every day with food and clothing, and overall, supply is meeting or exceeding demand. I would like to especially acknowledge Trey Bowman and his hunting clan; their reliability and consistency ensure a high quality of life for the people of the city.

Issler: Excellent. Thank you for your continued efforts to provide Isotopia with a strong, stable Marketplace. While we're on the subject of hunters, let's move to you, Trey.

Trey Bowman, Hunting Rep: Thank you, Madam Issler. Our squad leader, Allix Maris, tells me our newer hunters are exceptionally talented. With time to train and mature, I believe we will reap an even greater quantity and quality of meat and hides.

Issler: Thank you, Trey. I echo Ivy's appreciation for your clan's dedication. Natalya, any updates?

Natalya Corper, Healing Rep: My hardworking healers have made significant progress lately, discovering mixtures with promising medicinal properties. One recent mixture concocted by our leader Maxx Spike seems to be highly effective in treating Mad Rompogg Disease.

Mason Harding, Science Rep: Pardon me, Nat, but I have a growing concern I was hoping you could address. While your healers have made great strides in developing herbal cures for various illnesses, it appears they have also made available certain herbal mixtures with psychoactive properties, which seem to be highly addictive. For example, your new "Nectar" formula seems to be gaining popularity among the Youth and criminals of Isotopia, and I was hoping to learn what you plan to do about this issue.

Corper: Dr. Harding, I can assure you that your concern is unnecessary. First, the psychoactive herbs are highly therapeutic in the correct dosages. They are meant to heal the mind and calm the spirit. Second, the healing clan follows a strict code that no herbal recipes be released to the public, a code we put in place to ensure the more potent recipes don't fall into the wrong hands. Furthermore, Ivy Tikki and I communicate frequently to make sure her merchant stands only stock our safest products. The IES has also been extremely helpful in identifying individuals who obtain these mixtures unlawfully or use them inappropriately. We have no reason thus far to consider these types of beneficial herbs to be dangerous.

Issler: Thank you, Natalya. And thank you, Mason, for raising this potential issue. As of this moment, I am inclined to agree with Natalya. If something happens that leads us to believe the issue bears closer examination, we will look into it, but for now let us move on. Mason, what is the status of the scientists' current project?

Harding: I have some very bright and driven young scientists working on it, Madam Chairperson. Our mind helmets are already in the testing phase, and beta versions will be ready for select members of the IES very soon. These helmets will provide Isotopia with a significant step forward in understanding how the brain interacts with the body and its surrounding environment.

Tikki: What are you saying, exactly? That wearers of this helmet will have some sort of telekinetic power?

Harding: Preliminary proof-of-concept studies lead us to believe that might be possible, yes. In later versions, we may even be able to modify the relationship between one's body and physical surroundings, allowing the users to bend the laws of physics to jump higher, run faster, and even become stronger—all abilities that would greatly aid the protectors of our city in doing their jobs.

Corper: And what if this invention should fall into the wrong hands? This seems like a much greater cause for concern than the occasional reckhead who abuses our therapeutic mixtures.

Harding: Not an issue. As I said, we will only be releasing a limited number of helmets to certified IES detectives for testing to make sure they are safe. No one who hasn't passed a rigorous training program will be able to get his hands on a helmet, and the helmets themselves will be subjected to thorough testing. These helmets are not toys, and we do not intend to treat them as such.

Issler: All right, you two. As leaders of Isotopia, can we act as adults and set aside this pissing match for outside these meetings? Isotopia needs the balance of nature and science. Challenging each other is productive; fighting is toxic. Mason, it sounds as if your clan's research is showing much promise. I am sure that the rest of the Panel is as eager as I am to see the results of your hard work. Sands, is there any other business we need to discuss at this time?

Sands Graper, Chief Advisor: I believe we've covered everything on our agenda, Madam Chairperson.

Issler: Thank you, Sands. Everyone is dismissed. See you all here next week.

THE SCIENTISTS / CAM DIMLAN

Later that night, while the city slept, Cam Dimlan paced the floor of the lab. Long nights were nothing new to Dimlan and the rest of his clan, but he didn't mind. It was nothing a few puffs of stim leaf couldn't get him through.

"You know," said his lab-mate Nap as he took his puff and passed the herbarette to Cam, "as much as we bash those tree-hugging pseudoscientists, they sure know how to mix their plants."

Dimlan enjoyed nothing more than ribbing at the expense of the healers, and this comment made him cough up his toke, blowing out a puff of yellowish smoke as he laughed. "Can't argue with you there."

As the rette passed back and forth between them, Dimlan could feel the gears in his head turning faster. The stim put him on top of the world and provided the clarity he needed to push his research to the next level.

"It's pretty hard to believe what we're doing," Nap began, and Dimlan could sense another of his pointless rambles coming on. "I mean—here we are, just two young scientists, working on a helmet that makes the human brain more powerful than ever imagined. What's this thing even for, anyway? I mean, why is Dr. Adams having us build this?"

"Oh, I seriously doubt this project stops at our clan head. Adams has some brains but not much ambition to back it up. I'd guess this work is being pushed down from the top."

"The Panel?"

Cam nodded. "Haven't you seen Dr. Harding sniffing around?" Nap nodded, glassy-eyed but still following the thread. "And he's been working closely with Trey Bowman, possibly others."

"IES?" Nap asked.

Cam dragged on the rette, watching with amusement as each new tidbit penetrated Nap's skull. "Yep."

Nap glanced at their prototype and shook his head. "Wow. We still don't know what this thing is capable of. You really think it's wise to share this device before we know it's safe?"

Dimlan smirked. "Oh, Nap. It's nice to have you around; you're always good for a chuckle. Think about it. If we get this invention working to its full potential, it could stretch the limits of the human mind and body. People will do their jobs more efficiently, hunters will kill more effectively, and everyone will be able to protect themselves from the crazy Forgotten and man-eating forest lurkers of Isotopia. On top of that, we'll be famous! How would you like to be known as the man who revolutionized the world?"

Nap thought about this for a second. "Well, I guess it depends on *how* we revolutionize it—"

"Fuck that," interrupted Dimlan. "We are going to be superstars, my friend. We just need to stay on track and remember that *we're* the real scientists."

They both laughed as they sucked down the last of their herbarette, disposed of the ashes, and returned to work.

THE IES / DETECTIVE JAMES LASK

It was early, and a crowd had already gathered around the blood-stained street. Detective Jimmy Lask pushed to the center of the throng, where an old, seemingly homeless man lay splayed on the ground, a nasty gash running across the front of his neck.

This one's fresh. Lask knew not just by the lack of decay but because Lask had stood right here just yesterday, conversing with Koop at his stand. A short trail of blood led back to a pile of garbage bags along the curb, suggesting the body was dragged to the middle of the street after being attacked. *Why would the killer go to all that trouble to make such a scene of it? In fact, why bother harming this man in the first place?* The victim didn't look the type to have anything worth taking.

A second uniform appeared at Lask's side. "Huh. Apparently, someone doesn't like old people." Morty Paller. *Wonderful.* Paller never had the eyes to properly read a crime scene, but trying to teach the guy anything was a complete waste of time. "Maybe the geezer had enough strength left in him to get into a vicious fight over some pogg roast."

"Yup, it's possible," Lask answered, his gaze darting around the crime scene until he located Captain Ranger hustling toward the body with the sergeant hot on his heels.

"Kane filled me in," said Ranger. "Elderly victim, no signs of a struggle, clearly moved post-mortem. So, what do we think?"

"I think someone was trying to send a message, sir," replied Lask. "The plan seemed to work. It seems like all of Isotopia is gathered to see this."

"Yes, I'm aware," said Ranger. "So, here we all are. What's the message? What do you think we are all supposed to make of some Forgotten getting stabbed to death?"

"Probably just some reckhead junkie, acting out his rage on the only man he could take in a fight," suggested Paller.

"Then why go to the trouble of moving the body?" asked Lask. "I don't think this killing was random." He paused, taking another moment to consider Ranger's question. "What type of person would have the motivation to kill a nobody like this and put him on display?"

"Another nobody," answered Ranger.

"Maybe someone who felt like Isotopia wasn't giving his kind enough attention," added Sergeant Kane.

"Well, now we're really screwed," said Paller. "If it was some random Forgotten who killed this guy, it means he'll have no ties with any of the city's clans or organizations. It'll be impossible to find him. And until we do, anyone could be next."

For once, Paller was right. This thing could spiral out of control quickly.

"We need to spin this to the public as a struggle that ended in an accidental murder—that's all," Lask said. "In the meantime, we continue investigating. The last thing we need is for others to take up this cause and start dropping bodies in the middle of our streets. In my opinion, sir, we should get word of this to the Panel before things get out of control."

"Good thinking, Lask," said Ranger. "For now, let's increase late patrols and make sure nothing like this happens again. I'll handle damage control with Krakken."

Ranger turned to exit the crime scene, but his mention of William Krakken made Lask's ears perk up. He bolted to catch up to his captain.

"Captain, have you spoken to William Krakken since he became our new rep?"

Ranger paused but didn't turn around. "Uh, briefly. Why?"

"Oh, I don't know," Lask started cautiously. "I was just curious about the guy, you know, considering he's going to be in charge of us from now on."

"Seems like a good guy to me so far," Ranger said, clearly distracted. "Listen, detective, I gotta run. Stay with your sergeant and keep the people as calm as possible."

Ranger disappeared through the crowd of anxious Isotopians, and Lask was stuck with a million questions and no answers.

THE YOUTH / RAYNE HOBB

Rayne Hobb had nearly arrived at Sharon's stand for another day of his hopefully temporary job when he noticed the commotion. He pressed into the edge of the tight circle and jockeyed for a view of the activity at the center. No wonder all of Isotopia had gathered—it wasn't every day a dead body appeared in the middle of the Merchant Village.

A hand clamped down on Hobb's shoulder, and he turned to meet the awe-struck faces of his two closest friends, Jay and Len. "Whoa! That's a lot of blood," Jay said. "I hope they'll teach me how to paint my prey like that once I officially become a hunter."

"That's a human being you're talking about, Jay," Len chided. "I think all those expeditions in the forest are going to your damn head."

Jay glanced at Hobb for backup but quickly realized he hadn't scored any points there, either. It had been Hobb's dream since he first learned about the great clans of Isotopia to become a hunter. However, despite all his hard training and studying, he couldn't pass the barrage of tests to prove himself to Maris and the rest of the senior members of the clan. Soon after that disappointment, he flunked the entrance exam for the IES. Hobb tried to keep his spirits high, though. Working a merchant stand while studying up for the next round of hunter exams wasn't too terrible, just boring as hell.

"Sorry," Jay mumbled to no one in particular.

Len had already moved on, deep in thought as usual.

"This can't be a good sign for the city. Someone slaughtered that helpless old man and left him for all of Isotopia to see. I'd be surprised if this murder isn't the first of many in the near future."

Jay glanced at Len with wide eyes. "Damn, man, what are you, a detective? I thought you were joining the scientist clan."

Len rolled his eyes. "That's what scientists do, Jay. They observe. You could probably deduce things like that for yourself if you didn't devote so much of your attention to stroking your jumbo-root all day."

Hobb had to admit, it felt good to chuckle at Jay's expense. "Okay, hot shot," Hobb said to Len, "what's your theory?"

"Someone is pissed and wanted to show it; that's for sure. Probably some clanless reckhead."

Hobb nodded as he studied the corpse. The carnage was horrific and unforgivable, but he could imagine why someone on the outskirts of society might eventually reach a breaking point.

"It's tragic," continued Len. "It really makes you wonder about the whole clan system. There's a real tradeoff between the freedom of choosing your career and the possibility of falling through the cracks if you can't pass the exams"—Len put on the brakes, peeking over at Hobb—"because, you know, even the best of us could get screwed over due to sheer bad luck."

Hobb couldn't help but laugh at his friend's sheepish attempt to avoid offending him. "I think it works pretty well, all in all," Hobb said, hoping to comfort Len. "It gives us the chance to be who we want, and it makes us work hard to get it. If we don't pick the right clan the first time, then it lets us keep trying until we find the path that suits us."

Jay squeezed Hobb's shoulder. "You'll get it eventually, man. You have heart and passion like I've never seen." Hobb waited for the cheap shot Jay never could resist.

"You just can't shoot for shit, that's all!"

Hobb took a playful swing at Jay. They wrestled each other to the ground, laughing and exchanging vile banter, earning some nasty glares from their fellow citizens.

"All right, lovebirds," Len started, dodging flying fists as he moved toward them. "Either break it up, or go find a nice jumbo-root in the forest where you can get some privacy!"

Jay pulled himself to his feet and glanced at his Isodex. "Ah, shit—I'm gonna be late for my training session. We'll have to finish this up some other time! Later, my topies."

Hobb and Len watched their friend run off, then turned back to each other and erupted with laughter. "What a fucking nut," said Hobb. "Gotta love 'im, though."

"I just can't believe the hunters view him as a valuable addition." said Len. "He must be a better shot than Maris himself 'cuz that boy has got to be one of the dumbest clowns Isotopia has ever seen!"

"It's definitely a mystery," Hobb replied. Some time passed as they both reflected on Jay, the dead body, and the abnormally hectic city rush.

"So, Hobb, I know I probably ask you this far too often, but how's merchant life treating you?"

Hobb smiled to himself—that *was* a question his friend seemed to love asking him over and over—but he didn't mind. Len was just looking out for him. "It's fine, man. Sharon is a chill boss and talking with her passes the time. She knows I'm not built to be a merchant, so she's cool about not throwing too much responsibility at me so I can keep studying for my other stuff during the slower hours. A lot of the other merchants are cool, too. I just get worried once in a while that this is *it* for me—you know?"

If anyone in Isotopia believed in Hobb, it was Len. "Even though Jay was giving you a hard time back there, I think he accidentally made some really insightful observations about you. No one has the fire I see in you, man. Despite all your rough luck, you're never shaken by losing, and you're always ready to try harder the next time. If there's one thing I know about the hunters from talking with you and Jay, they value discipline above all else."

"Sounds like what Dr. Adams values in his scientist recruits from what you've told me."

Len was like a boulder rolling downhill once he got excited about something, one of the reasons Hobb always loved talking to him. "Exactly! Skills can be learned. Every successful Isotopian knows that. What truly sets the people with the highest potential apart from everyone else is their thirst for knowledge, their hunger for improvement, and their ability to learn from mistakes instead of wallowing in them. Those traits are rare, and you, my friend, have all of them. Maris will see it eventually—you just gotta stick with it."

"Thanks, man. I really hope you're right."

"C'mon. When am I not right?" Len didn't wait for an answer. "I need to run, too. One of the scientists wants to catch me up on their newest project. I'll see you later, man."

Hobb waved to his friend and walked toward Sharon's stand, replaying Len's speech and all the other pep talks he'd been given in the recent past. Hobb smiled to himself, appreciative for such a good friend who, Hobb had to admit, usually knew what he was talking about. Then again, Hobb was headed to the northern area of the Village for his day's work—a pattern that might continue well into his future.

THE HUNTERS / PATCH

Patch awoke, much later than intended, with a splitting headache. As he stood and pulled on his leathers for another day in the forest, he pondered how many fresh kills he could bring back to the merchants today despite his delayed start.

Five poggs minimum if I'm on my game, a few tissilisks if I venture higher up into the trees, and then maybe…

Patch's guessing game was disrupted when his reckover transitioned to full-blown nausea. The bile rose quickly, leaving him no chance to make it to the bathroom before projectile vomiting all over his floor. *Fuck*, that bright violet shade of regurgitated Nectar didn't mesh well with his red carpet.

Lumbering over to the sink, he caught sight of his disturbing reflection. *Holy fuck—are my eyes bleeding? How much of that shit did I take last night?*

Patch desperately tried to mentally retrace his steps, which aggravated his already extreme headache. *I guess I'm lucky I can even remember my name right now.* Somehow, he managed to find humor in this thought, despite feeling like a forest creature with a heat pellet shoved up its ass. Finally, he recalled a cloudy memory of being out in the forest for late-night shooting practice when he stumbled across his healer-drug dealer. *Ahh, right.* Cole—his favorite HDD. *Topie musta done me the beautiful favor of refilling my supply.*

Patch reached into his hide coat and pulled out the jar. Half full. *Ugh… I sure hope this thing wasn't topped off last night.*

Patch stared into the eyes of the reckhead in the mirror. How could he possibly hide his sickly state from Maris? Even if he could fool his squad leader, was Patch even capable of hunting right now? A violent stream of vomit doubled him over the sink.

Had this gone too far? Maybe Koop was right about the dangers of abusing these herbs. *Am I seriously fucking myself up?* Patch couldn't imagine he had caused any permanent damage. All the healers, including the great Maxx Spike, used Nectar frequently and were still perfectly functional. If those frail gardeners could handle themselves, Patch would certainly survive. *Fuck caution; I'm a damn hunter.*

The obvious next move was to re-fuel with a tiny drop of Nectar… just to combat the withdrawals. He unscrewed the top of the jar and felt nearly cured by the blissful aroma alone. He took a small swig and lay back on his bed to wait for his strength to return. The flashing Isodex on his nightstand caught his eye.

> Early this morning, the body of an unidentified male, approximately seventy years, was discovered in the middle of Merchant Village. IES Captain David Ranger characterized the incident as an isolated act of robbery turned deadly. Newly-confirmed Enforcement Advisor William Krakken has authorized late-night patrols for the safety of all concerned. The IES assures the good citizens of Isotopia that the streets of the city are as safe as they have always been and will now be even safer due to the presence of extra officers. However, the IES reminds you to stay vigilant when walking through the streets late at night, especially when alone. Despite the heightened security in

the city streets, it is always wise to be prepared.

Murders were fairly rare in Isotopia but not rare enough to be of any particular interest to the young hunter. *If anyone ever tries to fuck with me, they'll be the one facedown in a pool of blood. You can count on that.*

The Nectar had sufficiently done its job of repairing Patch's mind and body, leaving him renewed and ready to hunt. He grabbed his heat rifle and dashed out the door, eager to meet up with his squad and teach them some new tricks.

THE LIBERATION COMMITTEE

Bogue Issler, Chairperson: Thank you, everyone, for coming on such short notice.

Mason Harding, Science Rep: This news was quite a nice surprise. [*Laughter.*]

William Krakken, IES Rep: Yes—I doubt our mystery murderer knows the magnitude of the favor he did us. The wheels have been set in motion. However, we still need to proceed carefully. We're not going to get away with throwing everything into high gear just because one random Forgotten was killed.

Trey Bowman, Hunting Rep: The people have been assured they have nothing to be afraid of, but they're on edge. We need another murder in Isotopia.

Issler: Yes. A murder with such an obvious display of cruel intent and randomness that the IES cannot possibly deny our current security is inadequate.

Krakken: I'm on it.

Issler: Good. Our second kill will give us the momentum we need. Until then, stay close to the everyday operations of your clans and report back with any new information that may be useful in the near future. William—anything else?

Krakken: Yes, actually. I'd like to have a word with this mystery killer. Let's find him and bring him in alive.

THE YOUTH / RAYNE HOBB

The tail end of Merchant Hour approached with the setting sun. Hobb was hard at work, studying his *Basics of Hunting* manual between onslaughts of customers, when he looked up to see what had to be the most beautiful girl in all of Isotopia. Hobb shut his book and jumped to his feet.

"Hi there. How can I help you, Miss...?" Hobb tried to sound confident, but his voice cracked like a preteen's.

"Pan, and hey, yourself," the girl said with a smile that made him stir. "I'm here to drop off some herbal mixtures. This is Sharon's stand, right?"

"Yeah, I've just been helping her out. My name's Rayne. It's a pleasure to meet you." He hoped she didn't expect to shake hands, because his were drenched with sweat.

"I haven't seen you around before, Rayne, but it's always nice to meet someone new—it makes the day more exciting."

"Me too," stammered Rayne, hoping his response made any sense. "So, what have you got for me, P-pan?" *Get a hold of yourself. She's just a girl—an incredible, beautiful...*

"Oh, a whole bunch of stuff. Cooking herbs, headache relief tinctures, aromatic jumbo-root leaves—it's always a different mix depending on the weather and where in the forest I roam."

"Ah, you're a healer. Do you work with the infamous Healer Guru?"

Pan giggled, which gave Hobb some confidence. "Maxx is definitely a bit on the eccentric side, but he's a sweetheart. I love learning from him and hearing his loony stories. He's like a super-hip grandfather." She glanced down at Rayne's book. "A future hunter! How exciting!"

"I've been working toward it," said Hobb. "It hasn't been easy, but it's my dream, so I'm keeping at it."

"Well, I think it's great you know who you want to be, and you're doing what you need to get there," said Pan. It might have been wishful thinking on Hobb's part, but Pan seemed genuinely interested in him. "I actually have an old friend who hasn't been a hunter for too long. Have you met Patch?"

"I've seen him around during some of my assessments, but he wouldn't know who I am. He's an amazing shooter—something I haven't quite gotten down yet."

"I'll introduce you sometime. I'm sure he'd be happy to teach you—he's a little full of himself and loves to show off."

"That'd be great!" said Hobb. His day was getting better and better.

"Well, it was great meeting you, Rayne. I hope you're around here more often so I have something to look forward to when I make my deliveries. I gotta get back to the forest—see you around."

Pan spun away, leaving Hobb struggling to get his breathing and heart rate back to normal. *Meeting an angel can mess with a guy.*

THE HUNTERS / PATCH

Despite the nasty reckover, Patch managed to pull in quite the haul, and he was delivering the goods to Merchant Village when Pan crossed his path. His day always improved when he saw her.

"Linner! Gathering herbs today?"

"That's the plan."

"If the forest treats you half as well as it treated me, you're golden!" He turned to show off the impressive array of carcasses on his back.

Pan shook her head playfully. "You really think you're something special, don'tcha Patch? Which stand are you headed to with all that stuff?"

"Sharon's today," he responded. "Why?"

"Oh! I was just there, and I met a great new guy who was filling in. His name is Rayne, and he's studying to be a hunter. I gotta say, I think I'll be finding excuses to make extra stops to Sharon's stand from now on!"

This little confession made Patch's heart drop. He and Pan had always had some sort of special connection—whether it was romantic, he could not have said. He wasn't sure exactly what he felt toward Pan, but he had no trouble making up his mind about this Hobb character. Patch waved goodbye and began to move along when Pan called out to him.

"Oh, would you do me a favor and put in a good word for him with the clan? Maybe teach him a few tricks? He'd really appreciate it, and it would probably score me some points with him."

Patch, the master trapper, was cornered. "Sure, why not—I'll teach him a thing or two."

"Great!" Pan's reaction disheartened Patch even more. "Thanks, bud. I owe you one. See ya around!"

"Yup… see ya."

He had to think of something devious, and fast. Maybe just a small-scale prank to put the little shit in his place. An idea popped into his head that was more malicious than he intended, but it would have to do. While his brain was busy working out the details, his feet had carried him to Sharon's, and there he was. *Eh*. Whatever Pan saw in the guy sure wasn't clear to Patch.

"Rayne, is it? I'm Patch, but you probably know that already. Anyway, I just ran into our mutual healer friend Pan, and she tells me you have dreams of being a hunter."

Hobb shot onto his feet, a blush filling his cheeks. "Wow! Patch! It's great to meet you! Yes, I've seen you shoot, and you're incredible. Listen to me, gushing like a pathetic fanboy."

Patch smiled at him. "No worries, man. I'm used to it. Listen, I'm a little busy today for shooting lessons, but how about I let you in on a little clan secret to tide you over?"

Hobb's eyes widened, and Patch knew the stupid kid would take the bait. "I'd be honored! What is it, Patch?"

The young hunter looked around quickly, then pulled out the jar he kept securely fastened in his front pocket. "Nectar. It's a tradition among the hunters. You ever try it?"

"No, sir, I haven't. Honestly I heard that stuff can really mess with you."

"Who told you that, your mommy? Trust me, if you really wanna be a hunter, you gotta join in the holy ritual. Plus, it'll add some spice to your life as a merchant. I mean, you must be bored out of your mind doing this shit, especially if you wanna be out in the woods stalking prey and shooting poggs. Here, just try some. Start living a little more dangerously, kid. It's how we do things out in the forest."

Patch could tell Hobb was deeply conflicted, but he eventually grabbed the jar and tipped it until a drop of the juice landed on his tongue.

"Holy shit! This is amazing. Colors are brighter. Sounds are softer. I feel... invincible!"

"That's right," said Patch. "It's a beautiful thing. Just let me know if you want more." Patch slapped his carcasses on the counter and turned to leave. "Nice meeting you, kid. Best of luck with becoming a hunter."

Patch walked away with a grin on his face. *That's what you get for trying to steal my girl, you little punk.*

THE FORGOTTEN / SATO MAULER

The next night, as the sun went down and the city streets emptied, Sato Mauler dressed in a borrowed IES uniform and took his post in a well-hidden alleyway with a decent view of Merchant Village. He glanced at the Isodex on his wrist, which was tuned to a private channel so he could communicate in real time with his new employer.

WK: Sit tight until all the stands close.

Mauler rolled his eyes. He could be sitting around and waiting all night if no innocents happened to wander by his post. One last merchant stand was still open, and the young man who occupied it was deep into a book and seemed to have no intention of leaving any time soon. *What the hell is this kid waiting for?*

He scanned the area—at least no real IES members were in sight. *What's the deal with William Krakken and his mystery accomplices, anyway?* Back in the day, Krakken was just like Mauler—a dark soul who required violence for sustenance the way most people required food. What made Krakken truly stand out among the criminals of the city was his ability to lead. Krakken was always the smartest of the Forgotten, using his sharp tongue to infect the minds of other street dwellers with his own lust for terror and destruction.

After all these years without contact, Mauler assumed that Krakken had moved past his anger and onto bigger and better things. Clearly, he had been wrong. Krakken had been extremely vague, simply telling Mauler he was "starting up his old games, but on a whole new level."

38

That was enough to entice him.

Mauler stretched his neck to peer around the corner again, and to his extreme frustration he found that the boy had not moved from his stand. In fact, a hot little number was headed toward him, and it was pretty clear she wasn't there for a quick purchase. *Fuck me—I'm going to be here all night watching this kid try to score.* Mauler popped in the military-grade earbuds that came with his costume and easily picked out the lovebirds' sickening conversation.

"Pan!" shouted the boy. "I was hoping I would see you again soon, but this is a nice surprise."

"Well, I don't normally do this sort of thing, but I just couldn't stay away." She paused. "I *really* needed some late-night rompogg roast—it was an emergency!"

Their giggles curdled in Mauler's stomach like sour milk.

"You know," said the boy, "I've never, um, had such strong feelings for a girl I just met before."

Mauler stayed tuned in long enough to hear the girl tell him she felt the same way. A person with a soul might have found the whole exchange sweet. Mauler pulled the earbuds out. He'd have to find another way to pass the time while he waited for this little love affair to run its course.

WK: What's going on out there? Are you alone? Any potential targets?

Mauler brought the Isodex speaker up to his mouth and quietly briefed Krakken. "I have a couple of kids lingering in front of the last open merchant stand. We may have to abort and try again another night." The young couple were now sitting together on the counter and holding hands. *Fantastic.*

Out of the corner of his eye, Mauler saw something that jump-started his adrenaline—a robed figure emerged from the darkness and headed toward the merchant stand. Mauler smirked; only the homeless and the clanless wore such filthy and torn hides. *He'll ask them for food, and once he wanders off and turns the corner, he's mine.* He raised his Isodex again, eager to update Krakken.

"Potential target just appeared. Stand by."

WK: Excellent. Be patient. We can't afford any mistakes.

Mauler hadn't felt this alive since his old destructive escapades. In fact, he'd gotten so caught up in the excitement, he failed to notice the hooded figure had pulled out a large blade. By the time Mauler wrapped his head around what was happening, the robed man had sliced the young woman's neck from behind, drowning the merchant stand in a river of blood.

You've gotta be shitting me!

The boy opened his mouth to scream. The killer spoke some words Mauler couldn't hear. The boy shut his yap.

Mauler spoke hurriedly into the Isodex. "We have a situation here. Some robed man just came out of nowhere and sliced up the chick at the merchant stand before I could react. What do you want me to do?"

"It's our mystery killer! Don't let him get away. I want him alive."

Mauler's thoughts swirled. He was expecting somebody to die tonight, but not like this.

"What's happening?" snapped Krakken.

"It seems like he just wanted the girl," whispered Mauler. "I think he's about to slip away and leave the boy."

"Make damn sure the kid doesn't see you capture the murderer. You need to apprehend the killer and get both of you out of there before the kid contacts a real member of the IES and exposes us."

Mauler's heart thudded against his chest. Maybe he wouldn't get to kill someone tonight after all, but what a fucking crazy turn of events! Bringing this madman back to Krakken without being detected might prove to be almost as exciting.

He poked his head out into the street. Much to Mauler's growing delight, the murderer was headed straight toward him! He quickly positioned himself directly at the entrance to the alleyway, ears peeled for footsteps. He couldn't help but crack a smile as he snatched his blaster from its holster. After what seemed like an eternity, the robed figure entered the alleyway.

"Hold it right there, you murderous motherfucker," hissed Mauler under his breath, "and shut the hell up unless you want me to blow your brain to bits."

The man lowered his hood, revealing large, bloodshot eyes. This man had ingested enough reck leaf to kill a papa rompogg. "Go ahead and shoot me," he said. "I'm not afraid of the fucking IES." The killer paused to size up his new acquaintance, landing his gaze on Mauler's fabricated badge. "Or whoever the hell you are."

"As a matter of fact," Mauler replied, "I'm not with the IES, and if you do anything at all to try to attract attention from the IES, I'll blast your brains out right on the spot. I have a friend who's very interested to meet you, and that's only possible if we get out of here quickly and quietly. So, unless you want your days of murder and drug abuse to be over, you're coming with me."

LIBERATION HEADQUARTERS
INTERROGATION ROOM 1

Krakken: Here he is in all his glory—the infamous mystery killer. I thought I'd have to be much more patient, but my dream of meeting you has come true in just two short days! And you were even generous enough to give us your name.

Levol: I'm glad my presence can bring you such joy. And what's it matter if you know my name? There's not much you can do with it—especially since you're probably just gonna kill me right in this room.

Krakken: Oh, Levol, you have the completely wrong idea. I was hoping we could become friends.

Levol: No offense buddy, but I'm just not that into you. Can I go now?

[Prisoner attempts to leave but is subdued by Mauler.]

Krakken: Son, this may be hard for you to believe, but your escapades these past few nights have actually saved me a great deal of trouble. A few of my colleagues and I have been thinking a lot about Isotopia's future. We believe that, as it stands, our society has some fundamental issues that need solving. Unfortunately, the changes we have in mind are somewhat... *extreme* and won't be possible unless all of Isotopia feels the need for change. What do you think, Levol—how has society been treating you these days?

Levol: Well, let's see... I've got a cushy, high-ranking clan position. Anyone who's anyone knows of my power and kisses my ass every chance they get, and I go home to my gold-plated hut where I enjoy scads of blowjobs from Isotopia's finest whores. How could I possibly complain?

Krakken: All right. Considering you don't seem to have any difficulty expressing your frustration in the form of your spectacular killings, I know your anger, and I appreciate your methodical caution. However, you're seriously missing the bigger picture by insisting on "you versus the world." We were forced to dilute the symbolism of your first kill in the news, but every Isotopian with half a brain took one look at that pitiful old man and knew someone out there was sick of being invisible. I have to admit, you surprised me tonight, butchering that young, innocent girl. I guess you were pissed about how quickly the city put the first killing out of their minds, so you decided to raise the stakes? Maybe if you killed someone people actually cared about, you would finally get back at Isotopia for abandoning you.

Levol: So, you think you know all about me now just because I killed a couple people, huh? Anyone can kill somebody, you know. It's not that hard.

Krakken: If you knew who I am, you wouldn't waste your breath lecturing me about killing. The fact is I do know you, son, more than you give me credit for. I agree with you—anybody can just kill someone. But it was the way you did it. The way you used that Forgotten old man's blood as your paint and the city street as your canvas to pour out your own rage. I'm not one to ever mistake rage when I see it, because it's my rage, too. I fell through the cracks of the "perfect Isotopian society" a long time ago, and I know what it's like to trudge through life alone. Forgotten.

Levol: You? Forgotten? Then please, *brother*, explain to me why we're talking on property owned by the Panel, and you're wearing robes that equate to fucking royalty.

Krakken: Recently, I came upon an opportunity to make something of myself, and I took it—a position of power, which will give me a chance to have my say when it comes to what Isotopia is and how it functions. But you see, I'm still as cold and empty as when I terrorized the streets as a Youth. And I don't intend to restrict myself to the small fraction of power and responsibility that has been rationed to us. We're going to change Isotopia, Levol. We're going to change it in ways that no one will ever see coming, but we need help. So, son, what do you say, are you going to help us lead the charge?

THE MERCHANTS / KOOP

The next day, the sunrise illuminated the dark events of the previous night once again. The sense of dread and helplessness among the onlookers felt much more intense than when the city huddled around the corpse of the homeless man. It was as if the heavens shared grief with the societies they watched over.

This time it wasn't just some unfortunate killing of some unknown man. Instead, it was someone with a clan and a family, a contributing member of society who worked hard to heal the sick. But most importantly, the victim was a sweet, innocent, young girl who was adored by everyone who knew her. Who would possibly want to do such a terrible thing to such a beautiful soul?

Sharon stood just beyond the bloodstained cobbles, doing her best to comfort the immensely distraught young man talking with Detective Lask and his IES posse. Koop continued to scan the crowd, and sure enough, spotted all the healers off to one side, deep in mourning.

What Koop saw next made him shudder—Patch had arrived and was violently shoving his way to the center of the action, his face hotter than the pellets in his rifle. He probably couldn't have sorted out whether he was more furious or upset, and the Nectar had to only be confusing the matter.

"What the *fuck* did you do?" he yelled. Patch's outburst seemed to be aimed at the mess of a young man, who cringed with fear and ducked behind the detective for protection. "How could you let this happen to her?"

Lask wasted no time subduing Patch, who continued to thrash around as menacingly as one could with both arms locked behind his back. Patch spouted threats even as Lask dragged him away. "You're a dead man, Rayne Hobb! A fucking *dead man!*"

More officers swooped in to form a perimeter around the boy, who was now vomiting behind the stand. The IES wrapped up their conversation with the boy, and Captain Ranger turned to address the crowd.

"Fellow Isotopians, there is no doubt we are facing tough times. We won't sugarcoat this. Someone out there wishes to hurt our city and its citizens. Until we decide on further measures, security will be doubled. Please stay tuned to your Isodexes for updates, and do not be afraid. We will catch this murderer—whatever it takes. It's our clan's job to keep everyone safe, and we will not let this happen again."

The IES carted away Pan's body, and the crowd thinned out. The boy left also, dragging his body along like a pogg corpse. Koop took the opportunity to approach Sharon, who turned to him with an expression equally lifeless.

"Rayne was right here when it happened." She choked on every word. "Poor kid watched as Pan was sliced up right in front of his eyes. I don't know if a person can ever overcome that type of trauma."

"Not to mention that a hotheaded reck of a hunter just threatened to rip his heart out," added Koop. "Patch has never been one to share his feelings, but it wasn't hard to see his passion for that girl. He wore it on his face for all of Isotopia to see."

"Rayne Hobb is such a devoted young man," said Sharon, "the most reliable assistant I've ever had at my stand. Between serving customers, he buries himself in clan manuals. His dream is to become a hunter one day, and now one of them wants him dead. It would destroy me to see his entire world crumble."

"There are so few citizens of Isotopia with the loyalty and passion you attribute to this Rayne Hobb fellow," said Koop. "Listen—I have a relationship with Patch, and I think I can talk some sense into him. Let's make sure we don't have another death in Merchant Village if we can prevent it, hmm?" He paused. "As for Rayne... he's going to be in a dark place now. A place that few will understand but a place not so different from where I once was. Let me take the boy under my wing. He'll work at my stand, and I'll keep him close. Yes?" Sharon smiled. "Good! He starts tomorrow. Make sure he's not late."

THE HEALERS / COLE

Cole was perched on a jumbo-root where the rest of the healers wouldn't find him, toking on a fat herbarette of self-mixed bliss leaf. Patch had just left after a brief "business meeting," but Cole wasn't quite ready to rejoin society. The deep forest held territory the hunters didn't traverse often, and it was beautiful and soothing in its natural state. It was the only place he could mourn the passing of his dear friend and clanmate in peace.

Unfortunately, the rustling of some nearby shrubs interrupted his brief moment of solitude. Cole turned toward the disturbance and immediately recognized the shithead coward who had, according to Patch, let Pan die.

"Excuse me," choked the coward, in his shitheaded cowardly voice. "I was told I could find you here. I... I'm looking for some... I was told I could ask you—"

Cole huffed. "It's okay to say Nectar, man. I'm not IES." The healer-drug dealer took a long look at the timid little bitch in front of him and extended his hand.

"Hobb, right? Patch said I should expect to see you sooner or later." Hobb cringed at the mention of Patch's name. "You're in luck, my friend. It turns out I've just mixed up an entire new batch." Cole reached into his pocket and pulled out a jar.

"W—what do you want for it?" stammered Hobb. Cole couldn't help but crack a smile. This kid was just too pathetic.

"You know what, man? I'm just gonna let you have this one. I usually give out free samples when I mix up a new

48

batch. Plus, you must be having a pretty tough day, and you look like you could use it."

Hobb's face transitioned from despair to confusion to gratitude, and eventually he took the jar. "I really appreciate this. Are you sure you don't want anything in return?"

Cole peered straight into the kid's eyes and grinned once more. "The knowledge that I'm helping a brother out is all the payment I need. You just enjoy."

THE SCIENTISTS / CAM DIMLAN

It was getting late, and Cam hadn't moved from his computer screen for hours. *I could really use some fucking sleep. And where the hell is Nap? If that kid expects to take half the credit once I finish this project, he'd better think again.*

Although he rarely left the lab, Cam was fully aware of the dark events that had taken place in the city recently. Dr. Adams had been ramping up the pressure to finish the helmet prototype ever since Pan's death. *Some stupid healer gets her throat cut, and now I get no sleep. Yeah—that's fair.*

Cam sipped his stim leaf tea, which he preferred over rettes when working excessive hours, and scrutinized his program line by line. As he tinkered with the code, Cam allowed himself to revel in his genius. Sure, the original concept was relatively simple—enabling the device to isolate and amplify neural activity from sensorimotor brain areas—but there was no telling its full potential. It would all depend on the signal emitted from the brain. If very high frequency could be isolated, thoughts could be converted into text, which could then be transmitted to any Isodex or, even better, interpreted by another helmet. Low frequency amplification could increase mental capacity, improving memory. But the real question was, how much could one safely amplify brain activity?

It was this exact question currently keeping Dimlan awake, and after hours of debugging, he felt ready to do some testing. He activated the chip in the helmet and frantically moved through his configuration file, tweaking parameters of his code.

Let's try 30 MHz and 2X amplification. Cam flipped the main power switch, and a tingle rushed over his scalp. *All right. Let's see what you can do.*

He dialed his Isodex to the channel used to communicate with the helmet, then closed his eyes and focused on his favorite word. The lab was silent, and the world faded away as the helmet searched for the answer.

THE MERCHANTS / KOOP

Koop glanced at his Isodex and a fresh wave of disappointment rushed over him. He'd been open two hours already. *Where is this kid?*

Obviously, Hobb would need time to pull himself together. The kid had been to hell and back after Pan's death, and his issues with Patch weren't helping matters, but it didn't bode well that he couldn't even show up for work on day one. Koop had all but given up when he saw Hobb approaching.

"Ah, there's my new helper! Was starting to think you weren't gonna show. Good morning to ya."

As Hobb drew closer, Koop realized it was not, in fact, a good morning—not for this kid. His eyes had the same glazed-over look as Patch's, and Hobb's gait was far more impaired. The boy was messing with the same drugs as the young hunter, but he had just started, and he clearly couldn't handle his shit. Unlike Patch, this kid might be smart enough to take some advice.

First things first; Koop needed to protect the kid from making a complete fool out of himself in front of Head Merchant Katt and the others. If Hobb couldn't prove himself to them, how would he ever become anything more than a merchant's assistant? Koop flipped the "Open" sign to "Be Back Soon" and pulled out a stool from below the counter.

"Have a seat, kid, while you can still control where your ass is gonna land."

Hobb met Koop's eyes but looked past them as if they

52

weren't there. No smile, no tears—just *nothing*. He stumbled over and found his balance on the stool.

"She was a real sweetheart, wasn't she?" asked Koop.

Hobb turned a blank expression to Koop. "It's my fault. It happened right in front of me, and I just stood there and watched. Patch is right. I'm a fucking coward. I could never be a hunter." A tear rolled down his cheek.

"Listen, boy," started Koop, "I've known Patch for a while and can confidently say I know him better than he knows himself. He sees all his hunting talent and makes damn sure everyone else sees it too. But in the emotional department, he couldn't identify love and hate if they were his left and right testicles. The kid didn't realize how deeply he cared for Pan and couldn't admit to being crushed, so instead he made a show out of snapping at you. He'll realize he was in the wrong there, and if he doesn't figure it out on his own, then I'll help him find the truth."

Hobb let out a sigh that Koop chose to interpret as some form of minor relief.

"As for the whole 'it's my fault' thing"—Koop reached out and set his hand on Hobb's shoulder—"an old friend from the IES shared your official statement with me. Sorry for the invasion of privacy, but I asked because I want to help. By your own admission, the assailant was a giant. Even if you'd had the time to realize what was happening and tried to intervene, all that would have led to is a second dead body—and that one *would* have been your fault." Hobb processed for a few seconds, then mustered up the minimal energy to nod. "You're gonna be all right, kid. And you can trust me—I'm a wise old man. Ask anyone."

CHIEF ADVISOR SANDS GRAPER

As Sands Graper prepared to officiate the funeral service, he gazed out into the vast and diverse crowd, and warmth filled his heart. It was moments like these that made Graper proud to be Chief Advisor of such an amazing community. Was it a gloomy and tragic day for Isotopia? Of course. But here, too, was evidence of how the people united to face such trying times.

The funeral for the Forgotten had a much lower attendance, which was, sadly, to be expected. *This* event, however, was glorious and deserving of Pan's beautiful soul. The healers had picked a beautiful spot in the forest for the service. Pan rested in a casket handcrafted from the finest barks and roots Maxx Spike and his apprentices could find, topped with a rainbow of exotic flowers collected from deep in the forest. Stern IES officers maintained the peace along the perimeter of the ceremonial ground, delineated by the edges of a dome set up by the scientists to keep out poggs and pests. After the service, the mourners moved to the nearby feast, organized by the merchants and catered by the hunters. It was unfortunate that a tragic death was required to bring the city together, but at least it happened.

Not everyone had as much faith as Graper in the abundant freedom and choice of Isotopian society. He and Bogue had engaged in debates about the pitfalls of their clan system throughout his time on the Panel, but today Graper knew he was right. All were where they wanted to be; everyone had pitched in when it mattered most.

Confidence surged through him as he took the podium and addressed his audience.

"My fellow Isopeople, I wish we were together under better circumstances. Our hearts and our nerves have certainly been tested these last few days as we have seen innocent blood spilled into our streets. I can't say I had the pleasure of knowing Pan personally, but I have seen the lives she's touched, and I have heard countless stories describing her acts of immeasurable kindness—not just from her fellow healers whom she called family but from people of all clans and ages. There is one particular story about this young lady that her dear mentor, Maxx 'The Guru' Spike, told me, and I would like to share it with all of you today.

"When Pan was still a young girl, before she was an official member of the healing clan, a nasty plague that attacked the bones spread through Isotopia; the younger the victim, the more vicious the disease. Pan became infected and fell quite ill. There was no known cure for this disease, so she and the other children were merely kept comfortable with small doses of bliss leaf while Spike and others desperately searched for a cure. The future of these young people looked grim, but the healers did not give up, and neither did young Pan.

"Maxx and several of his apprentices discovered a root blend that had the effect of temporarily shrinking the bones; they hoped they could apply this compound to the inflicted and eventually starve the plague to death. Problem was, they had no idea what dose would be most curative. In fact, Maxx worried the treatment might actually accelerate the plague's devastating effects. Furthermore, the treatment would not only be very painful but would also render the patient extremely fragile and at high risk of breaking bones even after cessation. There was much disagreement among the healers about whether the blend was ready for human trials or whether it first needed to be tested on rompoggs. Tensions ran high between

Maxx and his students.

"Well, one day, a very sick Pan happened to overhear them arguing, and as frail as she was, she leapt out of bed to butt into the debate. 'Try it on me!' she famously demanded. The healers explained they didn't know if it was safe, that it could hurt or even kill her, but Pan wasn't having any of it. She told Maxx she'd heard him say it was riskiest for the younger children and pointed out that she was the oldest patient and, therefore, the perfect test subject. Then she told Maxx that he was a 'damn fool' if he didn't give it to her to save those kids and that she would steal it and inject it into herself if they didn't start treatment immediately!" The crowd allowed themselves a laugh at Pan's headstrong stunt, and Graper spotted Maxx in the front of the crowd, beaming as fat tears rolled down both cheeks.

"So, after days of facing excruciating pain and the very real possibility of death, Pan awoke one morning feeling well again. She continued to take the blend in various doses after she was cured to ensure even the youngest child's safety. That blend, which was promptly named Linner Leaf in her honor, has prevented countless children from falling prey to that disease. And of course, Maxx snatched her up into the healing clan as soon as she was healthy enough." More laughter from the crowd.

"Pan wasn't just a sweet girl; she was a guardian angel of Isotopia, and she will be dearly missed." Graper choked on those words and took a second to regain his composure.

"I want each of you to look around you today and see the love and trust within and among our clans. Every one of you has shown immense strength and bravery by uniting here on this trying day. Even in our roughest times, it is this bond that keeps us together and will continue to keep us together as we face future challenges. With that, let us all observe a moment of silence to wish our dear Pan a peaceful rest."

As Graper joined the crowd in reflection on the amazingly brave and stubborn young Pan, he was overwhelmed with pride in the citizenry of Isotopia, these people he helped lead.

THE IES / DETECTIVE LASK

Detective Jimmy Lask slumped into his office chair and focused all his might on not throwing up a profusion of pogg pie all over his desk. It was Isotopian tradition to stuff oneself with forest delicacies at a funeral feast, and as far as Lask was concerned, he'd conquered his obligation like a goddamn hero. But nausea wasn't the only thing Lask was feeling at that moment. He was also a bit puzzled.

In the past few days, Lask had noticed a parade of young, new detectives passing through the doors of IES headquarters. Yes, two innocents had just been murdered in cold blood in the middle of the street—in fact, Lask himself had requisitioned the increased patrols—but that didn't account for all the unfamiliar faces. Amid the hubbub, Lask picked out Ranger, striding across the squad room.

"Captain Ranger, sir!" Lask jumped out of his chair and pushed through the sea of newbies.

Ranger turned for a split second, then pressed forward. "Detective. I'm swamped. Is this important?"

"I was just wondering, Captain. What's with all these new recruits?"

"Krakken's orders," Ranger responded curtly. "Innocents die; citizens get scared; takes more of us to make them feel safe."

"So, these guys all passed the IES entrance exams?"

Ranger sighed. "Not exactly." A gnawing headache took hold at Lask's temples. "If a guy knows how to tie his

58

boots and shoot a rifle, he can pretty much wear a badge right now. No background checks, no studying for exams. Hell, the Panel even suggested suspending herb-testing on this latest bunch. Look, I gotta run, but we'll catch up soon. I'll need to brief everyone on our new security protocols. Stay vigilant." Ranger disappeared into the crowd.

No background checks? Something was definitely up.

"*Ayy*! Jimmy!" Lask recognized Paller's grating voice and scanned the crowd for the detective.

"Ah, there you are," said Lask, whirling around to face him. "Nice to find a familiar face among this shit show. What's up?"

"Afternoon haul. Check out the eyes on this one—you ever seen anyone look so recked? This kid should win an award or something! Anyway, you mind watching 'im for a sec while I go grab the paperwork?"

Lask registered surprise when he recognized the cuffed reckhead. "Hey, you're Koop's hunter friend, right? The one pretending not to be recked that first time I met you near his shop. What was your name again?"

The punk flashed that oh-so-satisfying "shit-I'm-busted" face for a split second before coughing up his name. "Patch."

"Yeah, that's right. I remember it sounding like some lame nickname."

"Y-you knew I was high that day?"

Paller chuckled. "I see you gentlemen have some catching up to do. Be back in a minute."

Lask beamed at Patch as his squadmate walked away. "Kid, I'm a detective. It's my job to notice, not that you make it all that difficult, walking around like you own the place because you think no one would dare stop you."

Patch looked confused. "Well, why didn't you? I mean, if you knew the first time."

"Koop seems to think you're a good kid, and I trust his judgment more than pretty much anyone else's in

Isotopia." Lask paused. "Don't go telling all your reckhead friends this, but personally, I'd rather spend my time apprehending murderers than herb guzzlers." Lask let that stew for a minute in the kid's head while pondering whether Koop was right about the hunter's potential. "But the old man did seem a bit worried about you. So maybe I should be too, huh?"

"Koop can be a bit of a worrywart."

"Mmhmm," Lask said. "Tell you what, Patch—why don't we step into my office where we can hear ourselves think?" Lask guided Patch into his office, closed the door, leaned back in his chair, and crossed his feet on top of the desk. Patch took a seat across from him and aimed his gaze down at the floor.

"Look, man," started Lask, "Koop says you're a kickass hunter, and I know you think that won't ever change, but just like anything else in life, you can screw it up if you're not careful." Patch shot him a look of disbelief, which Lask took as a challenge.

"Judging by that shade of red in your eyes, you're on Nectar. A relatively new concoction, but that slight twitch in your right hand tells me you've been using for at least a few months." Lask paused to make sure he had gotten Patch's attention before he continued. "To tell you the truth, Nectar itself doesn't appear to be all that dangerous, granted the user isn't an idiot about overdoing it. But that twitching will get worse if you keep abusing it like you do, and it'll spread too. This one dude we brought in a few months ago was tweaking so hard it looked like he was rave dancing. And I would be willing to bet your 'almighty spirit guide' Maris would catch on if his best hunter loses his perfect aim due to shaky hands and bloodshot eyes. Plus, I'm sure you've got some young hunters looking up to you, and if they see an addict as their role model, that's what they'll become. So, for everyone's sake, try to tone it down, kid—all right?"

Patch shifted his gaze back down toward his boots and

muttered a defeated, "All right."

Lask slid his legs off the desk, stood, and gave Patch a hard slap on the back that made him jump out of his chair. "Attaboy!" Lask said, as patronizing as possible, then opened the door to find Paller waiting outside.

"You two have a nice talk?" Paller asked.

"He says he's real sorry, and he'll never do it again. I think he learned his lesson, so you can probably let him go."

"You sure, Jimmy?" asked Paller. "He was pretty out of control when we found him."

"Aw, lighten up, will you? I'm sure you hate to see him go, but don't worry, Paller—he'll find his way back here soon. Besides, there're too many people here as it is. Place is a zoo."

Paller looked hard at Patch, then shrugged and took off the cuffs. "Lucky you got a friend in this place. Scram, kid. And lay off the drugs."

Patch glanced at Lask with a stupefied look on his face, then left while he had the chance.

"You do have a point, though. What's up with all the newbies?"

"No clue," said Lask. *But I plan to find out.*

THE SCIENTISTS / CAM DIMLAN

Full-clan lab meetings were rare, but for this special occasion—the demonstration of the helmet prototype—even Panel Rep Harding was present. As if Clan Head Hal Adams weren't intimidating enough on his own, Dr. Harding had absolutely no tolerance for mistakes. Cam Dimlan was doing the bulk of the talking—partly because he loved the spotlight but mostly because Nap was too busy fighting the urge to puke. No doubt, Nap was replaying a lab meeting a while back where one of the younger members was demonstrating a modified version of the Isodex, and it blew up in his face right on the spot. Harding proceeded to humiliate the loser until he pissed his pants and quit the clan.

"Each helmet has multiple interior chips," Cam lectured while pointing out each feature, "that interactively read and modulate various features of brain activity via electrical stimulation. Knobs on the outside of the helmet control the voltage to each chip, but those will likely not be necessary in future versions."

"And why is that?" asked Dr. Adams. Cam nodded to Nap, giving him the layup questions since he was too nervous to be of any other use.

"W-well, sir," started Nap as he tried to control his visible shaking, "we believe that with the installation of more sophisticated machinery, the user could theoretically change the activity level of each circuit through thoughts alone, rendering mechanical controls obsolete."

"An obvious next step," said Harding. "Why wasn't

that already implemented?"

Nap tensed, but his convictions overshadowed his nerves. "Our end goal is to grant the user perfect and intricate control over his or her thoughts while wearing the helmet, but trying to jump there in one step could be dangerous. If we don't first ensure that each individual function of the helmet works flawlessly, there could potentially be a scenario in which the user thinks one thing and the helmet does another. We couldn't afford that kind of mistake."

By Cam's standards, they were plenty ready, but Nap was always droning on about more thorough testing. *Pussy.*

Before Nap could shed any more doubt, Cam took over the presentation. "Each microcircuit inside the helmet is designed to modify a particular set of psychological and cognitive functions. This could be anything from improving memory and mathematical skills to producing euphoria. We're not just giving people the ability to perform at their best; we're allowing them to do *better* than their best."

Basking in the hot light of attention, Cam pulled the helmet over his head and turned one of the knobs. "Allow me to demonstrate. Someone give me a math problem—a difficult one."

One of the younger scientists yelled out, "4596 divided by 47!"

"9.635," responded Cam nonchalantly. "Now, someone give me a long series of random digits and letters. Don't go easy on me." Cam turned another knob on the helmet. Another list was rattled off and repeated back perfectly.

"The average human brain can hold roughly seven items in short-term memory. That sequence contained exactly thirty-three items." There were *oohs* and *ahhs* from the small crowd, but Harding sat back and crossed his arms.

"Impressive," said Harding coldly, "but I was led to

believe we'd see more than a glorified calculator today. How about we skip ahead to what makes this device worthy of taking the time out of my busy schedule to come down here?"

"I'm glad you asked, Dr. Harding," said Cam. "See these ports around the outside of the helmet? This is where the real magic happens. These babies both send *and* receive neural signals from inside the helmet, meaning not only can the helmets project cognitive states out into the world, but they can also be picked up by other users." Cam paused to make sure Harding was properly intrigued before moving on. "Allow me to give a brief demonstration."

Cam picked up a second helmet from the table in front of them and asked Nap to put it on. "All right, Nap. I'm thinking of a number between one and one billion. What is it?" Both men turned one of the knobs on their helmets.

Nap said, "One million, one hundred thirty-eight thousand, four hundred sixty-one."

"By golly, he was right!" announced Cam in a playful tone. "Don't worry. I know you're all skeptical scientists, and you require proof. Allow me to provide that for you." Cam pressed a button on the back of the helmet, and a beam of light shot out one of the ports, projecting the number 1138461 onto the screen at the front of the room for all to see. Applause filled the room, and Cam even detected a trace of wonder from Harding himself. *Wait till he sees this.*

"I think you can all imagine the possibilities opened by telepathic communication. However, I saved the best for last. You see, this helmet isn't limited to allowing the brain to communicate with other brains. It can also allow the brain to communicate with the environment." This was the part Cam had been waiting for all day and the reason he couldn't sleep last night. If this didn't impress Harding, nothing would. "It's quite simple, really. You have a thought such as, 'Gee, I really wish I had that pen over there.' That thought is expressed in terms of electrical signals that remain diffuse and essentially useless within the brain. But when the chips inside the helmet pick up this activity, they increase the amplitude of the brainwaves and the power of the signal. Finally, the exterior ports harness that energy, project it onto the outside environment, and"—the pen sitting on Harding's desk slowly stood on its tip, then launched across the room and landed in Cam's open hand—"*Voila.*" There was a collective gasp, followed by an eruption of applause.

"Nice work, men," said Harding, the edges of his lips curling ever so slightly into what could only be described as a snarl. It was probably the most ecstatic Cam had ever seen him. "What's the next step?"

"To push this thing to the limits and beyond," shot back Cam. "All we need are people willing to take a little risk."

Nap jumped in. "To be fair, the risk is potentially pretty high. We will, of course, need to proceed cautiously and not get ahead of ourselves."

Nap's warning did not dim the spark of fascination in Harding's eyes. Cam was happily reassured that caution wasn't high on Harding's priority list.

The meeting concluded with a round of applause. Cam reveled in the awe-stricken faces of the crowd as they filed out. Nap mostly looked relieved; his face had returned to its natural shade of pale, and he was no longer sweating profusely.

That's right, bitch. I carried us to success.

Cam's gaze followed Harding to the back of the room, where he greeted a man Cam had never seen before—a large beast of a man who definitely wasn't a scientist. Cam strained to hear their conversation, but all he caught was a name: *Levol.*

THE YOUTH / RAYNE HOBB

It was peak traffic time in the marketplace, and Hobb worked the stand while Koop foraged the food stands for something to eat. Normally, Hobb would have been overwhelmed and irritated by the relentless shouting and stampeding of the crowd, but lately he hadn't been feeling much at all. In fact, if anything, Hobb felt pretty good.

He reached into his pocket to examine his precious almost-empty vial of Nectar. *Enough to tolerate the world, but not enough for Koop to notice.*

Unfortunately, that amount had been slowly increasing over time, and Cole seemed to be raising the price at every visit. *Supply and demand, I guess.* But Hobb couldn't help but wonder what Cole charged his fellow healers or Patch and the rest of the hotshot hunters. Hobb wasn't special—in fact, he was as ordinary as could be—and that's how the world would treat him as long as he remained a merchant assistant. Just some nobody who had to pay more than he could afford to get his dose of synthetic happiness.

Hobb quickly looked around for Koop, popped open the stand's Isocoin box, and grabbed a small handful for himself. If Hobb was invisible to the world, he may as well take advantage of it. It's not like he was hurting anyone.

Hobb stuffed the coins in his pocket, then jumped when he looked up and saw Len standing on the other side of the counter. "Damn, dude! You scared me."

"Just wanted to come say hey," replied Len. Hobb knew his best friend well enough to read it on his face and in his tone: *He saw.* And Len wasn't the kind of friend to just pretend it didn't happen.

"Stealing from your own shop?" Len at least had the courtesy to keep his scolding to a whisper.

"It's not my shop," Hobb replied flatly. "I'm an assistant. And anyway, it's just a few coins to get some new clothes. Not a big deal."

"Not a big deal? Stealing is stealing, and you know it." *Goddamn buzzkill.*

"Look, Rayne," Len started in his superior tone, "I can't imagine what you've been going through. What happened to Pan would mess with anyone's head, but you've been a shadow of yourself since that night. And I'd be willing to bet you're not planning to spend those coins on some new shoes."

Hobb leaned over the counter, glaring into Len's eyes. "What are you implying?"

"That you're hurting," said Len, "and you may have found what you think is a quick fix. But it's a lie. Just a trick that fools the brain until the reality and pain come crashing back down even harder. It's no solution."

Hobb maintained his cold stare. "I don't know what bullshit tricks you're talking about, but whatever it is, I'm not doing it." Hobb paused for half a second to acknowledge to himself that he'd just lied to Len for the first time. There was no guilt—the Nectar washed it all away. "And besides, what *is* the solution in your smartass scientist mind?"

"To face the pain," Len said gently, "and realize you don't have to do that alone. Talk to me, man. I'm your best friend."

Just then, an older woman approached the stand. Hobb took a deep breath and backed away from Len. "I've got business to attend to. You should probably be getting back to the lab now anyway, yeah? Your clan needs you."

Out of the corner of his eye, Hobb watched Len leave as he turned and gave his customer a wide smile. "How may I help you today?"

THE SCIENTISTS / CAM DIMLAN

Cam lounged alone in the lab, with his ankles crossed on the desk and a stim herbarette in his hand. After all, he had impressed the great Rep Harding today. Cam strategically chose to hold this private celebration after-hours to ensure Nap wouldn't be there to suck the fun out of the room. Nap's fear of the unknown hadn't hindered the duo when they started out with more basic projects, but now that they were tackling uncharted territory, Nap was becoming an increasing liability. *If he keeps holding me back, he has to go. It's that simple.*

The door creaked open behind him. Cam whipped around in his chair to see none other than Rep Harding himself, accompanied by the same large man he'd spoken to after the meeting. *Shit.* Cam quickly snuffed out his herbarette, hoping the wafting herbal stench wasn't as obvious as it seemed.

"Don't worry about it, kid," said Harding. "You're one of the only scientists I've seen who actually has the mind for it, and I couldn't give a shit if you shoot up reck leaf to keep that up." Harding chuckled and elbowed the man standing next to him. "And that's saying a lot, because I've seen my friend Levol, here, slam some of that shit, and it's not a pretty sight." Levol grinned with his mouth, but his steely eyes stayed trained on Cam. Dude was intimidating as shit.

"All right then," replied Cam, trying to understand what was going on and hoping that this Levol monster wasn't about to snap his skinny neck. "What can I help you gentlemen with? Anything for you, of course, Dr. Harding."

"Funny you ask," said Harding, "because I actually do have a few questions for you. But first, I'd like to know if you're the right man to be talking to."

Cam was pretty sure by Levol's cold stare that the correct answer was yes, but this seemed like a question he did not want to guess wrong. "Sir?"

"This project is a joint effort between you and that partner of yours, but it also struck me today that you were the one presenting your work while your little friend was trying not to shit himself." Harding smiled, but Levol just kept glaring. "It appears that the more groundbreaking features of your invention have yet to be fully implemented, a problem which seemed to be more a lack of ambition than anything else. So, my question is, are you ready to stop dicking around and rise to your full potential?"

Cam's heart was beating a hundred times per second and his eyes were wide as a tigapogg preparing to pounce on its prey. "I'm your man."

"Well then, Cam Dimlan, I need you to make this helmet into the deadliest weapon in Isotopia, after which I will need you to teach my friends how to use it." Cam tried his best to contain his excitement but lost it when Harding added, "How would you like to be one of the most powerful men in Isotopia?"

Cam's smug smile lasted until he noticed Nap in the doorway. "How long have you been standing there?" Harding and Levol turned to face him, and the room suddenly turned icy.

"I knew this helmet couldn't possibly lead to anything good," said Nap in a shaky voice. "C'mon, man. People are gonna die because of this thing. Are you really okay with that?" Cam said nothing, because there was nothing to say, and Nap turned white and clenched his teeth while slowly backing away. "I'm not letting you guys do this.

Whatever fucked up plans you have, they stop now. I'm calling the IES."

Harding cackled. "I don't think the IES is gonna be too much of a help for you at the moment, kid." Cam wondered exactly what that meant. "In fact," he continued, "no one will." Harding nodded at Levol, who pulled out a silenced isoblaster and aimed it at Nap's head. Nap pissed his pants and dropped to his knees.

"*Cam*? You're going to let them murder your friend in cold blood just so you can go on to murder more people? Are you really gonna do that to Isotopia? To *me*?"

Cam walked across the room to stand next to Levol. He leaned down, towering over his partner. "You were always weak, never realizing our potential. This was inevitable; you did it to yourself. Don't look at me like it's my fault." Nap let out a wail of despair, and Cam turned to his new friend. "Do it, Levol."

THE HUNTERS / PATCH

It was the end of the day for Maris and his crew. Patch dropped back from his younger clanmates and found himself a sturdy tree to lean against. He pulled out the vial, unscrewed the cap, and held the Nectar up to his nose. The aroma alone lightened him, practically lifting him above the forest. Nothing and no one was more beautiful. Patch had just set the vial to his lips and tipped it back when Maris' voice cut through the shrubs.

Is that Bowman he's talking to? Patch lowered the bottle and listened. *What the fuck is our Clan Rep doing here?*

As far as Patch, Zap, and Arlo were concerned, Maris was the boss. Patch never much concerned himself with men whose jobs involved sitting indoors around tables, talking all day about quotas and economics—or whatever it was Panel members did—while the real men were out in the forest, bringing in the kills. Bowman had always seemed more like a concept than an actual person. Patch cocked his head toward the voices and listened hard.

Maris: "You're *sure* about this?"

Bowman: "I'm sure Bogue and company are planning something big and bad. I just don't know exactly what."

Maris: "And only the members of this top secret 'Liberation Committee' are in on it?"

Bowman: "Right. I hoped I could wait until something concrete was revealed so we could figure out how to prevent it, but the meetings are becoming fewer and farther between. And less detailed too."

Maris: "Hmm. Sounds like someone is holding secret meetings on top of the secret meetings. Who's leading the charge?"

Bowman: "Bogue sneaks off with Krakken every so often. It seems to have something to do with the IES. Getting the people scared enough to give the IES more power so they can do... something."

Maris: "That would account for the increase in IES presence in the streets recently. You're right; this doesn't sound good."

Bowman: "They're raising an army for something although I don't know how they're convincing the soldiers to act against their sworn duty to keep Isotopia safe. The IES takes that shit super seriously. Anyone who doesn't gets booted from the clan."

Maris: "Something's definitely up. What the hell are we going to do about it?"

Bowman: "That's the thing—I have no idea. I need to be extremely careful because they've already cut me out of the loop, which means my loyalty is in question. If the Committee finds out there's been a leak, they'll almost certainly turn to me first. The only other possibility would be Harding, but I get the sense he's on the inside, too."

Maris: "Hopefully, you'll get more info closer to execution time, and we can intervene quietly."

Bowman: "Until then, even telling Ranger is a risk since we don't know Bogue's angle on this thing. We need to make sure anyone who finds out about this can be completely trusted."

Patch tended to enjoy not giving a fuck about most people, but this seemed like something worth giving a fuck about. Plus, he hated to admit it, but he was pretty sure he actually knew someone in the IES who could be trusted. Sure, Lask had treated Patch like some random reckhead, but there was something about the guy—like Lask was the only one who could see the truth under a pile of bullshit, and he would fight to dig it out. The more Patch thought it over, the more the idea made sense to him: *I've gotta tell him.*

Patch sighed longingly at the vial in his hand. *I must be going crazy.* He took one last look at the sunrays passing through the sweet remaining Nectar, then chucked the whole thing into the forest and jogged off toward IES headquarters.

THE IES / DETECTIVE LASK

Lask surveyed the sea of black uniforms packed shoulder-to-shoulder on benches designed for half as many men. News of Krakken's first official address had spread like wildfire through the headquarters, it seemed. The hot, heavy air in the squad room—what there was of it, anyway—pulsed with an uneasy anticipation Lask could almost taste. Jammed in against the back wall, Lask was too far away to read Krakken's facial expressions at the podium.

"Good afternoon, gentlemen," started Krakken. "As I'm sure many of you veterans in the room have noticed, we have a high number of new recruits coming on board." *No shit*, thought Lask. *I can't even flex my dick without bumping into someone.* "Now, I know the IES has a long history of rigorously vetting new members and accepting only those who possess both the physical strength and the loyalty of a true soldier. I want to assure all of you these high standards will always be maintained and respected within the clan."

But...

"But there has been too much violence and too much fear among our citizenry to maintain order without change. I have been working in conjunction with Captain Ranger to expedite the recruitment process so we can get more uniforms out there, protecting our streets—and frankly, protecting your backs. You can all rest assured that these men are every bit as courageous and dependable as the best of you. I saw to that myself by personally interviewing each applicant to assess character and proficiency. Veteran officers, today you have many new partners and brothers, and I expect you to show them the same respect shown to each of you when you joined the force. Please, welcome your new clanmates." Applause filled the room.

"More soldiers will lead to less crime in Isotopia, but let's all be honest here—throwing more manpower at a problem can only get us so far. For this reason, we have been working closely with Science Rep Mason Harding and the rest of his clan to develop a breakthrough technology that will significantly increase the efficiency of our soldiers. The device is a helmet that acts as an interface between one's brain and the environment."

Okay, was not expecting that. What the hell?

"A select group will be notified individually that you have been chosen to beta-test the helmets, for which you will receive formal training from Dr. Harding and his bright young scientists. This team will learn how to use the helmets, test their limits, and eventually train other fellow IES members in their use.

"I'm sure you all have questions, but unfortunately, that is all I can share for now. We will pass along our findings as we are able. Thank you for your patience, soldiers. Live grand and keep safe. Dismissed."

The front rows cleared out first, like mourners at a funeral. The oxygen slowly filtered back into Lask's head while he worked his brain around the new information. *Definitely bad.*

"Detective Lask!" That hot-shit Patch was weaving between the uniforms toward Lask.

Oh, this oughtta be good. Lask smiled at the hunter as if they were old friends. "Come to turn yourself in today? Not the smartest move, but noble, I've gotta admit."

Patch did not return his smile. He leaned in and lowered his voice to a whisper. "Can we talk... somewhere less public?"

"Sure, kid." Lask led him into his office, shut the door,

and studied Patch more carefully. The vacant stare and bloodshot eyes were gone. "Wait. You're sober. Maybe the world's turned upside-down, after all."

Patch grunted. "Yeah, well." The kid looked serious, a little scared, even. "Listen, I just overheard Trey Bowman telling Maris all this shit about how that scar-faced hag—"

"Whoa, whoa. Slow down, man," said Lask. "Bogue Issler?"

"Yes."

Huh. Leave it to this arrogant kid to tell it like it is. Lask counted his lucky stars that his job description didn't involve looking at that woman's horrid face on a daily basis and wondered if the people who did ever got used to it. Those scars were deep and nasty. The herbals could hide the truth for a day or two, but most Isotopians knew at least part of the story—urban legend or not. Judging by the color and puffiness of the scars, the wounds were inflicted around Bogue's late teenage years. The *who* and the *why* were between Bogue and the unnamed, daring motherfucker who must have seen the evil in her even then.

"...and her new slave-boy Krakken are raising an army using the IES as a smokescreen." *Hence the uniforms coming at Lask from every direction.*

Lask sat on the corner of his desk, meeting Patch's eye level. "Who else knows about this?"

"Just Maris. Oh—and Harding, too. He's in on it somehow."

Lask's eyes widened. *The helmets!*

"And *you*," Lask added. *Damn*, this kid had put himself right in harm's way.

"Yes, but they don't know I overheard their conversation."

"What else did they discuss?"

"They wanted to bring this to someone at IES," replied Patch, drawing a slower breath. "Bowman was considering Ranger, but nobody knows who to trust right now, and I thought, well..." Patch's eyes met Lask's for the briefest moment before darting away.

Well, hell. Lask prided himself on judging people from first impressions, but he'd really missed the boat on this one. Experience had taught James Lask to never trust an addict, but there was something about Patch—something in those pleading eyes—that made Lask want to make an exception.

He placed his hand on Patch's shoulder. "You were right to come to me with this. I've known something was off ever since Krakken was appointed, but I haven't been able to put the pieces together. None of the other guys, not even my superiors, seem to notice or care. In fact, they seem almost complicit." Patch raised his eyebrows. "I mean... they don't *know* they're involved, but Krakken is smart, and he's trying to play us all—but it won't work." Lask waited for Patch to nod, then gave his shoulder a squeeze before letting go. "Were you here in time to hear Krakken's speech?"

"No."

"I'll give you the abridged version. One—there will now be a shitload more IES members who can basically just walk into the clan if Krakken wants them to, and two—a small subset of us will be testing out some new sort of weapon built by Harding and his scientists."

"Are you one of the testers?" asked Patch.

"Something tells me that's not gonna happen," responded Lask. "I have a feeling Krakken will be cherry-picking from these new members he essentially smuggled into the clan."

"Shit. What do we do, officer?"

Lask cracked a grin. "Actually, it's *detective*... but you can call me Lask. And I'll tell you what we're gonna do. You sit tight and see if you can drop in on any more secret meetings between Bowman and Maris. Report back to me if you get any new intel. We'll figure this shit out and stop it before a lot of people get hurt."

Patch nodded.

"Look, Patch," started Lask, "I've seen kids pulled through these doors day in and day out, recked out of their minds. For the most part, they're all the same—addicted to the drugs and addicted to escaping. The first couple of times I saw you, I gotta admit that's what I saw, but I was wrong. It's not the drugs that make you tick. It's the drive to be the best, no matter what it takes. I'm right about you, aren't I?"

Patch blushed. "Yes, sir—er, Lask. I mean, I think so."

"You're one of the good ones, and Isotopia is going to need you." said Lask. "Probably sooner than you think."

THE SCIENTISTS / LEN

Not for the first time, Len acknowledged that his days and nights would have been a whole lot easier if he'd chosen a more "traditional" line of inquiry for his clan initiation research project. Despite the not-so-gentle urging of Dr. Adams to explore a topic "within the realm of scientific objectivity"—his clan leader's kind way of directing Len away from the sheer folly of explaining human personality—Len persisted. Curiosity burned within him: what made Len a scientist, Jay a hunter, and his best friend Rayne lose himself along the way? Did any of them, as Youth, truly choose their own paths, or was destiny already written in their DNA?

He had already uncovered preliminary proof of consistent patterns differentiating the "ideal" archetypal brains from each clan. Hunters, for example, were found to have high levels of noradrenaline receptors in their brains, explaining their ability to track prey in the forest. What if scientists were scientists simply because of an excess of certain chemicals that make one seek logic and truth?

Len sat at his desk, occupying his mind with lines of code while his imagination skittered down every disturbing corridor. If his hypothesis was right, if whatever made someone a "fill-in-the-blank" was a purely physical occurrence in the brain, then this new mind helmet could almost surely manipulate the process. What if you could turn a scientist into a healer or a healer into a hunter with a tweak of the helmet? Where might that all lead?

Ever since Len and his buddies reached clan declaration age, it seemed obvious that Hobb would always have a disconnect between what he wanted and what he could achieve, but Hobb's passion had always bridged the gap somehow. Pan's tragic death seemed to have stolen that fire away, leaving Hobb vulnerable and lost.

Look at 'im now. Snatching Isocoins from Koop's merchant stand. Getting recked at work. But the most worrisome and terrifying change was the void of emotion.

Hobb's life was crumbling down around him, and Len didn't have a clue how to intervene without making everything worse. It was a delicate situation, and Len wished he could just focus on his damn project.

THE HEALERS / COLE

Cole's favorite spot in all the explored Isotopian forests was a small clearing surrounded by tall, thick trees. At its center was a fallen jumbo-root log that made for a perfect place to take in the overwhelming beauty of the forest and puff away the troubles on his mind. Since the death of his dear friend and clanmate, those troubles felt bigger and heavier by the day. He took his first hit, lay back, and let the forest envelop him in its warm embrace. For now, he just wanted to forget.

A rustling in the nearby shrubs alerted Cole his short-lived moment of peace was over. The clearing wasn't just Cole's oasis for reflection and tranquility; it was also one of the many spots his customers knew to find him.

Ahh, and here comes one of my quicker success stories. Cole and Patch had made a reckhead junkie out of Rayne Hobb in no time. Deserved it, too, if everything Patch had told him was true, how the kid could've stopped Pan's murder but wasn't man enough.

"Hey, man," called Cole. "Take a seat in my office." Cole patted next to him on the log, and Hobb sat down.

"Whaddaya got there?" asked Hobb, pointing to the herbarette.

"It's bliss leaf. Give it a try." Cole leaned over and passed the rette. Hobb took a drag and got that dumb look on his face like a kid who'd just seen his first pair of naked boobs.

"Shit's amazing, man," said Hobb. "I feel floaty. Much appreciated."

"No problem, my topie." Cole took a look at his smoking buddy and decided to indulge his curiosity: "Hey, Hobb, I know it's a touchy subject and all, but if you don't mind me asking... what was it like being there?"

"Being where?"

"You know..." Cole hesitated. "*There*. When she died." The expression of ecstasy faded from Hobb's face, and his eyes opened wide.

"People always say it all happens so fast, y'know, when describing a near-death experience. Like as soon as the moment passed, it was swept away. But that's the exact opposite of how this went down." Hobb took another drag off the rette before he continued. "Every time I close my eyes, I see it in perfect detail. Like each fraction of a second was branded into my memory. I can't sleep."

"How close were you?"

"I was behind the stand and she was sitting out on the front counter. By the time I realized what was happening, it was over. I should've been quicker, and I should've been braver. I should've been able to protect her."

Cole felt like a pile of shit. "Dude, there was clearly nothing you could do. You can't put that all on your own shoulders. And I owe you an apology because I thought you were just some pussy who left her to save yourself."

"Apparently that's what a lot of people think. I know Patch does. Now the guy hates me, and I've probably lost all hope of ever becoming a hunter."

"Listen, man," said Cole, "Patch and I are tight, so naturally, I believed his version. But you know what I think? I think you were just some dude who found himself in the wrong place at the wrong time. Life is raw and organic and random, and bad shit happens we can't control sometimes. Let me talk to him. I'll straighten it out."

"Really? That would mean a lot to me. Thanks, Cole."

"No problem. Hey, man, did you enjoy that bliss leaf? I'll give you a special discount if you wanna snag a batch."

THE PANEL / CHIEF ADVISOR GRAPER

Sands Graper loved the marketplace, especially at peak hours. Life and energy surged through the crowds as everyone ran their errands or caught up with friends. Outside Merchant Village, this type of intermingling was rare. Clans tended to cluster together and focus on their own tasks; in fact, certain members of the Panel believed that productivity improved when the clans kept to themselves.

This lack of diversity among Isotopians troubled Graper greatly. Isolation reinforced the ongoing hostility between the clans, especially the scientists and healers, and he used his influence as Chief Advisor to try to improve the situation every chance he got.

Graper's old buddy Koop offered him a wide smile and his customary cheerful greeting. "A pleasant good afternoon to you, my friend!"

"And you," Graper answered. "How's business? Are you taking good care of your stand?"

"Oh, don't you worry! I treat my shop like a beautiful woman—gently and passionately." Koop gestured at the young man beside him. "Meet my friend, Rayne Hobb. He's been helping me out the past couple weeks. Hobb, I'm sure this old fella needs no introduction?"

The kid glanced up at Graper with soulless eyes and smiled with the left half of his mouth. "Of course. Honor to meet you, sir." Hobb didn't seem too interested in conversing, which was fine by Graper.

"So, Koop, you know this city like no one else. How

do people seem to be holding up with all this killing?"

"I see some ragged faces and weary gaits, but overall, not too bad. We partially have you to thank for lifting our spirits with that speech a few days ago. I sense people feel comforted by Krakken's promise for more troops on the streets."

Graper was relieved to hear about the well-being of the city; Pan's death had really hit hard. "Glad to hear. And what about you, Koop? How are you these days?"

"To tell you the truth, not so great."

"Oh?"

"I've recently seen good people get themselves into bad things, and it makes me worry that some people just can't recover from emotional trauma." Graper wondered if Koop was referring to the emotionless boy standing next to him. "Plus, I look around at all these new officers surrounding the city, and all I can see are guns. I have this pit in my stomach, like something bad is gonna happen."

"I'm sorry to hear you're feeling this way."

"There's this detective who stops by every so often to keep me company. Really bright guy, wise enough for twice his years. Anyway, he thinks something fishy is going on with Krakken and all this increased security." Koop leaned in and lowered his voice. "I knew Krakken when he was much younger; he was a cunning and violent boy. I think you might consider keeping an eye on him."

Graper truly hadn't given Krakken much consideration, but hearing this warning from his old friend made him queasy. Come to think of it, Bogue had been acting distant ever since Krakken appeared.

"I'll tell you what; I'll watch more closely and intervene if necessary. If that man intends to cause any harm to anyone in this city, it sure as hell won't happen on my watch."

Graper said goodbye to his friend and continued to make his way through the wondrous and thriving marketplace.

THE IES / DETECTIVE LASK

Lask didn't know how or when, but shit was most definitely going down—unless he could prevent it, of course. Everything was changing too quickly with all the new troops and helmet bullshit, and no updates were coming in from Captain Ranger or the sergeants. Lask would need more information to stand a chance.

He surveyed the squad room from his office doorway. He needed someone young, new, and stupid. *Ah, got one.* Lask moved across the room and approached his target.

"Hey, man. Are you one of the people testing out that rad new helmet?"

"Yeah." *Yep—idiot. Let's hope he continues to impress.*

"Oh, perfect. Listen dude, they just threw me into the group today but completely neglected to tell me when and where the training sessions meet. Can you believe that incompetence?" The young guy stared blankly. "Anyway, if you could just fill me in on that, it'd really help me out."

"Yeah, sure man. Eight o'clock in this big-ass field about three miles west of the city border. A bit of a hike, but there's a path through the forest."

"Cool, thanks, man. Anything else I should know?"

"Not much. Other than you do *not* wanna show up late."

"Got it; thanks again. See ya there, buddy."

Lask beamed to himself as he walked back to his office.

THE HUNTERS / JAY

It was hunting time, and Jay's veins pumped battery acid as he desperately tried to keep pace with his crew. Up ahead, barely within shouting distance, Maris and Patch led the charge as always. Zap and Arlo flew through the forest with a level of grace and dexterity that put Jay to shame. *I wish Hobb was here so I wouldn't look like such a pussy.*

Rumor had it Hobb was a mess over Pan's death, blaming himself. Drama wasn't Jay's thing. He felt for his friend, but he'd wait this one out.

"Are you ladies keeping up?"

Jay rolled his eyes at the latest predictable, twice-a-minute check-in from Patch, and refocused on not hyperventilating or tripping on a root. Patch hadn't been this annoying in a while. In fact, Patch seemed to have lost interest these past few weeks in the charming mix of hazing and life lessons he usually enjoyed delivering to Jay and his young hunter companions. Maybe that had something to do with his struggle to keep up with Maris.

Whatever had been bugging Patch seemed to have cleared up; he was back at the top of his game and annoying as ever. *I bet Maris scolded his ass for not showing enough discipline.* Jay managed to crack a smile between his heaving breaths.

Mercifully, the hunters came to a stop. Jay struggled to smooth out his ragged breathing. Any sign of weakness would invite humiliation from Maris and Patch, and as the newest member of the crew, Jay was already their default target.

The crew fell silent as Maris pointed out a pogg hidden in tall reeds up ahead, its snout lowered to drink from a small pond. Zap raised his heat rifle—it was his turn to make the kill—and took aim. The forest stopped. The hunters held their breath and so did the wind; all the animals around them seemed to freeze in their tracks. The pogg turned to look down the barrel of Zap's gun as if challenging him to make the shot. Jay willed his pounding heart to quiet.

Zap pressed the trigger. In a flash, life resumed. A pellet erupted from the chamber, torpedoed toward the pogg's eye, and pierced the center of its pupil. *Apparently, Patch's constant negative reinforcement pays off.* All expression drained from the pogg's face, as if its soul had already left its body.

"Nice shot, Zap!" Arlo slapped his friend on the back.

Maris offered a quiet nod of approval. Even Patch chimed in with, "Sweet kill, man."

Jay needed to say something before his silence became obvious. "Hey, good job!"

Luckily, everyone was too absorbed in Zap's victorious moment to notice Jay's lame compliment—but then, he'd always been a bit of an outsider to the crew. The five of them had been dashing through the forest together every single day with a clear chain of mentorship that allowed everyone to learn from each other. Within the brief time Jay had been a part of the group, he'd witnessed Zap's transformation from a novice to a confident sharpshooter. Through all the hazing and exhaustion, Jay had begun to develop into not only a hunter but a real man, a man who had the skills to kill and cook his own dinner; a man who followed a code instilled in him by his clan; a man who had the fire to be as good as he could be and always sought to be better.

"On this happy note," Maris said, "you are all dismissed for the day."

Patch trailed behind with his younger companions,

offering his "daily dose of wisdom" on the way to the city gates. "All right guys, listen up. That was good shit today from everyone. Obviously, Jay needs to lose a few pounds to keep his ass up with the rest of us, but we are on fire." The guys laughed, and Jay cracked a sheepish grin. "Maris is a great hunter, and you will learn a lot from him, but one thing he will never teach you is how to be a warrior. The man believes in pacifism and balance above all else, and the fact is, that's all we need most of the time. But every once in a while, you come across prey that doesn't go down easy, prey that fights back. And when that happens, it's no longer a hunt—it's a war."

"I appreciate the advice," said Arlo. "Now I know I shouldn't run like a pussy if I encounter some big-ass, never-before-seen creature in the forest."

"Yeah, yeah, I know. It seems dumb to say," replied Patch. "But think about these recent murders and that endless line of IES soldiers walking the streets. All I'm saying is, everything was once jolly and good here in Isotopia, but that doesn't mean it will always be so. If that day comes when Isotopia needs to defend herself, it will be up to us to be at the front lines, leading the strike."

As the pep talk came to an end at the city gates, an IES officer gestured for Patch to follow him.

Has to be the drugs, thought Jay. *That explains the paranoid doomsday speech.*

THE IES / DETECTIVE LASK

"Where are you taking me?" asked Patch as he and Lask marched deeper into the forest. "I'm hungry, man. Are we gonna get back in time for dinner?"

This kid asks a lot of damn questions. Still, in a matter of days, Patch had managed to hop from Lask's shitlist to valued informant. Plus, it wouldn't hurt to have a skilled hunter by his side.

"Your boys Bowman and Maris were right. I figured out where they're holding those training sessions. We're gonna go in there and see what they're up to." *And hopefully you won't screw anything up with your big mouth.* "Should be right up over this hill."

Lask located a tall tree with sturdy branches and good leaf cover, and they climbed to the top. "Here," Lask whispered, nudging Patch with an extra pair of binoculars. "These are for you."

"What are we looking for exactly?"

"Anything that appears shady and dangerous."

"Over there!" Patch pointed toward an open field in the distance. "Definitely shady."

Lask shifted carefully on the branch and trained his binoculars on a cluster of roughly thirty men, some IES but others he didn't recognize, standing in a combat formation. Two smaller-framed men stood off to one side. Everyone wore a helmet.

"The fuck are they doing down there?" asked Patch. "Having a moment of silence?" Patch was right; no one appeared to be saying anything. Definitely odd.

Without notice or warning, the soldiers stepped in perfect sync to form a straight line and lifted their rifles in an eerie unison. Lask panned outward in the direction of the rifle barrels to a row of human-shaped targets standing about fifty feet from the pack, each directly lined up with a soldier. "Looks like target practice," he whispered.

The guns fired simultaneously, producing a single, spectacular *BANG*! Patch lurched forward, clutching the branch just in time to avoid falling out of the tree.

"Whoa!" Lask clasped his hand around Patch's wrist. "Steady there. Y'okay?"

"I'm good," Patch answered. The color had drained from his face, but he was not the type to show weakness. Lask could appreciate that.

With a brief nod, Lask looked through his binoculars again. *Damn*! Every single target had a hole right between the eyes. The soldiers lowered their weapons and eased into a neutral stance.

"Can you explain what the fuck is happening right now? Because I am confused as shit over here," Patch said.

Lask answered, keeping his eyes trained on the activity below. "The soldiers don't need to speak in order to communicate. They must be receiving commands through their helmets somehow." An army with perfect coordination and absolute stealth—not the kind of enemy Lask would ever want to encounter. "We have to figure out what they're saying."

"Well, how 'bout this: we wait till one of the guys steps out to take a piss, beat the crap out of him, and steal his helmet."

"Good idea, genius," retorted Lask, "except the instant we touch the guy, everyone else wearing a helmet will know exactly what happened. Game over."

"Well, I don't hear any ideas from you, *detective*." Patch was a pain in the ass, but he was right. Lask was stumped.

"Keep watching. We need as much information as we can scrape up."

The session seemed to be winding down. The soldiers moved out of formation and filed out of the clearing. On the way out, the soldiers picked up their respective targets and lifted them over their heads. *Damn, those things must weigh twice as much as they do. How are they...?*

Lask desperately surveyed the scene in the little time he had left, picking up as many clues as possible. At this point, even the tiniest detail would be better than what they had—nothing.

"What the—? Is that Maxx Spike over there?" Lask pointed toward a cluster of trees across the way.

"Holy shit, it *is* Maxx. The fuck you think that old healer's doing up here?"

"Probably the same thing we are. Trying to figure out what the hell is going on with those helmets."

"Let's go find out what he knows." Patch handed his binoculars to Lask and clambered down to the ground. Lask followed, and the two of them intercepted Maxx just outside the city gates.

"Mr. Spike, we haven't officially met. I'm Detective James Lask, and this is my associate, Patch."

"Very fine to meet you, detective," Maxx said, returning Lask's handshake before turning a warm smile on the hunter. "Patch, how are you, dear friend?" Maxx took Patch's hand between his own. "We healers used to see a lot more of this fellow when Pan was still around." This comment provoked a few seconds of depressing and awkward silence that felt like an eternity. "Anyway," continued Maxx as he turned back to Lask, "what can I do for you gentlemen?"

"We saw you spying," replied Patch. "We were doing the same from the treetop over there."

"Ah, yes," said Maxx. "This is actually not the first time I've seen them out here. I keep returning to the spot and trying to wrap my head around what's going on, but I haven't figured it out, and I wasn't sure who to go to about it."

"Please, whatever you do, don't go to the IES," said Lask firmly. "All of those soldiers are supposedly my clanmates, and even I have no idea what they're doing. This mystery would be a little easier to crack if the bastards actually talked."

Maxx furrowed his eyebrows. "What do you mean?"

"I mean they're going to be hard to stop if we can't hear them."

"You"—Maxx's confused gaze shifted back and forth between Lask and Patch—"couldn't hear them?"

THE MERCHANTS / KOOP

The city was finally winding down as people retreated home from the Marketplace. Koop and Hobb were closing up shop when three of Koop's good buddies emerged from the forest border.

"Well now," Koop boomed out, his ever-present cheer spreading across his cheeks in a wide grin. "A hunter, a soldier, and a healer! All we need now is a scientist, and we'd have one of everything right here!"

"You're missing a Forgotten," remarked Hobb in a sarcastic tone as he continued boxing up inventory. The group met this comment with uncomfortable laughter.

"It's funny you mention a scientist, because that's exactly why we came to you," Lask said. "We need someone we can trust—and fast."

Koop was intrigued. "What have you fellas gotten yourselves into?"

"You remember we discussed those experimental helmets?" Koop nodded and Lask continued. "We've discovered the soldiers' training ground, or at least one of their sites. Patch and I watched them drill. We thought it was strange we couldn't hear the orders the soldiers were responding to—"

"Which it *was*," Patch cut in.

"Yes," Lask continued, "but not nearly as strange as the fact that Maxx could hear them perfectly."

Koop's eyes widened as he studied Maxx. "I always knew The Guru to have a magical aura, but are you tellin' me this old bonker is a certifiable mind reader?"

"A drug-induced mind reader, to be exact," responded Patch.

"Maxx, here, has been up to his usual shenanigans, mixing herbal cocktails left and right," explained Lask. "One or some combination of all those chemicals he's ingesting must be enabling him to hear at the frequency broadcast through the helmets. Trouble is, there are *so many* drugs involved"—Maxx gave them all a sheepish shrug, which brought a resigned chuckle from Lask—"we have no way of knowing what's what."

"Why not just take the cocktail?" asked Koop.

"Not a great plan to ward off the super-psychic soldiers while recked out of our minds," Lask answered, causing Patch to snort.

"I see your point," Koop said.

"What we really need," Lask continued on a more solemn note, "is a trustworthy scientist to sort through all of Maxx's shit and figure out what's causing the heightened senses. Issue is, the scientists are heavily involved in all this, so we don't know who to approach. That's where you come in, my friend. You know more people than anyone in Isotopia, and I trust your judgment. So, will you help us?"

"Of course," Koop responded. It wasn't every day a merchant was called upon to help the IES with a matter of grave import. "Though I must admit, I've never gone much out of my way to interact with the scientists, Maxx and I being long-time friends and all. I'm not sure how much help I can be, but I'll definitely keep my eyes open."

"Len Krossling," mumbled Hobb.

All eyes turned toward Koop's apprentice. "Did you say something, Rayne?" Koop asked.

"Talk to Len. He's a friend of mine, a new member of the scientist clan. He's a great guy, smart as a whip, too. He'll help you with whatever you need."

Lask and Koop locked eyes. *Could Koop vouch for Hobb?* In the short time Koop had worked with Hobb, the kid had proven himself reliable. Koop gave Lask a nod.

"Perfect. Thanks for the info, man," said Lask. "Tomorrow we'll find this Len and have a talk with him."

"Good plan," said Maxx. "In the meantime, this old man is pretty burnt out from the day's herbal activities. Time to head home."

"Sounds like an excellent idea," Lask answered. "Patch, I'll be in touch."

Lask and Maxx broke away from the group, and Koop turned back to his daily sales tally when Patch's voice stopped him cold.

"Hey, Hobb."

Rayne's head snapped up, eyes wide and frightened. "Yeah?"

Oh, hell no. Koop stepped to Rayne's side, fully prepared to tell Patch where he could stick his aggressive bullshit.

Ignoring Koop's death glare, Patch plowed ahead, his tone oddly devoid of its usual conceit. "Listen, forget about what I said to you that day—after Pan died. I was just pissed and took it out on you. It wasn't your fault." Koop felt the tension seep out of Rayne like a tire that had just picked up a nail. "And I remember Pan telling me how badly you wanted to be a hunter. In fact, your buddy Jay is in my hunting group, and that kid won't shut up about how ambitious you are. So just keep working at it, okay?"

Hobb looked up with the expression of a man risen from the dead. "That means a lot to me, Patch. Thank you."

THE SCIENTISTS / LEN

The sun still shone bright in the sky, but Len could barely keep his eyes open. Generally speaking, most scientists did not sleep well, what with questions and possible solutions rolling around in their heads all night. The further Len delved into his work, the more trouble he'd had falling and staying asleep.

His initial hypothesis had turned into a beast of a project. If we really are born as certain archetypes due to slight variations in our brains, how far can that concept be stretched? Are our moods and thoughts, and even our behaviors, controlled moment to moment simply by fluctuations in neurochemicals? The questions flooded his brain more and more every day. The implications were almost too huge to contemplate.

Len's thoughts were disrupted by three strangers barging into his office. He jumped to his feet, fully alert now. There was at least one murderer on the loose in Isotopia, and Len didn't like his odds.

"Hello, can I help you?"

"We needed to consult a chemistry expert. You came highly recommended by your friend Hobb," one of them replied.

My friend Hobb. Len held back a frustrated sigh. Was Hobb high when he sent these people? Did he give a shit that Len had *real work* to do? "Mind if I ask who you folks are?"

A man in an IES uniform nudged the first guy out of the way. "Forgive my friend Patch, here; his manners are a little rough." Patch harrumphed and rolled his eyes. "I'm Detective Lask, and this is Maxx Spike."

Maxx Spike, in the flesh. Not just *a* healer, *the* healer. Len could hardly believe the Old Guru was standing right here in his office, requesting a favor of a *scientist*.

"Look, Len," the detective said, "I'm going to get right to the point."

"Please," Len replied. *I have a deadline to meet.*

"It appears that those helmets coming out of your shop are being used for something that is most likely really dangerous for Isotopia."

Patch cut in. "We have reason to believe some of your scientist friends are involved—likely the ones who were heavily involved in the process of developing the helmet."

Cam. So Len's suspicions were true. "I really hope you guys figure out what's going on and stop them as soon as possible," said Len, his stomach tied in knots. "Every day, my research shows me how truly powerful that helmet can be, and you can bet that if I know its capabilities, Cam definitely knows. Do not underestimate that kid."

"Well, how fast we can stop them may be up to you, Len," replied Lask. "The helmets seem to allow the soldiers to communicate without talking." Len nodded. *Tip of the iceberg, fellas.* "Thing is, we, uh, stumbled upon an alternative means of access."

"Into the helmet network?" Len asked. "But it's a closed system. How did you—?"

Lask and Patch both turned to face Maxx, who gave Len a sly wink as he dropped the bomb. "Psychoactive herbs."

"You have got to be shitting me," Len said. Leave it to the healers to slip in through the back door.

"Nope." Maxx pulled a clear packet of chopped herbs and roots from his pocket and dangled it in front of Len. "Somewhere in this concoction is a chemical that modulates auditory processing to an extent that was previously *unheard* of." The Guru's horrid attempt at a joke was met with absolute silence.

Lask sighed loudly and regained control of the conversation. "We need to isolate that chemical. That's where you come in."

Len grabbed the pack of herbs and took a cursory look. "Holy hell! Talk about looking for a needle in a haystack."

"Can you do it?" Patch pressed.

Zero patience. Aggressive. Direct. *Hunter*, Len guessed.

"You guys gotta give me some time."

"How much time?" Lask asked.

"I'll have to get back to you, Detective."

Lask looked like he wanted to object. *Not a man accustomed to waiting for others to get things done but wise enough to know when pushing won't help.* "One more thing," said Lask. "See if you can get any information out of your friends. Even the smallest tidbit might be of use."

"I'll see what I can do," Len promised.

His visitors thanked him and left Len to his endless mountain of work. The only good news was that he could probably synthesize a year's worth of stim leaf from the bag sitting in his lap.

THE PANEL / CHIEF ADVISOR GRAPER

Another Panel meeting, repeats of the same bland promises from the clan reps, more of the tiresome, inevitable head-bumping between Scientists and Healers. Graper was beyond weary; he was worried.

He'd noticed a shift in his talks with Bogue. They were no longer the passionate, post-election discussions the two of them used to have about how to make Isotopia great. Lately, their conversations felt curt and empty, and Bogue always had somewhere to rush off to. In fact, an undercurrent of tension seemed to be picking up strength ever since the new IES Rep William Krakken had joined the Panel. After a week of trying to read between the lines at the committee meetings, Graper still had nothing.

He glanced around the conference room at the faces of his peers, the same people who'd worked every day to make Isotopia safe and productive, feeling as if he didn't know whom to trust. If something really was going on with Bogue and Krakken, others could easily be involved. Anyone could be an enemy.

His gaze landed on an old friend, Mason Harding. Their friendship had begun on shaky ground, given that Graper started in the healing clan before moving up to his role as Chief Advisor. And yet, despite the animosity between the scientists and the healers, Graper and Harding's friendship persevered. They'd met for the occasional lunch during the Marketplace rush. Sure, Harding could be an insensitive prick, but he was the smartest guy Graper knew. More importantly, Graper had always trusted Harding to be his voice of reason.

"If you've nothing to add, Sands?"

"Hmm?" Graper's attention snapped to Chairperson Issler, whose cold stare reminded Graper of being called on in class when his mind had wandered off. "No, nothing."

"Then, we are dismissed," she said.

Graper jumped up quickly and caught up to Harding. "My friend, can you spare a minute?"

Harding spun at the hand on his shoulder. "Uh, of course! How have you been, Sands?"

Graper checked to make sure no one was in eavesdropping range. "Honestly, a little uneasy."

"Oh, really? And why is that?" Harding seemed distracted.

"I've been hearing some scary rumors. They're probably garbage but worrisome nonetheless. Have you seen or heard anything suspicious lately? Possibly regarding, say, Bogue or Krakken?"

"Hmm. I don't think so." Tiny beads of sweat gathered along Harding's forehead. "Although now that you mention it, I guess Nat has been acting odd."

"Nat? Odd *how*?"

"Don't you think she's strangely apathetic about the murders? Especially considering she lost one of her beloved healers?"

Nat Corper was anything but apathetic. Graper searched his recollections for anything that matched up with Harding's comments, but all that came to mind was the bickering between Corper and Harding at the last meeting. The conflict between healers and scientists was hardly new, but it was enough to stir an uneasy feeling like a gathering storm in Graper's belly.

"Hmm, I suppose Nat could be more upset than she's letting on," Graper said cautiously.

Harding shook his head. "I think there may be something more behind it."

Huh. Why was Harding working so hard to throw Graper off Bogue and Krakken's scent? If Harding really hadn't noticed anything lately, wouldn't he have just said so? The bastard knew something, and he was hiding it at all cost.

"Sands? Are you all right?" Harding's beady eyes were laser-focused on Graper's every twitch and the quake of his hands. Graper wouldn't have been surprised if Harding could see his heart beating right through his shirt.

"I'm fine." That was twice Graper's mind had taken a hike and twice he'd been caught. "You know, I must be imagining things. Comes with the territory when you get to be our age, right?"

The men shared a fake laugh that convinced neither.

"Get some sleep, Sands," said Harding. "You'll feel better in the morning."

THE YOUTH / RAYNE HOBB

Near the center of the Healers' village, situated next to a waterfall feeding into a quiet spring, there stood a small, unassuming building known as the Mind Spa. The facility had a solid reputation for delivering the type of help Hobb needed, not that he'd ever looked for that help before today.

For the first time in weeks, Hobb was starting to feel better. Patch's apology, if you could call it that, had eased Hobb back into studying for his clan exams. When Koop noticed his progress, he encouraged Hobb to take advantage of his improved mental state and do everything in his power to promote the healing process. Hence, the stare-down with the slogan at the front entrance: "There is no such thing as a typical case." Hobb supposed the motto was meant to instill confidence. It didn't—not even with the cheery daisies-and-sunshine mural in the background.

He hesitated for a second to listen to his instinct—*this place is full of shit*—but shook off his doubt and moved through the doorway. He'd promised himself he would give it an honest try.

Hobb crept toward the front desk where a girl about his age was frantically thumbing through reports and spinning around in her swivel chair to ask questions of the colleagues surrounding her. She smiled without looking up. "How can I help you?"

"Uh... my name is Hobb... Rayne Hobb... and I was just wondering if I could schedule an appointment to talk to someone."

"You a new patient?"

"Yes."

"All right," responded the girl, reaching for a small stack of papers. "Fill these out, and in the meantime, I'll see who's available."

"Thank you."

Hobb sat down with his shitload of paperwork. Most of it turned out to be putting a checkmark next to "NO" for about fifty redundant questions per page.

Have I ever felt suicidal? No.

Have I ever felt the strong urge to hurt a friend or coworker? No.

Hobb was beginning to wonder if he should even be there. After all, he was really just a healthy kid going through a rough patch.

Have I ever stolen from my family or friends? Eh, technically, not really...

He turned in his paperwork and stared at the wall for a while until the girl at the front desk finally called him up. "Dr. Balter has an opening now if you'd like to see him."

Hobb shrugged and followed her through a maze of hallways to a door marked *Ash Balter.*

"Here we are," said the girl. She knocked lightly on the door and skittered away.

The knob slowly turned, and the heavy door made a screeching sound as it gradually opened, giving way to a large, dark-skinned man with glasses, a beard, and a kind face. "Rayne Hobb is it? Nice to meet you. You can call me Ash."

"Nice to meet you, too."

Hobb made a quick survey of the room. The walls, painted a green as vibrant as the spring leaves of the forest, were lined with photographs. A gallery of family photos filled one entire section; the rest were either group photos of healers or artistic close-ups of herbal concoctions.

Hobb caught a glimpse of Pan in one of the pictures, and a chill shot down his spine, snapping him back into the moment. He took a seat where Ash indicated, and the doctor sat across from him in a chair way too small for his frame.

"So, Rayne, what brings you here today?"

The question flustered him—not that he hadn't expected it, but Hobb's negative emotions felt like they were in the past. In fact, the more Hobb thought about it, the more okay he felt, making him wonder once more what the hell he was doing there.

"Well, *today* I actually don't feel bad, but I've had a rough month."

"Were there certain things that happened to cause your rough month?"

Hobb glanced at the picture again, and an ache rose in his chest. "It started when Pan died."

Ash's face fell; of course, Pan's death would have hit him hard as well. "Pan was such a sweet girl. A true angel of Isotopia who lit up the lives of everyone she knew. I can understand why things have been tough for you. There has been a lingering feeling of grief among all of the healers since we lost her, one that will never fully go away."

"I was with her when it happened," Hobb said. Ash said nothing and didn't seem particularly surprised by Hobb's confession. "The murderer was hidden in the darkness of the night, and I didn't see him until he already had his arm around Pan's neck. He ordered me not to move, but even if I had, there was no possible way to leap over the stand and intervene. It was too late."

"I'm sorry. That's a terrible thing to have to carry with you," Ash said quietly.

"It didn't help that Patch flipped out on me the next day."

"Oh! I recall witnessing some kind of nasty encounter that following morning. What was that all about?"

"Apparently, this hotshot hunter, Patch, had feelings for Pan."

"I see."

"Yeah." Hobb sighed. "And he blamed me for her death, so he cursed me out and told me I would never be a hunter." Shame washed over him again, and Hobb had to look away from the doctor.

"This Patch's opinion matters to you," Ash noted gently.

"I've wanted to be a hunter for as long as I can remember. So yeah, Patch was somewhat of a role model, I guess."

"That must have hurt, having your dreams shaken like that."

Hobb risked a glance at Ash and was met by a kind expression that encouraged Hobb to open up. "I didn't take it well. I shut down so I couldn't feel the pain, but I ended up not feeling anything but hollow inside." *Should I tell him about the Nectar?* There was a very real chance Ash would turn him away if he learned that Hobb had abused drugs. He decided to skip that part. "Patch and I kind of worked things out recently. I've actually started studying for my hunter clan exams again."

"Well, that's great! It sounds like you're already on the road to recovery. It's a very good sign you've returned to activities you're passionate about. So other than that, how have you been feeling?"

"I think Pan left some sort of hole in me that I can't fill no matter what I do. It's hard to focus. On top of that, I'm stuck working as a merchant assistant until I can get into the hunter clan or the IES, so life is incredibly boring. The worst part is that while I'm stuck behind that stand, my friends are off in their new exciting clans. My buddy Jay is a hunter, and my best friend Len is a scientist." The memory of the painful conversation with Len brought a lump to Hobb's throat. "Len is a really good guy, and he's going to be a top scientist one day, but we haven't talked recently."

"Why is that?" asked Ash.

"I sort of alienated him the last time we saw each

other."

"What happened?"

Hobb's insides churned as he realized how horribly he had acted. At the same time, he wasn't ready to tell this man he'd just met about the fight over the drugs and stealing. "He noticed I was off and tried to help. I pushed him away."

"There are times when we all need space. What happened between you and your friend is perfectly natural. That said, you're clearly hurting, and I think you might feel a whole lot better if you and Len were able to clear the air."

"You're right. I'll do that this week."

"Perfect—we've already established your first homework assignment. You sound as though you're on the right track with the studying and your day job; both of those will keep you moving in the right direction. Now, as for your fatigue and inability to concentrate..." Ash turned around and rifled through his drawers. "I can give you a mild medicinal herb combo to help with that." He set a bottle on the desk. "This is called Afternoon Delight. One capsule in the morning will keep you up and alert through the entire workday. The hope is, you save your dozing for nighttime. I think we should start you on this and see how it goes."

The meeting was over. They scheduled an appointment for next week to follow up. Hobb left the office feeling hopeful and relieved.

THE SCIENTISTS / LEN

Lask knocked this time before bursting into Len's lab with Patch and Maxx Spike.

"I'm glad you're here," Len said.

Lask strode over to Len's desk. "You sorted out the chemicals?"

"Before we get to that," replied Len, "I need to run something by you."

"What's that?" Lask asked.

"I haven't been able to locate the two scientists responsible for the helmets. Cam, I can understand; he's out in the field, training the soldiers. But Nap... I don't get it. I've spoken to every scientist I could find, and *nobody* has seen the kid for days. I even asked Dr. Adams—"

"Adams? Who's that?" Patch interrupted.

"He's our clan head. All he said was, 'I don't know, but you can tell your friend he's in some serious shit for missing all this lab time.'"

All eyes turned to Lask as he processed the new information. "Sounds like whoever these people are, they needed Nap out of the way."

"You think they *killed* him?" Patch asked. Not the most delicate guy Len had ever met, but if Len was honest, he'd been thinking along the same lines himself.

"Anything is possible," replied Lask.

Len's gut twisted. "So, what do we do now?"

"Well, it's going to be a bit of a balancing act," said Lask. "We want to find out what happened to Nap, but we don't want to raise any red flags. If word gets out that we're investigating the disappearance of a young scientist, panic levels in the city will spiral out of control. Len, obviously you have the best access to the inner workings of your clan. Keep your ear to the ground," Lask said, turning to Maxx and Patch. "The three of us will continue to monitor the training sessions for any intel we can pick up."

Lask paused and took a deep breath. "Gentlemen, what's developing here is a race between the good guys and the bad guys. We need to figure out their plan and stop it before they destroy Isotopia. Thing is, our side is basically just the four of us plus a couple extras like ol' Koop. We have no idea how many are in with Bogue and Krakken, especially within the scientist clan. We also don't know if the helmet soldiers are aware they're training for some kind of revolution. Either way, our enemy is formidable. If we're to have any chance of beating them, we'll need our own army. Hopefully, Len will have the chemicals analyzed soon. That may just give us the leg up we need."

Patch fired back at Lask. "Are you suggesting we just unload this information on a bunch of random people and hope for the best? Do you understand what could happen if our suspicions make it to even *one* person who's connected to the wrong side of this?"

"You're right, Patch," replied Lask calmly. "Our situation is far from ideal, but our time and our options are severely limited. And no, I'm not saying we rely on random citizens."

All things considered, Len agreed with Lask. If Bogue's plan turned out to be as scary as they feared, a preemptive strike might be their only option.

"Assuming you're right, Detective," Len cut in, "who *do* we tell?"

Lask gave him a somber nod. "Only the people you trust *completely*. One degree of separation *maximum*, only best friends and clanmates who could be of help. As we start widening our circle to recruit friends of friends, we'll have to be prepared for anything."

"Good luck preparing against whatever it is those helmets can do," said Patch, as if the group needed reminding of that dreaded detail.

"True," agreed Lask, "but if Maxx and Len, here, can isolate and mass produce the right herbs, we could give almost anyone the ability to fight for the cause—which brings me back to where we started. Len, have you worked out the chemistry?"

"I believe the soldiers are essentially sending and transmitting signals by transferring them through the helmets at sound wave frequencies outside the typical human range, like channels on a walkie-talkie. My original hypothesis was that whatever Mr. Spike ingested amplified his auditory capability to detect those frequencies, which would explain why he could hear the soldiers' thoughts but not vice-versa. Since he wasn't wearing a helmet, he wasn't transmitting a signal.

"So, I basically ingested small doses of each chemical on its own, then struck a tuning fork at a frequency lower and higher than the typical human range. I figured once I hit upon the right compound, I'd hear something. A bit oversimplified but given the time constraints..."

Patch cracked up. "You, sir, are a brave soul for trying all the drugs Maxx takes. Or maybe just incredibly stupid."

Len shrugged. "Everyone thinks science is about methodical genius, but sometimes, it's just about having the balls to ingest a ton of psychoactive drugs."

"So, what happened in your little experiment?" asked Lask, growing more impatient by the moment.

"I actually isolated the substance that worked!" Len's hands shook as he pulled a leaf out of the sack Maxx Spike had left with him. "Tell me about this one, Mr. Spike."

"Please—call me Maxx," he said, chuckling as he studied the leaf between his fingers. "This, gentlemen, is called crimson leaf, and it happens to be one of the most plentiful plants in the forest. Crazy that out of all possible herbs, *this* would be the one that grants superpowers."

This was precisely the type of discovery that made Len believe anything was possible in Isotopia. The healers would have had no reason to explore the effects of crimson leaf beyond the psychoactive qualities they were after, and the scientists had no reason to study the leaf at all prior to Maxx's accidental discovery.

"So, we can listen in now!" Patch, as usual, had leapt ahead.

"Even so," replied Maxx, "everything I've heard so far was focused strictly on the drills. There was no talk about any large-scale plan."

"It's quite possible that using this leaf won't bring us any new information," noted Lask, "but we have to try if there's even the smallest chance."

Patch grinned. "Are you saying you're going to take drugs, detective?"

"There's a first time for everything, I suppose," Lask answered. "Let's meet at the city gate at eight tonight."

"Time to put these power-hungry assholes in their place," Patch replied with a fist pump.

Adrenaline buzzed through Len's veins. It was almost too much for his delicate system.

THE SCIENTISTS / CAM DIMLAN

Life had taken a definite swing in the right direction for Cam Dimlan. The helmet program was progressing more quickly than anyone had imagined, and Cam was the star of the show. Soon, he'd be running the place—Commander of Isotopia—and its citizens would be his slaves. The thought quickened his steps to the training field.

But Cam was no fool. He had a back-up plan stashed away, a secret helmet, specially customized to be more powerful than any of the others—just in case.

"Cam!" shouted a distant voice.

He spun around to find his Panel Rep jogging toward him. Cam waved to Dr. Harding and waited for the man to close the gap. "Evening, sir."

Harding bent to catch his breath, hands on his knees. "You're doing good work, son," Harding said, when he could finally speak. "Without you, none of this would be possible."

"Thank you, sir. Sometimes I feel bad about what happened to Nap," said Cam, with no attempt to conceal his bald-faced lie.

"Don't worry about it, Cameron," said Harding. "It's no one's fault, and I'm sorry you lost your friend. But it had to be done—you know that."

"Of course."

The two continued on for several minutes in chilling silence before Harding sparked another conversation. "So, tell me, Cam. What's your angle?"

"Sir?"

"Come on. Why are you in on this?"

He'd caught Cam off guard. Harding wasn't known to have deep personal conversations, and his questions felt like a fishing expedition in choppy waters. Cam gathered his thoughts and regained his footing before answering.

"I want to be the brains behind the revolution. I want everyone to remember what we did together. What *I* did." He couldn't tell whether he'd given Harding the answer he wanted, but he'd given him the truth.

"I like you, kid," said Harding. "You know when it's time to make your move and take things to the next level. Most importantly, you don't let emotions cloud your judgment."

Cam felt an actual stir in his pants. Did Harding just *praise* him? "Thank you, sir," he answered. *That's one step closer to the top.*

The two men swept aside the tall grasses in their path and entered the training ground. A new, dangerous question popped into Cam's head: *Could I be a better Panel Rep than Harding?*

THE IES / DETECTIVE LASK

Detective Lask didn't hate how he felt right now, and he wasn't sure that was a good thing. He shimmied up the tree in what felt like record time, but that might have been the crimson leaf talking. Maxx and Patch seemed to be taking it all in stride. *Practice makes perfect.*

As the crew settled in among the branches, Lask picked up the faint sound of radio static. "Hey, do you guys hear that?" he whispered.

Maxx nodded, a knowing grin spread across his face.

The static gave way to chanting: "Left! Left! Left, right, left!" Lask felt the presence of a large group seconds after he'd heard their unspoken communications.

"This is insane," said Patch. "I gotta hang out with you more, Maxx. I would kill to experience your lifestyle, even if just for a day."

The soldiers filed into the clearing and followed the simple battle orders broadcast through the helmets. It didn't take long for Lask's patience to wear thin.

"Maxx, is this all there is? Just these boring movement commands?"

"Pretty much. I couldn't even tell you if the helmet soldiers know what they're doing here."

"Well, let's hope they 'think' about something juicy this time," replied Patch.

The group halted their conversation as an unfamiliar figure entered the scene along with the two civilians Lask had noticed last time. *A woman*, Lask deduced, though she wore a long cloak and a pogg-hide hood that fell over her eyes. "You've seen her here before, Maxx?" asked Lask.

"Can't say I have," Maxx answered.

The woman stepped in front of the civilians and lifted her hood. A collective gasp arose from the lines of soldiers as they recognized their chairperson.

Bogue Issler. Here!

The soldiers removed their helmets and saluted in perfect synchronicity. Enthusiastic applause ramped up among the men. Lask's stomach dropped like a sack of bricks thrown off a tall building.

"Thank you. Thank you," said Bogue to her audience.

Lask rolled his eyes. "So much for the crimson leaf."

"Well, detective," started Patch, "if you're ever looking for something more interesting, I'd be happy to hook you up. Just say the word."

"Cute," replied Lask.

Lask and the others fell silent once Bogue started speaking. "These two scientists tell me that the progress of this group has been superb so far. I wanted to see all this for myself and to thank you personally for your time and effort in this endeavor. Due to your stellar performance, we should be ready for action in a matter of weeks." The soldiers gave themselves a round of applause at Issler's request.

"That's all you need to hear from me," she continued. "When it's time for the rollout, General William Krakken will take over as your commander. He is the best military mastermind you will ever work with, so consider it a privilege to serve. Please, Dr. Harding and Mr. Dimlan, resume business as usual."

Issler pulled the hood over her head and filed away. There was nothing of interest shared after her departure, and it seemed unlikely that any future monitoring of the helmet chatter would produce anything significant.

THE PANEL / SCIENCE REP HARDING

Sands Graper's questions weighed heavily on Harding. He wanted to confide in Bogue, but what if he'd misread the situation? Casting doubt on her Chief Advisor could be political suicide—or worse. People were disappearing, and Harding didn't want to be next.

He listened intently during the Panel meeting, paying close attention to the dynamic between Bogue and Sands. By the end of the meeting, Harding had made up his mind. He waited for the crowd to thin out before sidling in close to Bogue—not an enviable position, but confidentiality was critical.

"We may have a slight problem, ma'am."

"Oh?" She spun around, bringing her mutilated face inches from his. Harding fought off the instinct to recoil. Bogue hated weakness. "And what would that be, Dr. Harding?"

He'd gone too far to turn back now. "After our last Panel meeting, Sands and I had this… weird moment. He started to ask me about some rumors he'd heard but stopped himself."

Bogue's mouth tightened into a scowl. "I've known Graper for a long time. He's a smart man, and it's not good he's suspicious."

"I tried to put him on Corper, but I don't think he bought it."

Bogue barely hesitated. "We're going to have to get him out of the way."

"Graper is a good man. We can't just—"

115

"We can, and we will," interrupted Bogue with an ice-cold hiss. "We've come too far to be brought down by a single man."

This was ultimately Bogue's decision, and she clearly had made up her mind. "What do we do?"

"This needs to be done the right way. It has to be untraceable—we don't need to rouse any further suspicion at this point. We'll need to be patient. I'll have Krakken put his best man on it. Was there anything else?"

"Hmm? Uh, no, ma'am. Have a pleasant night."

THE YOUTH / RAYNE HOBB

It was lunch break, and Hobb had decided to try out Dr. Balter's advice and make things right with Len. Hobb gripped the doorknob outside Len's lab, took a deep breath, and creaked the door open.

Len was at his desk, back to Hobb, focused intently on his computer screen.

"Hey, Len," Hobb said softly.

His friend turned around and beamed as if all was already forgiven. "Good to see you, man."

"Yeah, same." Hobb was leaking sweat from every pore.

"How've you been?" Len caught Hobb's gaze and held it for a beat too long.

Hobb couldn't blame Len for checking to see if he was rekked again. He debated telling Len about Dr. Balter and the Mind Spa, that he was getting help and working hard at it... but there were other, more important things he needed to say first.

"I'm okay... I just..." *Say it already!* "I apologize, Len. I was a dick to you for no reason. I shouldn't have dismissed you like that."

"Eh, don't worry about it."

"Just like that?"

Len laughed. "Life just gets too hard to handle sometimes. It happens to all of us."

Hobb released a long breath and finally felt his chest unclench. "So, how's your research project going?" Hobb peered over his friend's shoulder to see what he was up to.

"I wish I could tell you about some genius breakthrough I've made in my work, but for now, all that's on the back burner—thanks to those men you sent to see me."

"Sorry about that, too—"

"Don't be," Len assured him.

"You're really not mad? About any of it?"

"Course not. I'm glad you're back so I can tell you what's been going on. I swear, if I had to keep all this to myself much longer, I would probably explode."

"*Damn*," said Hobb. "What is it?"

Len got up out of his chair and grabbed his hat. "Not in here." The two buddies walked outside to find a place to talk.

THE HUNTERS / PATCH

The words had been rolling around in Patch's head all morning, but they weren't coming together any easier, and he was fresh out of time. The squad would be tracking their next target any minute now.

"Maris?" The veteran turned his head and Patch continued. "There's something I need to tell you"—Patch jutted his chin toward the younger hunters resting on the log—"in private." Maris followed Patch out of hearing range from the others.

"You don't look too good," said Maris.

"Yeah, well you see... there's this thing I know about that I know I'm not supposed to know about... and now that I think about it, I probably should've let you know earlier that I know what you know about."

Maris gave Patch a blank stare. "Kid, I've got absolutely no idea what you're trying to say."

"Well, sir, I hadn't really planned out the phrasing."

"How about anything that's not complete gibberish?"

"Okay, okay. Let me just spit it out." Patch let out a deep breath. "I overheard you talking with Rep Bowman the other day. I know what's going on." He paused. "Well, I know as much as anyone else what's going on."

Maris put his palm to his forehead and looked up at the sky as if it were to blame. "You weren't supposed to hear any of that. And what the hell do you mean by 'anyone else'? Have you had the nerve and shortsightedness to tell *other people*? You know nobody can be trusted."

"Sir, that isn't true. I went discreetly to someone in the

IES I know I can trust. And we have a couple other people helping us, too, who are just as trustworthy—a scientist and a healer. It's a solid group, sir, and we've learned a little more about what's going on."

"Oh yeah?" said Maris. His voice was still dialed up, and he took a breath before continuing. "What did you and your spy friends find out?"

"We know where they train. We know the potential enemy is a group of IES soldiers with some 'super helmets' the scientists created. And we also got confirmation last night that Chairperson *Scarface* is at the top of it all, along with Krakken and Harding."

Maris sighed. "You're right. You should've told me sooner."

"I know, sir. You're right, and I'm sorry. But I don't think it will be long before these soldiers do whatever they're gonna do, so we need to stick together and think of whatever we can to stop them."

Maris shook his head. "All these young leaders these days. None of them like the world the way it is, and they'll do whatever they think is necessary to 'fix' it. To be frank, I'm surprised we've gotten so far without any major incidents. Even an optimist like me knows some sort of violence is overdue."

"So, what's our role as hunters?" asked Patch. "What are our orders, boss?"

Maris stared off into the distance. "If at some point the IES can no longer defend Isotopia, then it becomes our duty to protect the citizens. We have to hunt down our enemies like poggs racing through the forest."

"At least we know who our enemies are," replied Patch. "The real trouble seems to be the helmet soldiers. One of the scientists told us that the helmets had the potential to significantly enhance humans, both mentally and physically. If the soldiers realize that potential, there could be real trouble."

"You and your friends don't have the bandwidth to

handle this on your own."

"What do you suggest?" said Patch.

"First, I fill in Bowman on all this new intel, so maybe he can penetrate the defenses Bogue and her followers have put up. Second, we need more intel gatherers. Tell only the guys you can trust. Have them talk to any of their friends in the other clans and report back to you. We're going to be on top of this every step of the way. You did right bringing this to me, Patch."

Patch grinned as he realized he was wrong about Maris. He was a warrior after all.

THE PANEL / CHIEF ADVISOR GRAPER

Chief Advisor Graper's heart pounded through his chest as he paced back and forth on his shiny marsh-wood floor. Harding was one of the bad guys; even worse, Harding knew that Graper was onto him. What started out awkward was now lethal.

Graper had to act quickly, aggressively, and relentlessly even if it earned him more enemies. But where to start? Graper had no clue how pervasive this uprising was or if there was anyone left he could trust. His engagement with Harding had proved that much.

Hell, maybe Harding wouldn't have been a good choice under any circumstances. There was no denying Harding's bias against healers even if Graper wanted to give the man he used to regard as a friend the benefit of the doubt. Friendship could transcend flaws, Graper had always believed. It was a smack in the face to realize how wrong he'd been.

Surely, there must be one Panel member I can confide in? Healer Rep Corper popped into Graper's mind. Nat had been a healer for almost her entire life. She might not be privy to the details of the unfolding drama, but Graper could be fairly certain she would not betray a fellow healer.

At this hour, Corper was likely to be home, unwinding with a cup of bliss leaf tea after a long day's work. Graper grinned, walked over to a drawer in the back corner of his bedroom, and opened it, revealing a dust-covered bag of raw bliss leaf. *Just in case she's running low.* Graper wasn't going to miss this opportunity to live like a healer again.

He grabbed his wind cloak and raced out the door.

The fastest route to Corper's home involved a cut-through of the "abandoned"—a flowery term for "filled with Forgotten and creepy as hell"—South City Park. Over recent years, the Park had transformed into a repository for Isotopia's outcasts, who roamed the park like zombies, provoking rumors that the place was haunted. The Youth would test their bravery by seeing how far they could venture into "Forgotten Island" without running out screaming. Activists sometimes gathered by the entrance to "expose the atrocity of the pitfalls of the modern clan system," but even they were afraid to help these humans discarded like so much trash. What if one of them had a gun?

Graper hesitated when he reached the border, but walking around the park would require more time than he had tonight. He took a deep breath, then stepped into the cold abyss. True to Isotopian lore, a sinister blackness sucked out the meager light of the moon and stars.

This place was truly an abomination, and of course, Sands wished it didn't have to be so, but it would have been naïve not to acknowledge its necessity—and Sands Graper did not have the luxury of naïveté. Given the imperfections of human nature, someone had to take the fall. Forgotten Island was the unfortunate price Isotopia had to pay to enable the freedom and autonomy of its clan system; the city's Forgotten thieves, murderers and madmen were, at the same time, her unsung heroes.

Everyone knew Graper's immovable stance on the issue. Year after year, enough Isotopians agreed with him to continue voting him into office. But so, too, was Bogue Issler elected, and she most definitely did not share Graper's views. After their first violent disagreement on the subject, she'd dragged him here, to this very park, and ordered him to "see what he'd done." The truth was, most Forgotten started out just like Sands, Bogue, and everyone else in this world. Through an all-too familiar pattern of failed clan exams, their lives spiraled downward, and the pain-numbing herbal mixtures only added to the feelings of worthlessness. One by one, loved ones and friends would pull away, until the Youth (or sometimes older) finally accepted the streets of Isotopia as their home.

If it troubled Sands that the Forgotten couldn't vote, he assured himself that the majority—and lifeblood—of Isotopia decided what was ultimately for the greatest good. The clan system enjoyed such popularity among the Panel and the citizens of Isotopia, not even the Chairperson could change it. Hence, the sweeping of the Forgotten under the rug, and on Graper's good days, off his conscience.

A small radius of light highlighted the stagnated green ground below Graper as if lit from above, but all else was dark and quiet. He'd expected the usual assortment of nearly-starved, dirty individuals spanning all ages, all of whom wanted "just a couple Isocoins, brother" to get back on track, some making their "requests" while waving around a knife or a shard of a shattered Nectar bottle. The most depressing part was that none of them ever would get out of this shit hole. This is all they would be— zombies, lusting for spare coins or a cheap reck session until they rotted away in this very park. It wasn't uncommon for a week-old corpse to be detected by an unsuspecting citizen halfway across the city due to the stench of dried blood and decaying human innards.

He stopped and looked around through squinted eyes. *Where is everyone?* Normally, a passerby would have to watch his every step to make sure he didn't trample one of the Forgotten. It was especially bad for Graper when someone recognized him. Those encounters would haunt his nightmares and jar him awake in a cold sweat, panting for air. Grateful for the lack of contact, he was nonetheless even more spooked by the eerie emptiness of the place. Graper picked up the pace until Nat's house came into view.

He arranged a smile on his face, shoved the "Forgotten issue" from his mind, and rang the doorbell. It wasn't until the door creaked open to a soaking wet, towel-clad Corper that Graper realized he probably should have called first.

"Sands?" Concern clouded her face, where Graper strained to hold his focus.

If only he didn't remember what lay beneath that towel. *Keep your mind on the task at hand.* "Hi, Nat. Look, I'm sorry to just show up like this..."

"Come in," she said, stepping behind the door as she pulled it open for him. "Let me go throw on some clothes."

Graper walked into the main room through the once-familiar main hall, a passage lined with some of the rarest and most beautiful woods from the forests of Isotopia. Graper had always appreciated that Nat had built her own home, an expression of herself to the outside world. You could know someone instantly by walking into the space—though Graper never could make much sense of the art Nat chose to hang on her walls.

His gaze landed on an object in the back corner of the room—a picture that made his heart lurch: the young Healers, Sands and Nat, wearing a pair of smiles that jumped out of the frame. Eyes slightly glazed over from the fat bliss leaf herbarette in Graper's hand and Nat's fingertips grazing his cheek. Graper had the very same picture in his nightstand drawer, and some nights when he couldn't sleep, he would take it out and reminisce.

As hoped, Nat returned with a cup of tea in each hand. She extended one to Graper. "The Chief Advisor is still allowed to have a bit of bliss leaf now and then, right?" asked Nat with a wink.

"I believe I can manage," replied Graper, as he pulled his own bliss leaves out of his pocket. "In fact, I brought us a little extra." Graper handed two leaves to Nat and kept one for himself. The friends dropped the leaves into their drinks and clinked the cups together.

"So, what's going on, Grapes? I can't even remember the last time you were here."

"Nat, I unfortunately come bearing some troubling news." Graper summarized the recent happenings of the Panel and, as delicately as possible, described the possible danger he was in.

"Yes, Maxx already filled me in," replied Corper in a monotone voice. "Apparently, there's a small group trying to be heroes."

Graper's eyebrows leapt. "Wow! Sounds like you're the one who should be filling *me* in. Tell me more about these brave souls."

"It makes me sick we even have to plan for this," Nat said with a sad sigh. "But we're healers, and we have our role to play."

"What kind of role?" Graper asked, not at all sure he wanted the answer.

"We've started mixing poison cocktails, just in case."

"This whole thing has been developing right under my nose, and I had no idea!" Graper sank into the sofa cushion and took a long draft of his bliss leaf tea. That— and Nat's company—helped calm his nerves.

Nat wasn't just the most passionate mixer Graper knew; she was also one of the most resilient. It seemed the healers were always under attack from skeptics and science sympathizers, and Nat never backed down from a battle. Graper loved her fire. They spent the rest of the evening bantering back and forth, inventing increasingly outrageous conspiracy theories to explain Isotopia's dire situation. Meanwhile, that first cup of bliss tea turned into two... then four.

Graper took a sobering breath. "Listen, Nat, given what's happening, and that they're onto me, I probably shouldn't spend the night at my place."

"I totally agree. That would not be a smart idea."

"So... maybe I could stay here tonight?"

"I suppose." Corper kicked off her shoes and snuggled

close to Graper on the couch. "I guess we should have a bit more tea if we're gonna be up for a while. What do you think?" she asked with a giggle.

Yes, Graper thought, *let's dose up this warm-from-the-dryer blanket feeling with more of that aphrodisiac bliss leaf.* "Certainly couldn't hurt."

THE SCIENTISTS / DR. HAL ADAMS

Hal Adams didn't like being kept in the dark. He'd always regarded the helmet project as nothing more than a flashy display of scientific puffery, but judging by the conspicuous lack of scientists in the labs recently, he could no longer ignore that there was some giant party going on that he wasn't invited to. Time to go get some answers from the boss man.

In his rush to confront the clan's Panel Rep, Adams tripped over his lab coat. A hard metal desk broke his fall.

Whoa. The work station was littered with papers, diagrams, and notes scrawled in Cam Dimlan's handwriting. Maybe Adams didn't need to go to Harding for answers, after all.

"Are you okay, sir?" asked Len.

Adams turned sharply. Since Cam had basically gone off doing whatever Harding had him doing and Nap had disappeared altogether, Len had become Adams' go-to guy. The kid's chipper attitude could be a bit grating, but he seemed bright enough and eager as hell to please.

"Yeah, yeah, fine. I'm just trying to figure out where Cam is. He say anything to you?" Adams turned around to face Len, who took a suspiciously long time to answer such a simple question.

"Uh, I haven't seen him, sir. But I'll let you know if I hear from him."

"You're sure you don't have any information on Dimlan?"

"Positive." The kid would've lit up a lie detector with

his answers, but Adams had bigger fish to fry.

"Okay, then." Adams resumed his search, digging through the piles and drawers with Len's gaze drilling two holes in his back. Buried in the bottom drawer of Cam's desk, Adams found a small box that piqued his interest. *And what might we have here?*

Inside the box was a carefully folded piece of paper, which Adams promptly opened. *Hmm.* Adams spun the paper until he recognized what he had stumbled upon: the design schematic for the mind helmets. Now, why would Cam go to all the effort of folding up the drawing and hiding it in the back of the drawer? The helmet design had been shared throughout the scientist clan; there were no secrets. Except—

What the hell is this cylinder attached to the back?

Adams studied the drawing until he could make sense of the extra feature—an external battery! A battery so enormous, in fact, it could power all of Isotopia for years or amplify the abilities of this helmet beyond anything they'd already seen. Adams recalled the moment during the helmet demonstration when Cam moved a pen across the room with a wave of his hand. And that was *without* this big-ass battery. *Imagine what could be done if...*

Had Dimlan already brought this battery-boosted helmet technology to life? Adams clutched his stomach and leaned back in the chair, drawing in several deep breaths.

"Sir? Are you okay?" Len was now hovering over him, grossly invading his personal space.

Adams took a second to collect himself, then without turning around said, "Thanks for your concern, kid. I'm fine."

THE IES / DETECTIVE LASK

Detective Lask leaned against the counter of Koop's stand, shooting the shit with Maxx and Patch while the Market closed down for the day. The sun sat on the horizon like a fat egg yolk, sending out one last mighty pulse of green light before retiring until morning.

"Maxx, I gotta ask you something," said Patch. "Seriously, how do you hold your shit together with all that stuff you're on all the time?"

"Years of practice, kid." Maxx stared off into the distance, his eyes nearly blacked out with telltale swollen pupils. "You see that tree over there?"

Patch and Lask followed his gaze to an unremarkable tree. "Sure," Patch said with a shrug.

"It's pulsing with breath," Maxx said, ignoring the chuckles of his friends. "The leaves are changing color right before my eyes."

"Damn!" Patch squinted and tilted his head comically.

Maxx grinned. "Yep, I've seen a lot of crazy shit, but it never ceases to amaze me."

Lask shook his head. *Clowns!*

A curious spectacle drew Lask's attention to the center of the Market: a lone soldier in full military gear and mind helmet, marching toward the forest. His heavy footfalls echoed through the empty streets.

"Yo, guys," whispered Lask sharply, his eyes wide and glued to the soldier. Enthralled by their nonsense, Maxx and Patch clearly hadn't heard him. *"Guys!"* They both finally shut up and followed Lask's pointed finger.

"Why would they be coming through here?" whispered Koop.

"Looks like it's just one of 'em," said Lask.

Patch turned to the detective. "You think shit is about to go down?"

"Nah," replied Lask. "I think this guy is just a dumb ass fool who was too lazy or cocky to stay out of sight on his way to training."

"We're just gonna watch him walk by?" asked Patch.

"Unless you'd rather we blow our covers and get our asses killed." Lask fell silent and kept a tight watch on the soldier; Maxx and Patch followed suit.

But Isotopians were a curious lot, so Lask wasn't completely surprised to hear a merchant across the way call out, "Hey, guy! What's with the helmet?" The soldier ignored him and kept walking, but the merchant wouldn't back down. He ran ahead and placed his hand against the soldier's chest to stop him. "Hey! I asked you what that helmet is for."

Lask's heart pounded into the tense silence. This guy was going to get himself and maybe a whole lot more folks killed.

"Get off!" The helmet distorted the soldier's voice into a low, menacing growl.

The merchant held his ground. "Not until you answer my question."

Without further warning, the soldier delivered a punch to the man's stomach that sent him rocketing ass-first into the ground. The man howled in pain.

"Fuck, dude!" said Patch, his chest puffed and ready to charge.

Lask pushed Patch back with a frantic, "Stay here!" and raced into harm's way, forming a human barrier between the soldier and the merchant. Patch's muttered *"Oh, fuck!"* carried across the still air to Lask's ears. The last thing Lask needed was that arrogant kid rushing in.

Lask established eye contact with the soldier through

the tinted helmet visor. "I'm IES. Lask," he said, tapping the badge on his chest. "There a problem?" The entire Market froze for a short eternity as the two faced off.

"No problems here," said the soldier in his artificially low voice.

"Good," replied Lask. "How about we move along then?"

The soldier leaned forward so Lask was sure to get an eyeful of his evil grin, then nodded and resumed his path toward the forest. Once he was out of sight, the entire Market heaved a collective sigh of relief. The downed merchant brushed himself off and convinced everyone he was okay. Lask relaxed his shoulders and drew some slow breaths as Patch approached him and patted him on the back.

"Pretty badass there, dude," said the hunter.

"That was close." Lask turned back to the stand to see Koop and Maxx staring with their jaws dropped. "Well? What are you guys waiting for? We have a training session to attend."

THE FORGOTTEN / LEVOL

Where did this fucker disappear to?

Over the past few days, Levol and Sato Mauler had turned Graper's home and office upside-down and even roamed the streets hoping to run into him, but no luck. Krakken would not be happy with their inability to follow his direct order. Luckily, Isotopia was small, but the Chief Advisor was onto them—Levol was certain of it now—and that could make him one tough old fart to locate.

Sato had left to patrol the city gates, leaving Levol hunkered down at Panel Headquarters. Huddled in darkness against the side of the building, Levol couldn't help but question the competence of Krakken and the others who'd recruited him. Graper wasn't some random Youth or Forgotten; he was one of the most powerful men in Isotopia, and he undoubtedly had other high-ups he could trust. The circle of people turning their spotlights on Krakken and Bogue could be widening by the day because these amateurs couldn't keep their shit locked up.

Levol fired up a rette, releasing an orgasmic sigh as waves of warmth and energy rushed through his body. *Just show yourself, Graper. I will suffocate you with two fingers.* A flash of movement caught his eye. Levol scrambled to his feet and raced around the corner of the building, craning his neck to make sure his eyes hadn't deceived him. There he was, right on cue! It was moments like this that made Levol okay with the fact that he had no home or friends to go back to. All he needed was the comfort of the silent night and a weapon in his hand.

Levol grabbed the blade strapped to his left boot. Adrenaline shot through him, clearing his head and readying his body. He crouched, flexed, and prepared to pounce.

That's when he saw the woman on Graper's arm.

If she'd been some random citizen, Levol could have easily killed them both without challenge or conscience. Healing Rep Natalya Corper was no random citizen. Levol had never met her personally, but he'd heard more than enough about her to know she was a hippie feminist bitch. As much as Levol wanted to slaughter them both right on the spot, he remembered Krakken's strict orders: a silent, untraceable kill. Isotopia had to believe that Chief Advisor Graper died of natural causes—preferably a heart attack. Somehow, that wouldn't be possible if Levol left a bloodbath of two Panel members at the door of their headquarters.

Levol ducked back behind the corner and spoke into his Isodex. "Yo, Sato. You there?"

Static, then a response. "Find 'im?"

"I did, but there's a problem. He's with Corper."

"Krakken gave us strict orders. Do *not* engage the target."

Tell me something I don't fucking know. "What do you suggest?"

"Follow them. Watch where they go, see what they see, who they meet. We need to know exactly what they know about us."

Levol rolled his eyes. He was a cold-blooded killer, not some desk-cowboy detective.

"You got that, Levol? Strict orders."

"Yes. Fine. I'll get back at you when I have something." Levol lowered his Isodex and poked his head out again to see that they had just gone into the building. He slipped inside behind them before the door closed. Making his steps as light as possible, Levol followed just close enough to see what the two Panel members were up to.

Levol had spent enough time at HQ with Krakken to know that the building was a maze of interconnected hallway loops with no dead-ends, making it quite the mind-fuck to navigate, but also allowing Levol to follow his targets from a safe distance. The darkness wasn't even a consideration to the creature of the night. If Levol stayed on his game—and the reck leaf should help with that—he could weave around Graper and Corper's path and intercept them if necessary.

As Levol turned corner after corner, keeping up with the whispers of his targets, he scoured his mind for potential security risks. What if Harding or Krakken had left incriminating evidence lying around? Surely, the most sensitive documents would be secured in Bogue's office. It was likely Graper had clearance.

If Graper and Corper stuck their noses where they didn't belong, Levol might have no choice but to pop them—orders or not. Levol's heart rate spiked as the couple turned into a stairwell that led directly to the Chairperson's office.

THE PANEL / CHIEF ADVISOR GRAPER

Perhaps not the most romantic of dates, but Natalya held tight to Graper's hand as he led her through the pitch-black hallways of Panel headquarters, straight to Bogue's office. As second-ranking leader of Isotopia, Graper had access in case of emergency—and this siege on his city definitely qualified.

Sands and Nat turned the last corner and screamed bloody murder as the dark outline of a hooded man hopped in front of them. Nat squeezed Graper's hand so hard he could have sworn he felt bones cracking.

"Oh, hello, lady and gentleman," said the hooded figure. "Sorry to startle you two lovebirds. I assume, since you must have security clearance to be here, you aren't up to any trouble?"

Graper and Nat exchanged bewildered looks, then slowly turned back to the mysterious figure. "Uh, yes," Graper answered. "And who might you be?"

"New security, hired by Madam Issler herself. Just making sure no one's here who's not supposed to be."

Graper wasn't sure whether he was more frightened, relieved, or just plain confused. "Oh. Well, I suppose it's a good thing we're staying so... secure."

Awkward silence.

"Anyway," continued Graper, "I forgot something in this room earlier, and I was about to see if I could find it. I have my own key. See?" Graper dangled his key card, hoping the hulking guard would see the wisdom in stepping aside.

"I'm very sorry, sir. I'm sure you're a very important man, but I'm under strict orders from the Chairperson not to let *anyone* in here, no matter who they say they are. I'm going to have to ask you to come back at another time when Madam Issler is here to confirm your authority."

Game over—at least for tonight. Whether this new "security guard" recognized them or not, the man was a stone wall they were clearly not going to pass through. Bogue would learn soon enough they'd tried to breach her office tonight, but that would only confirm what she already knew: Graper was onto her.

"Okay, sir, I understand." Graper smiled and grabbed Nat by the hand again. "We'll come back later. You have a good night, young man."

"You too," replied the shadow.

Graper and Nat walked until they turned the corner, then bolted for the exit.

THE YOUTH / RAYNE HOBB

Hobb squinted hard against the mid-afternoon sun. It had been a particularly crazy afternoon, and Hobb slaved away beside Koop serving one customer after the next. If not for the "Afternoon Delight" blend from Dr. Balter, Hobb would have been face down on the street by now. He couldn't imagine how any normal human being could survive the onslaught of hungry Isocoin-waving citizens without a little boost.

By some stroke of merciful luck, the two merchants found a few seconds' rest between hordes of customers. Hobb plopped onto his stool and wiped the sweat from his face with the hem of his shirt. "Hot enough to melt a brick out here today."

"Yes, it sure is," responded Koop cheerfully. Years of hard work seemed to have given Koop some kind of immunity to even the most brutal of suns. "Say, Rayne, how are your sessions going at the Mind Spa? That doctor any help to you? Can't say I've ever been over there myself."

"They're all right. I'm just so bored though. All the time. I feel like I'm trapped in myself. No healer's gonna fix that. The only thing that *will* fix it is making something of myself."

"Well, you better stop complaining and keep studying, then!"

The next wave of customers brought Hobb and Koop to their feet. Sweat streamed down Hobb's back, but there was ol' Koop, leaning against his stool, joking easily with his customers while somehow managing to serve twice as many. Hobb actually felt bad for the customers who got popped out of the queue onto his side of the stand; he had a feeling most people shopped here just to check in with their good pal, Koop. The man was certainly a character, no doubt about that.

A familiar face at the front of the line sent a jolt through Hobb's system. There stood Patch, dripping with pelts and freshly-killed meat. Hobb managed a greeting. "Evening, Patch."

"Gentlemen," Patch answered with a wink. He spun around to the line behind him, cupped his hands around his mouth, and yelled, "This stand is closed! Come back in ten minutes!"

Koop shot Patch an irritated look as his customers dispersed. "What the hell, Patch?"

Patch faced Koop and splayed his hands onto the stand. "Sorry for the inconvenience! I've got some fresh inventory for you."

Patch slid the carcasses off his shoulders and pulled several dead forest dwellers from his sack. He slapped them onto the counter, one perfect kill after the next, the only blemish on each a pellet mark right through the pupil. Patch truly was a hunter prodigy.

Hobb could barely work up the courage to speak, but he didn't know if he'd get a second chance. "Hey, man... I know things are a little hectic right now, but will the public exam session still be held next week?"

"To tell you the truth, kid, I hope we'll all be alive to *see* next week." Patch seemed to soften at Hobb's wide-eyed reaction. "Sure, if we're all still breathing, I think they'll be held as usual. Why, you planning on taking it?"

"I've been studying, and I think I'm ready," said Hobb.

Patch locked eyes with Koop, not turning back to Hobb until the old man gave him a nod. "Let's go for a walk, kid," said Patch as he stepped away from the stand.

Before Hobb could ask Koop's permission, the old

man shooed him away. Hobb raced to Patch's side. The hunter stretched an arm around Hobb's shoulders and pulled him in.

"All right man, listen up. As you already know, I think you're a good dude, and I have heard from everyone I know about your enthusiasm for joining my clan." Hobb's heart hammered in his chest as Patch continued. "As you know, the hunters are *extremely* selective. I'd say the only clan harder to enter is the IES. To make top detective, you need to be highly intelligent and proficient with a handgun. To be a hunter, you have to be able to adapt to your surroundings and understand how to actually *be* a killer. So, if you ask me, being a hunter is the most prestigious clan.

"The hunters have always taken their high standards very seriously. Now, from what I've observed from your previous field trials, your technique and quickness in the forest need *significant* improvement. You're going to have to be willing to work harder and put in a lot more time than the other new recruits."

Wait, what? Hobb did not dare raise his hopes again, but that sounded an awful lot like...

"Does that mean you believe I'll pass the exams this time?"

"Kid, as you may have noticed, recent events unfolding in Isotopia could lead to lots of people getting killed, and we need all the help we can get. I'm taking you under my wing."

Hobb's stomach growled with either a victory scream or a vomit warning, and he didn't know which. "Are you saying I'm a hunter?"

"According to Allix Maris, hunters are going to play a vital role in the event of an Isotopia-wide emergency. Plain and simple, we need to expand our clan, and that means easing up on our requirements for joining."

"Like the IES is doing with their new helmet soldiers?" Hobb had overheard enough conversation at Koop's stand to understand the danger.

Patch stopped walking, turned, and gave Hobb a nod heavy with something that felt like respect. "So, you know?"

"Yeah. You were saying... about expanding the clan?"

Patch smiled and patted him on the back. "You're in."

Hobb tensed every muscle in his mouth to keep from grinning. Had his lifelong dream really, *finally*, come true, just like that? Mercifully, Patch didn't give Hobb a chance to make a fool of himself.

"Meet me at the city gates when the sun comes up tomorrow. We've got a lot of work to do. In the meantime, get your ass back over to that stand and help out your poor old partner." Patch said this loudly enough for his old merchant friend to hear, and Koop flipped him the bird. "I'm out for now, Hobb. Remember—tomorrow at sunrise."

"Wait!" yelled Hobb as Patched retreated. "Do I need to bring anything?"

"A hell of a lot of heart. You're going to suck at first, so you'd better get some damn good sleep tonight, kid."

Koop beamed at Hobb as he made his way back to the stand. "Well, looky here, will ya? I think my young hunter is finally growing up!"

THE PANEL / CHIEF ADVISOR GRAPER

Graper leaned back in his favorite chair, feet propped up on his desk, a sip of Jollyman's Tea at his lips. The doorknob turned, and the relaxing effects of the Jollyman's dissipated in an instant with the Chairperson's appearance. Graper lurched forward, bobbling the mug until it came to a safe landing on his desk.

It was time to put all his cards on the table.

"What are you doing, Bogue?" Graper's heart pounded, but he kept his composure and shook his head like a disappointed father. "Are you planning to let hundreds or even thousands die?"

"You've known me for a while, Graper," replied Issler, appearing not the least bit daunted by his attack. "Do you really think I would let something happen that wasn't for the good of Isotopia as a whole?"

Graper had been asking himself that question for a while now. Once upon a time, Bogue was stunningly sexy and electric, brilliant and promising, but even then, she'd kept her emotions locked up. Now she was nothing but a cold, hardened monster, from her tragic wreck of a face to her violent, bloodthirsty soul. The truth was, Graper had never fully trusted her.

"I wish I could say no, Bogue. Thing is, even if *you* believe you're making Isotopia a better place, I sure as hell can't figure out how we benefit as a society from murdering innocent people!"

A hulk of a man swept into the room and aimed an excessively large weapon at Graper's head. A shaky sigh escaped Graper as he spoke to the open end of the rifle barrel.

"I suppose if you wanted me dead, you would have already shot me, so how about you get that big gun out of my face?"

The man holstered his firearm and leaned against the wall without speaking. Graper drew an easier breath but couldn't help wondering which of his words might make the man draw that gun again. "Wait! I know you! You're the guy who stopped me from getting into Bogue's office last night, right?"

The man just stared at Graper before shifting his gaze back to Bogue.

"He's not a big talker," retorted Bogue without looking behind her. "Now, let's not get sidetracked by my friend, here."

"Oh, *right*," started Graper as he brought his tea to his lips again and took a sip. "You were just in the middle of telling me how you're going to save Isotopia by slaughtering everyone."

"Your only smart move here is to leave us to our business, Sands. It would make life easier for everyone if you trusted me. Plus, do you really want to see what my friend will do if you don't cooperate?"

Nothing was going to get resolved on the spot; Graper would play nice for the time being. "I apologize for my suspicions against you, Miss Chairperson. It was out of line, and it won't happen again." He glared into the assassin's eyes and all he could see was pure evil.

Bogue stared Graper down with her piercing, fiery eyes; Graper answered by sipping his tea. She nodded, sealing what Graper assumed was a very *temporary* peace agreement. Unless they wanted a bloody mess all over Graper's office, there wasn't really another option.

"Apology accepted," she hissed. "As for your little investigation last night... don't try to pull that shit again. You're not a spy or a hero; you're an old man whose days left on this planet are numbered, and you'll have even fewer if you fight what's coming."

Graper could hardly believe his ears. The woman he was elected to advise on leading Isotopia had just threatened his life! What was this poor, cursed world coming to? He managed a tight nod.

"Good," Bogue replied. "We understand each other. Have a good day, *Chief Advisor.*"

"I've been your supposed right-hand man all these years," Graper said, halting Bogue in her tracks, "and you know what's even crazier than the fact I didn't realize you were plotting against me and all my friends?" Graper unleashed the wicked grin he saved for special occasions.

The Chairperson cocked her head and waited.

"That I've never been privy to a fundamental piece of information about you. If you're about to kill me," said Graper coolly, "why not at least show some mercy on my soul by finally relieving my curiosity about *those?*" He pointed at the hideous scars covering her face.

Bogue stomped right up to Graper's desk, smashed her fists down on the wood surface, and set her face so close to his that Graper could smell the death. "*That,*" spat Bogue, "is *none* of your *damn business!*"

The two top leaders of Isotopia stared at each other for an eternity. Bogue slowly backed away from Graper's desk and out of his office. Her thug followed without a backward glance.

Graper might have known more of Issler's scheme than she gave him credit for, but she was still the one with the army and the power. He sat back and took another sip of his tea while trying to plot his next move. Obviously, he wasn't about to back down, and even more obviously, Bogue wasn't going to let him off scot-free. Despite his herbal treat, this sick little game left Graper feeling nauseated and anxious.

THE SCIENTISTS / LEN

Len knew a desperate man when he saw one. Watching Dr. Adams rifle through Cam's desk, Len couldn't help but conclude that the man still hadn't dug up any useful information on the whereabouts of Cam or Nap. But why would Harding and the others leave the head of the clan in the dark—especially when Adams had always been the one pressuring Cam to finish that helmet? The only explanation that made any sense to Len was that Dr. Adams was simply carrying out clan directives from above. Everyone knew Mason Harding was a Type-A asshole, and obnoxious demands from the top tended to trickle down the ranks. If Len's hypothesis proved correct, Adams and Len could help each other.

"Excuse me, Dr. Adams," started Len. "I don't mean to butt into your business, but—"

"But *what?*"

Len ignored the animosity; frustration and fear would do that to a man. "I think I know what you're looking for, and you're not likely to find it in any of those drawers."

Adams' frenetic hands halted. He looked up, jaw set in a tense clench that barely allowed for speech. "What is it that you think you know, kid?"

"The reason you haven't seen Cam or Harding lately is because they're training newly-recruited IES members to use the helmets to their full potential. They have some sort of plan that could very likely lead to the loss of innocent lives—*many* innocent lives. That's all we really know at this point." Len braced himself for an explosion, but Adams took a deep breath and answered him calmly.

"How do you know this?"

"A small group of, um, people approached me for a scientific consult. We've been tracking the activities of the helmet soldiers in the hopes that we can stop this madness before anyone else gets hurt."

"Damn, Len! Why didn't you speak up sooner?"

Sweat fogged Len's glasses. "To be honest, sir, I thought you might be in on it. I needed to be sure before approaching you."

Dr. Adams stared into the distance as if he were spooling through the past for answers. "So, the information skips a rank. Why the hell wouldn't they fill me in on this?" He turned to Len as if the young scientist had a clue.

"I have no idea, sir. It's alarming, for sure. Might be best to stay away from Harding and Cam as much as possible for now, just in case."

A dark chuckle left Adams. "That shouldn't be hard. I haven't seen those two for days." Adams' gaze dropped to the floor as he shook his head, defeated. "By the way," he said, his expression suddenly twisted with grim comprehension, "where the hell is Nap?"

THE HEALERS / COLE

"I'm pretty sure bliss leaf falls under the 'not on the job' category." Maxx delivered his reprimand with a gentle smile, but Cole still felt guilty for disrespecting such a great man.

"Ah shit, I'm sorry, sir." Cole snuffed out the rette against the log and tossed the butt over his shoulder. "I was just thinking about Pan, and I—"

"It's been a rough couple of months for all of us," said Maxx. "Hey, you're friends with Patch, right?"

"I, uh..." Cole could hardly deny his reputation as one of the top Healer Drug Dealers in Isotopia with the bliss leaf cloud hanging heavy in the air. "He's a customer. Why? What do you know about Patch?"

Maxx sighed wearily, sank onto the log next to Cole, and looked over his shoulder in a way that made Cole's skin prickle. "We've been working together on... something."

Something? That might explain why Cole hadn't seen Patch in a while. No one in Isotopia loved a quality Necreck more than Patch. "He okay?"

"You might've lost yourself a customer. I imagine what he's going through would adequately distract him from his herbs."

"You think Patch has stopped using?" The realization stung. Patch was more than his top customer; he was Cole's favorite drug buddy. This must be some deep shit he'd gotten himself into. "What the hell's going on, Maxx?" Even as he asked, Cole was pretty sure he didn't

147

want to know.

The old guru lowered his voice, even after craning his neck to make sure they were still alone. "We think Krakken and Harding are heading up some sort of hostile takeover."

And I'm sober. "There's gonna be a war?"

"We can't say for sure, but they have an army and some highly advanced technology on their side."

"How do you know all this?" Cole asked, hoping against hope the old man was losing his mind.

"A few of us stumbled upon their training sessions, and we've been watching their movements very carefully."

"Who are they? What do they want?"

"We don't know that yet. They're doing a good job guarding their secrets."

"You're scaring me, Maxx." Cole regretted tossing away his rette—he could've really used another hit. At the risk of sounding like a pussy, he asked, "Are we gonna be okay?"

"I honestly don't know, son."

Cole stared up at the treetops and tried to absorb the news. If they were going to be attacked, they'd better fucking be ready for it. "We're gonna fight to the death if it comes to that, right?"

"You know how I feel about violence, Cole," Maxx answered, his mouth twisting into a grimace.

Cole leapt up from the log. "What if a bunch of innocent healers, or *any* innocents for that matter, get shot up tomorrow, and we could've stopped it?" Maxx would oppose him, but Cole had to try. "We have poisons—untraceable, lethal mixtures." Maxx looked up, startled, but Cole railed on. "We have to take a stand against this, or at least be ready to fight back when the time comes!"

"Whoa, whoa, whoa. Slow it down, son. We still don't even know for sure we're in danger," replied Maxx in a maddeningly calm tone. "We need to know more before we take any action."

Cole nodded but fought to hide his frustration over his mentor's passivity. "Okay... so, we tell the rest of the clan." Cole meant for it to sound like a question, but it came out closer to a command.

"I wish we could, but we don't know how broad the effort reaches. There's a possibility that even some of our healers could be in on it."

Cole swallowed over the hard lump in his throat. "Well, I personally am going to make sure we do everything we can to stop it. Even if you won't." Cole could see from Maxx's eyes that his last statement stung more than he intended.

Maxx shook his head and stood up, placing a firm hand on Cole's arm. "Never in my life have I seen a conflict well resolved with violence." His tone was so gentle, his words melted into the forest air as he spoke them. "This is a delicate situation, Cole. We can't afford to do anything foolish."

THE RESISTANCE CREW / PATCH

Maxx was late for their nightly spying session, but Patch didn't mind waiting when he had Lask and Koop to keep him entertained—even if their quick, familiar banter sounded like pure nonsense to Patch's ears. As their jib-jab floated past him, Patch's gaze swept the slowly-clearing marketplace for good-looking women, landing instead on Cole, charging straight at him.

"Hey, Cole!" Patch called, greeting him with a cheery wave. "What's—"

Cole's fist slammed into Patch's nose. Blood spurted in a sickening arc as he dropped to the pavement. The crowd gathered quickly, surrounding Patch with gasps and murmurs and greedy curiosity.

"Here, let's get you up." Koop's voice cut through the fog of stunned disbelief as he helped Patch to his feet. "Are you okay?" Koop's anxious gape blurred a bit, then shifted back into focus.

"I'm fine," Patch answered, craning around Koop to make sure Cole wasn't about to pop him again. Not a chance—Lask had him pinned from behind.

"It's all right, man," Patch said to Lask. "I mean, *he's* all right." He said it louder this time, spinning a three-sixty to address the whole crowd. "He's my friend."

Lask huffed. "Some friend. So, what's going on here, guys? Trouble in the sack?"

Patch rolled his eyes, then racked his temporarily scrambled brains. "No idea." He turned to Cole. "Dude. What the fuck?"

"If anyone should be asking that, it's me!" shouted Cole. Lask tightened his grip, and Cole kicked and squirmed.

"Whoa, buddy," Lask said smoothly, "how about you give it a rest? You have the man's attention."

Cole jerked his shoulders once more, but it seemed more for show than an actual threat. He nodded at Lask, who let him go, but not before Cole flashed them both a look of disgust.

"So... *what*, Patch? You stop coming by, and now you're trolling with the IES?"

Patch had barely thought about Nectar the past few weeks, let alone Cole. Sure, they'd shared plenty of good times, but Cole was his HDD first and his friend second. "Look, man, I'm really sorry I haven't been around. I've been extremely busy lately—"

"Save your breath. I know all about your little escapades with your new friends. How could you just bail on me? Am I nothing to you but a bottle of Nectar?"

Patch shot daggers at Cole, but the damage was done.

Lask let him have it. "Ah! So, this 'friend' is your drug dealer! And you've been buying Nectar off him for how long, now?"

"Shut the fuck up!" Patch yelled at Lask.

Lask grabbed two fistfuls of Patch's shirt and yanked him forward. "Don't forget about my badge just because we're working together, you damn degenerate."

"Let go of me!" Patch pushed Lask's hands away. "What, you think you're better than me because you're IES? And just who do you think is going to hunt down our enemies when chaos erupts? I'll give you a hint: the hunters."

Lask chuckled. "Have you ever even *seen* the IES in action? Have you witnessed an operation? Seen our weapons?"

"See this?" Patch jabbed his thumb toward the heat rifle strapped to his back. "This thing can kill and flash-cook a full-grown pogg before you can even whip out your damn hand gun!"

"Oh, well that's perfect! When shit starts getting heavy, we'll all hang back and let you *cook* our enemies for us! Because that's exactly what we need—cooked terrorists!"

"Hey!" snapped Koop, who'd been swiveling back and forth, trying to keep up. Patch and Lask stopped arguing and took a cautious step away from each other. "Remember who our enemy is, men. Seriously, if *you* two can't hold it together at a time like this, then how the hell is the rest of Isotopia supposed to?"

Lask forced out a frustrated sigh. "Koop's right. We got a little distracted there. How about we get ourselves back on track?"

Patch nodded, then turned to Cole. "Maybe now you can understand why I kind of forgot about my life for a while?"

"Yeah. Sorry I got so heated."

Maxx entered the marketplace just then, greeting his friends with a cheery "Good evening" the group wasn't quite ready to return.

"Looks like it's time for one of your classified spy sessions," said Cole, his tone edged with sarcasm. "I'm coming."

Lask glanced at Patch, then shook his head at Cole. "Look, kid, that's really not a great idea."

"Agreed," Maxx added, giving Cole a long, hard look. "We discussed this, Cole."

Patch jumped in before Cole could get in another word. "Listen, man, Maxx is right. Even three is too many, so how about we let these two cover the training session? Maxx is in good hands with Lask"—Lask acknowledged Patch's compliment with a nod—"and that leaves you and me free to go on a little mission of our own."

Cole's eyes lit up. "What mission?"

"A parallel, covert operation. We know the people behind this, and we're gonna go dig up as much intel as we can on them."

"Sorry, Patch, but that sounds like another bad idea," interrupted Lask. "These people are incredibly dangerous and the last thing we want to do is run right toward them."

"*Run*? Listen, Lask. I get you're a soldier, but I'm a hunter. An assassin. As long as Cole stays close and does as I tell him, we'll be just as safe as you two. And if things do get heated, Cole is quick enough to keep up with me. No offense, but I'm not sure you can say the same about Maxx, here." Patch felt a little guilty for picking on Maxx until the Guru glanced down at his stubby body and shrugged in agreement.

"That's the problem," replied Lask. "*All* of this shit is completely unsafe."

"Well," started Cole, "you guys have clearly opted into this danger already. And I'm opting in now. So, let's do it."

"I'm pretty sure you're not gonna convince him otherwise," said Patch with a grin.

Lask deliberated for a moment, then threw up his hands. "Go! Maxx and I are heading into the forest."

"Okay, then," said Patch. "We'll convene here tomorrow and catch each other up?"

Lask shrugged, not saying what was written all over his face: *If we all don't get ourselves killed before that.*

Patch swung his arm around Cole's shoulder and led him away from the stand.

THE RESISTANCE CREW / LASK

Whatever disaster was approaching, it was coming fast. Krakken had taken over training the soldiers, pushing the scientists to the sidelines and dramatically increasing the intensity and complexity of the drills. He'd divided the helmet soldiers into three squads of ten, performing entire synchronized battle sequences that always ended the same way—with one bullet from each soldier's gun penetrating the exact center of its target.

"These guys are getting good," Maxx whispered to Lask.

Both men had taken their usual dose of crimson leaf before the session, but Krakken had reduced communication among the group to an occasional one-word command.

"These soldiers aren't training anymore," said Lask. "They're rehearsing."

"Sounds like they're just about ready to go with Operation Question Mark."

"The only time I've ever seen military sequences this complex was a few years back, when a gang of Forgotten organized a series of small-scale attacks on the city. The IES finally defeated them with surgical attacks on multiple targets at once." Lask had been a wet-behind-the-ears recruit at the time, but he vividly remembered watching the IES counter-offensive through the city camera feeds at HQ.

"You think that's what they're planning?" Maxx asked. "Some sort of multi-pronged assault?"

"Unfortunately, yes."

"Then we better damn well hurry up and figure out who's behind this," Maxx said. "I sure don't know of anyone in the healing clan who's in the loop on this."

"How well do you know Natalya Corper?"

Maxx's head snapped up. "Nat? We go way back. I can promise you she cares about nothing more than the health and safety of Isotopia. That's why she took the job of Healer Rep in the first place."

Lask pressed once more. He suspected ol' Maxx might have a blind spot where Nat was concerned. "You do realize it's mostly Panel reps who are on the inside?"

Maxx shook his head sharply. "If Nat knew anything, she would be doing everything in her power to stop them. Plus, with Harding and at least some of the scientists in on this, we healers probably don't stand a chance."

"Don't you worry, Maxx. We've got your back." Movement at the edge of the training ground caught Lask's eye. He trained his binoculars on a jeep rolling into view. "Huh. Looks like they've got company."

Krakken jogged over as the car pulled to a stop. Captain Ranger stepped out of the jeep, saluted Krakken, and marched behind him to the men standing in formation.

"Fuck."

"What is it?" asked Maxx.

"It's my captain." Lask hadn't seen that one coming.

Ranger shouted an order; the soldiers responded in perfect precision. He tested out several more voice commands, all with the same impressive results. Lask couldn't help but be moved by the awesome display of skill and power, exactly what had inspired him to work to his full potential and become one of the youngest IES to make detective in the history of the clan.

"I'll tell you what," Lask said, thinking out loud. "Ranger doesn't know shit. He thinks he's out there commanding a highly trained army with his voice. He has no clue about those helmets."

Mild alarm crossed Maxx's face. That would be the crimson leaf tamping down the terror they should both be feeling.

Lask rubbed his eyes and let the binoculars rest on his chest. "Okay, what else do we know? Len told me earlier today the Head Scientist—what's his name, *Adams?*—is out of the loop."

"I really hope Sands isn't in danger because of his strong ties with the healers. He would never cause another human harm. Bogue must know that after working with him for this long."

"Weird," said Lask.

"What's that?"

"The head of Isotopia knows, but her right-hand man doesn't. The IES Rep knows, but the IES Captain doesn't. Scientist Rep Harding and Cam know, but Scientist Head Adams doesn't. We even know from Patch that Hunter Rep Bowman knows while Hunter *Head* Maris only knows because he stumbled on the information."

"They're targeting clan heads?" asked Maxx.

"Not the clan *heads,*" responded Lask. "I think they're targeting the clan system itself."

"Why would they want to do that? It sounds reckless and foolish." Neither man could come up with an answer to that one.

Lask's hands balled into tight fists. "We've got all we're gonna find out here. Let's go."

Lask stretched his leg to the branch below him. His boot slipped just as he was transferring all his weight to the lower leg. He lost his footing and tumbled through the branches, flailing his arms for anything to stop his fall, but all he could grab onto was air. He plummeted to the ground and continued to flip and roll from the top of the hill, a ball of completely useless arms and legs. The harder he fought to slow his momentum, the faster he rolled.

The ground flattened, finally, and Lask staggered to his

feet. His vision was blurred, head still spinning, but he could see clearly enough to know he was deeply and truly fucked. He was surrounded by helmet soldiers. The fact he wasn't wearing his badge was his one and only saving grace.

His dizzy mind raced, working out an escape route. "Oh... hey, guys. Nice hats."

Silence. Not even a thought.

"Sorry to interrupt your... whatever." Lask whipped out some of the extra crimson leaf in his pockets. "I was just tokin' on this heavy shit up there and happened to see you guys from a distance. I thought the helmets were badass, so I took a step closer to see better and *boom!* Did I mention I'm wasted?"

Krakken used his helmet to order his soldiers not to fire. One of the soldiers stepped out of line, toward the detective.

"I've seen this man before," said the soldier in his deep, modulated voice. He took a step toward Lask and leaned in closer. After a few chilling seconds of inspection, the man stepped back. "Yeah! Yeah, it was this guy! He told me a couple weeks ago he was a new recruit and needed directions to the training site. He's IES!"

Lask threw his hands up as an army full of rifles cocked and aimed at him.

"Hold it!"

Silence took over again as Krakken pushed his soldiers aside and wedged his body between Lask and his accuser. Lask held his breath, afraid to move a muscle. Krakken removed his helmet and studied Lask at close range.

"Hmm," Krakken said after a painful few seconds, "I can't say I know the man myself." No one dared to say or think a word. Krakken spun slowly to face Lask's accuser. "Tell us again, soldier. Exactly what happened with this man?"

"A couple weeks ago, he came to me asking for the location of the training site and I—"

"And you *told* him." The platoon was eerily silent. The soldier didn't answer.

Without a thought or word, the two soldiers on the ends of the lineup aimed at the snitch and fired in unison. One bullet pierced his left eye; the other, his heart. He dropped to the ground with a dull thud.

Krakken spun to face his army. "Which one of you rats thought that was *your* order to give?"

"That would be me." If Cam was afraid of Krakken, his voice didn't give him away.

Krakken paced toward Cam, a lion stalking its prey. "And what makes you think you have any power here, kid?"

"Oh, I don't know. How about *this*?" Every soldier pointed a gun at Krakken's head. Harding inched away from Cam's side.

"Whatever childish game you think you're playing, it's over now," Krakken said. "You really think my men would turn against me?"

Cam smirked. "Of course not. Not if it were up to them."

Krakken actually looked shaken for the first time. His voice was filled with a false bravado that might have fooled the soldiers but not Lask. "You're smart, but you're just a kid," Krakken said. "In fact, you're a kid we don't need anymore. Thanks to your nerd sessions, these guys are pros now. What did you think was going to happen at this point, we were going to make you king of the universe? Nah, kid, you're nothing but a stepping stone. And we've used you." Krakken turned to address his men. "Kill the kid."

This time, two soldiers in the middle of the lineup fired, sending a bullet clean through each of Krakken's hands. He howled in pain and fell to his knees.

"Actually," started Cam, as he approached Krakken with an arrogant strut, "I pictured taking over at this point, seeing as I know all your military plans." The soldiers pointed their rifles at Krakken's boots. "But let me know if you're not convinced yet, and I can try again to make myself clear."

Krakken raised his bloody hands in surrender. "You'd better not fuck this up, kid, because this plan is bigger than the two of us."

"Maybe yours was. I'm in charge now."

Even Harding registered surprise at Cam's audacity. So, they weren't in this together.

"*You* three, take this *spy*"—Cam rounded on Lask with a cold-hearted glare that made his skin crawl—"deep into the woods and execute him. Leave no trace." Lask had an almost irrepressible urge to beat the cocky little shit to the ground, but he wouldn't give Cam a reason to put a bullet in his head. Lask's chances against three soldiers in the forest were better than an entire army in the clearing.

Cam pointed to another pair of soldiers waiting at attention. "*You* two, guard the gate just in case this soon-to-be dead detective brought his friends."

Fuck! Maxx was out there somewhere, utterly defenseless. Please don't do something stupid, old man.

Turning what he probably thought was a charming smile on the platoon, Cam fired off his last orders. "Everyone else, go home and get some sleep. You're going to need your energy. Dismissed!"

There was a flurry of activity as the soldiers packed up. Lask ducked into the crowd to make his escape but met up with the barrels of three rifles pointed at his face. "Halt!"

"Hey, fellas. How 'bout we talk this out?"

A swift blow landed so hard on Lask's jaw, his world went black.

THE RESISTANCE CREW / PATCH

"Where are you taking me?" asked Cole.

Patch answered without turning around. "We know several Panel members are behind this, so we need to get into their building and do some snooping. We're goin' in there." He pointed down the road to the Panel's headquarters.

As the two reached the fence surrounding the building, Cole threw a stiff arm across Patch's chest. "Listen, man," said Cole, "we're heading into some serious shit. I think it's best if we're as sharp as possible."

"Agreed. Keep your focus up and have my back, and I'll have yours."

"That's not really what I meant." Cole searched through his sack and whipped out a rette. "I think we should stim up first."

Patch sighed. This was why he always considered Cole his HDD first, friend second. "Dude, you know I've been clean for a while. I'm trying to keep that going, but you do whatever you gotta do."

"All right, man." Cole lit up the rette and took a first toke, closing his eyes as that rush Patch knew so well was surely coming over him. For the next few hours, Cole would be stronger, faster, and sharper than anyone in Isotopia—at least in *his* mind. "Will you at least chill out here with me while I finish this?"

"Of course."

"And, as always, if you want some, just say the word."

"Cole, c'mon dude."

"Okay, okay! No more drugs for Sergeant Patch. Got it."

They stood in silence as Cole took his puffs. "So, what's it like being sober? I can't remember the last time I was completely clear. I mean, I can go days with lower doses or lighter blends, but I'm always buzzin' one way or another."

Patch didn't really want to think about that buzz, and Cole's usage pattern made him a little sick to his stomach, but he entertained the question. "It sucks, man. Lately, I've been so occupied with all this 'world is ending' bullshit, I haven't had time to think about it all that much. But sometimes when I can't sleep, or I start thinking too much about what might happen to Isotopia, it makes me crave like a bitch."

"I hate to say it, but the one thing almost all of my customers have in common is that no matter what they tell me or themselves, they always come back eventually. I fully support you in your decision, but I'm just warning you, it's a rough road."

"Once an addict, always an addict," Patch said. "Koop said those exact words to me when he learned I was on the Nectar. I think he's right. It's like gravity; no matter how far I run to get away from it, it tries to suck me back in." Patch watched the orange glow eat up the rette. It was about halfway gone. "Sometimes, I have dreams where I chug a bottle, and I wake up high. It's the only taste I ever get anymore. It only lasts about fifteen seconds once I wake up, so I close my eyes again and savor the living shit out of those fifteen seconds. Make them the longest damn fifteen seconds in the world, y'know?"

"Damn, that sounds dark. If I woke up with a fake high, I'd take a swig from the bottle on my nightstand and replace the fake high with a real one with no time in between." Cole sure as shit wasn't helping—a true professional dealer—but at least he had the grace to change the subject when he saw Patch's frustration.

"Look, I'm a healer, man. I know no other lifestyle. You're a hunter and a killer, a man of discipline. I've heard about your clan leader Maris and all his spiritual mumbo-jumbo. I'd put much more faith in *you* to quit over any of my other junkie customers."

"Are you calling me a junkie?"

"Err, no, I meant *most* of my customers are junkies. But you're not, which is why you'll succeed!" Night was closing in around them, but Patch could clearly see the dark blush on Cole's cheeks. "Oh, dude, I forgot to tell you. I'm glad you changed your mind about Hobb and took him on as your trainee. He's a good kid."

"He is."

"Not only that," Cole barreled on like a runaway train, "I'm very happy to report that Hobb is also an *ex*-customer of mine. Yep, he kicked the Nectar too. By the way, that was a cruel trick you played on him, getting the kid hooked like that."

Cole took a large puff off his rette, roughly a quarter of it left now. *Every puff he takes is one I can't have.* Patch tried his best to focus on his HDD's words, but all he could do was stare at that burning stick, cooking away the end of its life. The spirit drained from Patch, too, as if his soul had fused with the rette. The certainty kicked him in the gut: *I can't just sit and watch it die.* His body screamed for it, blood pumping hard through his veins. *GIVE IT TO ME NOW!*

"Hey man, can I actually get a puff of that?" *Keep it cool.* The words came out louder than intended, but softer than the voice in Patch's head. It could've gone worse.

"Are you sure, man? Now I'm feeling like to be a good friend to you, I need to support your efforts to stay clear."

It was far too late—Patch had made up his mind. "Yeah, of course, dude. Staying clear, yeah. Most of the time. But, uh… you're right about this. We're about to go in there, potentially the most dangerous place in Isotopia right now, and I've gotta be at the top of my game." The rette burned shorter. *Just wasting away. It was a tragedy. A fucking catastrophe.*

"*Please*," said Patch, this time accidentally revealing desperation in his shaky voice. "Gimme a puff. I want a damn puff!" Patch no longer cared how he came across— he would've sucked Cole's shlong for a toke right now.

Cole, wide-eyed, threw his hands up in surrender. The poor guy probably thought Patch would beat the shit out of him if he didn't hand it over. "There's not much left. Just go ahead and finish it off, man."

"Yeah. Yeah, I will." Patch took hold of the rette as if handling a newborn. His hands shook; if he dropped it, it would burn out, never to be lit again. *Dead, forever.*

Patch closed his eyes and inhaled gently at first, quickening his breathing until he achieved optimal herb burnage. He couldn't help but grin: *I still got it.* He dragged on the rette until it burned his fingers, then sucked up as much shit into his lungs as possible. When he couldn't hold his breath any longer, Patch leaned his head back and blew out a series of thick, white smoke rings.

By the time the last ring dissipated, so had Patch's guilt and worry, and he was a new man. The tingling euphoria crawled from his pounding heart down to his stomach, legs, and feet. "You're right, Cole. We're facing what could be a serious threat to our entire society. We need to perform."

Patch sensed a flash of concern in Cole's eyes, but it passed as quickly as it came. "Now you're talking, buddy. Just remember, you're using it for this one, extreme situation, then you go back to being clear. It definitely makes sense, man; I just didn't wanna push you into it."

"There's no more 'reckhead Patch' here anymore, hell no! We save everyone, then it's right back to *sober* Patch!" Just then, Patch's Isodex buzzed. He whipped it out of his pocket to see Maxx's distress call: **Lask captured! Get back here now!**

THE RESISTANCE CREW / MAXX

Maxx was hysterical by the time Patch and Cole arrived.

"The fuck happened?" asked Patch. "Apparently we can't split up. I leave *one* time, and we lose our IES detective."

Maxx had predicted Patch's reaction almost word for word. "They're gonna kill Lask if we don't move, you self-important ass. They went that way. Let's go!" Maxx grabbed Patch and, as fast as his old stubby legs would allow, waddled over to the spot where Lask disappeared into the trees.

Patch took over, the skilled hunter in his element. "This branch is bent to the right. I count four sets of footprints. This way—quick!"

But there was something off about Patch. He was acting weird—goofy, almost. *Dammit*, he was definitely on something. Had Cole turned him back into a reckhead in such a short time? Maybe those two *should* be kept apart. Extremely high on a potent blend himself, Maxx huffed and puffed to keep up with Patch. If they couldn't retrieve their lost friend, there would be plenty of bigger problems to worry about than Patch's relapse.

"This way. Let's go, let's go, let's go!" Patch maniacally—yet effectively, Maxx had to admit—slashed hanging branches out of the way with his machete as he followed the trail of Lask and his kidnappers, with Cole two steps behind. Every time Patch paused for a second to track, Maxx reached into his bag for a stim leaf, popped it into his mouth, and chewed. *Gotta keep up. Gotta keep up.*

"Seriously though!" yelled Patch back at Maxx. "How did they get him?"

"He slipped out of the tree and rolled all the way down the damn hill!"

"Why didn't they just kill him on the spot?"

Was Patch going to keep it up with the questions? Because ol' Maxx didn't have enough oxygen for running and shouting. "That scientist kid took control of everyone. They shot Krakken! I'll explain when we stop!" No more talking until Maxx found himself a nice log to rest on.

"*Dimlan?* Shot Krakken? Wow!"

Maxx pushed through more huffing, sweating, bug-filled hell before Patch finally stopped and put a finger to his mouth. "We're here," whispered the hunter as he gestured Maxx and Cole in closer. Patch pulled back a thick branch and revealed Lask on his knees, his face bloody and bruised, three soldiers standing behind him with their guns trained on the back of his head.

Maxx bent to catch his breath while Patch snuck closer to Lask. Taking cover behind the branch, Patch craned his neck, searched left and right, then slipped back toward Maxx and Cole.

"Okay guys, listen up," said Patch. "Shit's gonna go down right now so brace yourselves. I have two guns and one knife for the three of us. Can both of you shoot? Because frankly I don't trust either of you with a knife."

"Hell yeah, I can shoot," said Cole, as he snatched the heat rifle and jumped into a ridiculous battle pose.

"Me, too, although it's been a while," said Maxx, as he cautiously accepted the hunter's hand cannon. *A very long while.*

"Here's the plan," said the hunter. "Get up here." Patch moved into the danger zone again, placing all three of them into position. "Maxx at my left, Cole at right. On my count, you two shoot the man directly in front of you. Aim for the upper chest. Cole, careful with that rifle, it kicks back like a motherfucker. I'll go for the middle one as you take out the others. Ready? Here we go, bitches."

Maxx had never been more scared for his life. He lifted his rifle and aimed at the target as Patch began the countdown.

"Three... two... one... *FIRE!*"

Maxx shot his guy square in the chest, killing him instantly. *Not bad for an old healer.* Patch threw his knife just barely above Lask's head, piercing his target's throat and sending blood gushing out as the corpse dropped to the ground.

Cole missed wide. A sharp recoil in the forehead knocked him to the ground. His target lunged for Cole, but Lask threw his cuffed hands over the guy's head and tightened his grip. After a short struggle, the last soldier was dead.

Maxx wondered if he would ever sleep again.

THE RESISTANCE CREW / LASK

Out of immediate danger, Lask surrendered to gravity and flopped onto the forest floor. "You guys were *this* close to being too late."

Patch and Maxx dashed over to help him up. "We always got your back," said Patch. "Just remember that I was the one who found you."

"Yeah, yeah, yeah. Hunters are awesome. I'll admit it and feed your ego—you actually deserve it for once. As do you, Mr. Spike. Aren't you full of surprises?" Lask asked with a grin.

"Thanks," Maxx said, handing his gun to Patch as if it were burning a hole in his hand, "but I think I'll keep my day job."

Lask dusted himself off, wiped some blood off his cheek, and gently touched his left eye where one of those assholes had smacked him with his rifle. *That is gonna be quite the shiner.* He tipped his chin toward the body sprawled out on the ground a few feet away. "Is Cole okay?"

"He's relaxing over there for a minute—it's all good," Patch answered. "Turns out he's not much of a shooter, after all."

Lask sniggered. "No, I guess not. Well, boys, it looks like we've got ourselves some helmets."

"How long till they find out what we did?" asked Patch.

"I don't know, but we have to get out of here as soon as we can. The range on these helmets is probably at least as far as an Isodex message. It can shoot across the entire city in half a second."

"Let's go!"

Cole woke up just in time to see Patch toss one helmet to Maxx and the other to Lask. "Hey, what about me?"

"Sorry, dude," Patch answered. "It's only fair that the 'original three' get the helmets. We'll find one for you soon; don't worry."

Cole's face contorted in protest, but all he could manage was a nod.

"Whoa, whoa, whoa! Wait a minute," said Maxx. "Are we actually planning to use these hideous weapons?"

"They're only weapons in the hands of someone with violent intentions," Patch replied.

"We don't even know if we *can* use them yet," said Lask as he flipped the helmet around and examined it up close. "Each one could be wired to only respond to its intended user. Not to mention we just watched Cam control other helmet wearers with his super-human mods. No, we stash these somewhere safe until we can disable Cam's. Then we use ours only if we absolutely have to. It's too much power for one man."

"So, we bury 'em?" Patch asked.

"Not yet," responded Lask. "First, we have to buy ourselves some time."

"How?"

Lask tapped on the helmet. "If these soldiers don't report back to Cam and tell him I'm dead, he'll know what happened here and throw the switch on his operation early out of panic."

Patch shook his head. "Are you back to saying we should put them on? Right after that entire speech about how dangerous that could be?"

"I'll do it," said Lask. "Only one of us needs to do it, and being IES, I know how they talk. I've got the best shot of convincing him."

"What if he makes you? He could order you to shoot

us all!" Maxx looked like he'd had about all he could take.

"I know how insane it sounds, Maxx, but we have to risk it," Lask said. "We're in no position to protect the city from those soldiers yet, and we need to delay Cam as much as possible. Plus, the troops have just been ordered to sleep. We have to do it now; it's our best hope." Lask put on his helmet with shaky arms and waited for the inevitable call.

"Okay, he bought it." Lask said with a deep sigh of relief as he wiped the sweat off his eyebrows. "New plan. We bury two of the helmets and bring the third to Len. Dig, men."

Cole made up for his poor marksmanship by locating some quality jumbo-roots and digging like a champ. They made quick work of burying the two helmets, then sprinted through the forest to the science hub, a journey that was much longer than Lask remembered. When the men finally emerged from the grasp of the trees and shrubs, they were covered head to toe in dirt and tiny forest crawlers.

"I feel like I have a small tree shoved up my ass," Cole complained.

"Better than getting shot by helmet soldiers posted at the gate," Lask said.

Patch backed him up. "Agreed. I vote for the scenic route back to the city."

Lask's Isodex buzzed. Len, *finally*.

"Hey man, I'm sorry—I know it's incredibly late and you're probably busy with your research, but we need you. *Now*."

"Understood," Len answered. "I'll meet you at the front door."

THE RESISTANCE CREW / LEN

The ragtag group covered in pods and leaves didn't exactly inspire confidence, but these were the only good guys Len could count on for sure. Helmet tucked under his arm, Detective Lask strode through the door, recounting the group's recent adventures all the way to Len's desk.

"May I?" Len asked, and Lask set the helmet into his hands. Len held it up to the light and examined it carefully from all angles. "This is the first time I've actually touched the finished product. It's incredible."

"You haven't seen one of these yet?"

"No," Len answered, meeting Lask's eye. "Top secret means top secret. Even Dr. Adams didn't know what Cam was doing with the mods, and he was furious when he figured it out. He went rifling through Cam's desk and drawers, as you can see." Len pointed at the whirlwind of papers and books on the floor. "There are blueprints and half-completed user's manuals mixed in there somewhere. I didn't find much, but you can take whatever you think might be helpful."

Lask dove into the pile. "Damn! He's certainly put a lot of time into this." He waded through the papers, flipping each one around as if trying to figure out which direction was up. "So, what can you tell us that we don't already know?"

A shaky breath left Len. "I've been unable to sleep for months, imagining what a relatively well-meaning, intelligent human could do with *this* helmet. Add to that the modifications you're talking about on Cam's... he made sure his would end up the most powerful."

"Clearly," said Lask. "I'd consider *mind control* pretty damn powerful."

"It's horrifying," Len said. "His helmet has a custom battery rig. More input current—*much* more. The amount of potential energy attached to his helmet could supply an entire city for months. Now, you take a human brain, which is already extremely powerful and energy efficient, amplify that by running it through the helmet, then supercharge *that* through the battery; it basically makes his brain the most powerful weapon Isotopia has ever seen. The only thing we know for sure is the kid can't be underestimated."

"No shit," said Patch. "We just witnessed him shoot William Krakken and crown himself king of the army. We need to do something about that little fucker."

Maxx piped up for the first time. "I think we can all agree about that."

THE RESISTANCE CREW / LASK

Lask was standing outside the science building trying to digest everything he'd just seen and heard when the helmet vibrated in his hands. He yanked it over his head in time to catch the end of the thought message from Cam.

...information out of the detective before you killed him?

Lask inhaled deeply before sending back a mental message. *The guy was IES, too smart to say anything.*

I figured as much. Pause. *Emergency meeting at headquarters. Get back here ASAP.*

Still digging the grave. Will leave after we cover our tracks.

Lask shrugged out of the helmet, eager to be free of the metal cage and any possibility of being compromised. Patch stepped in front of him, anxiety written all over his face. "What's he want now?"

"Says to meet up at headquarters."

"Headquarters!" A grin stretched across Patch's face. "We've got those fuckers all in one place. We could actually cause some real damage."

"You think they have a separate HQ we don't even know about, or was he referring to the Panel building?"

Patch shook his head. "In the clearing where we saved your ass, I saw tracks heading deeper into the forest and didn't even think about it. Everything was happening so fast, and we were focused on getting out..."

A shiver shot down the detective's spine as he recalled his near-death experience. "Are you suggesting that those three soldiers stopped in the middle of the path to their headquarters to kill me?" Lask shook his head. "Real IES

172

soldiers would never make that mistake."

"The helmets seem to control the army of brutes on the whole," Patch said, "but we've seen instances where the soldiers can, and have, made mistakes."

"Yes!" Maxx became animated suddenly, and all eyes turned to the old healer. "Cam and Krakken are both smart guys, but clearly they're divided, and Cam clearly doesn't have all the information. Remember when Krakken told him, 'The plan is bigger than both of us'?"

"Cam is young and cocky," said Patch, ignoring Lask's eyeroll. "I think all he basically ever wanted is power and for everyone to know how smart he is."

Lask, somewhat of an expert on the minds of rebellious youth, agreed this was very likely. "He saw his opportunity and pounced. We still don't know the endgame or whether Cam will be enough to stop it."

"*If* he wants to stop it," Maxx interjected. "We need to know Krakken's plan."

Lask searched his mind for any details he may have overlooked. What underlying constants produced the appearance of such a random shitstorm they were viewing from the back end? *Think motive*, his training told him. What did he know about Krakken? A conversation with Koop came back to him—the first thing he'd ever heard about William Krakken: *he was a Forgotten*. Probably a very long time ago, but history is character is motive.

"What if all the helmet soldiers are Forgotten… a whole army of Forgotten?" Lask's theory picked up momentum as the puzzle pieces fell into place. "I don't think it's a group of people they're after; I think it's Isotopian society as we know it."

Patch, Cole, and Maxx nodded quietly as Lask's conclusions sank in.

"How does that explain Bogue's involvement?" Maxx asked.

"That is a very good question," Lask said. "Still, I believe we now know the face of our enemy. It's a lot to process, but we have no choice. We need to throw everything we have at these bastards right now before Cam catches on to us."

"Yes," Cole agreed, "the clock is ticking."

"Yeah, but you said they'd probably need a couple hours to figure us out, right?" Patch asked. "Possibly more if the soldiers are off-duty for the night?"

"Yes," replied Lask, hoping for, but not expecting, the hunter to have a real idea.

"Okay, so, very soon they'll send out a search team for their missing soldiers," Patch said. "I say we handle them the same way we handled those other helmet-wearing dick-bags in the forest."

Maxx voiced his reservations about the use of violence, but Cole had already forgotten about his battlefield injury and was thirsty for war. "I get that you don't like getting your hands dirty, Maxx, but let me remind you we're talking about the monsters responsible for Pan's murder."

The Guru couldn't argue with that. After all, the increasing craziness threatening Isotopia could all be traced back to that dreadful, bloody night.

Lask could taste his friends' lust for revenge. "We're certainly not short on reasons to kill these bastards. Let's go, before they reach the same conclusion about us."

PATCH

The crew stopped to catch their breath behind a building near the city's main entrance, where two more helmet soldiers stood guard. If they had known the fate of their three dead brothers-in-arms, they wouldn't be waiting around—they'd be stomping down every wall in Isotopia until they found the IES detective who'd threatened their operation.

"What's our plan of attack here?" asked Cole.

"For starters, *you* sure as hell aren't getting the heat rifle this time," replied Lask. "We're lucky there was no harm done except that big-ass bruise on your forehead."

"*Fine.* The recoil stung like a motherfucker," Cole said. "Is everyone happy now?"

Patch and Lask grinned at each other, but they all had better things to do than yank Cole's chain. Patch reached back for his bow and motioned for Lask to grab his pistol. He placed a finger to his lips and Lask attached the silencer.

Patch counted down with a hand signal—*3... 2... 1*—and they both fired. The guards collapsed to the ground on top of each other. The night remained silent. Lask waved Cole and Maxx through the gate, then threw up a signal to halt.

"We have no idea what we're walking into here," said Lask. "If we intend to strike tonight, we should call in all the help we can. I'm contacting my captain and the few IES guys I can still trust."

"I'll see who I can round up from the cavalry," said

Patch.

Maris turned out to be no help, leaving the decision to Patch to decide which of his squadmates were deemed "ready for battle." Patch was flattered by the trust from his mentor but overwhelmed by the responsibility. *Who's ready for this?*

Zap and Arlo had been training for months now, and Patch was confident they could handle themselves. Jay was still new to their squad and had plenty to learn, but he deserved the chance to prove himself.

Which left the hardest decision for last: *Hobb*. With Isotopia collapsing around him, Patch only just now remembered—with an accompanying pang of guilt—the practice session he'd promised Hobb for this very night. Despite the kid's fire and numerous hours of training in the forest since being recruited, Hobb simply wasn't ready. If anything should happen to Hobb in the conflict, Patch would never be able to live with himself.

Patch put in the calls to Zap, Arlo, and Jay; all three hunters grabbed their gear and headed straight to the gate. Patch had to make Jay swear to keep the news from Hobb.

"What about people outside the IES and hunting clan?" asked Cole. "Just because someone isn't trained doesn't mean they couldn't grab a gun and help out."

Lask squinted his eyes at the young healer. "*Grab a gun?* How does that even work?"

"I dunno, man," replied Cole. "Maybe your IES friends could bring extras?"

"Do I really need to remind you *again* what happened when you had a gun?"

Cole brushed his fingers across his self-inflicted wound and frowned.

"Imagine having five or six of you," continued Lask. "We may as well all shoot ourselves now."

Patch knew Cole wasn't good at taking jokes and felt kind of bad for the kid, but he couldn't help cracking a smile at Lask's comment—though he at least turned away so Cole couldn't see it.

"Yeah, yeah," said Cole. "What about lookouts or something? Other people can still help."

Lask shook his head. "It's too dangerous. In fact, it makes me extremely nervous that you're going to be joining us, but I know I won't be able to stop you, so please for fuck's sake, be careful." That was enough to shut Cole up for the time being.

"What about Len?" asked Patch. "His knowledge might really come in handy in the heat of battle."

"Call him," said Lask. "He's not setting foot in the forest, but maybe he can help us from a safe distance."

Patch nodded and pulled up Len on his Isodex. After a quick briefing on the situation, Len was all too happy to play a part in the battle. He offered to pilot a small drone and provide surveillance from above.

The resistance crew, such as it was, began to take shape. It hit Patch like a bullet between the eyes—this operation was likely to produce some dead bodies. The only question was whose.

LASK

Lask furiously bit his nails as more and more people showed up and merged into the crew. Every person who joined them was another soul Lask had to keep safe. For starters, he moved them all out of plain sight, into a busy area outside the city gates.

Lask surveyed the crowd, clusters segregated by clans: Patch and his fellow hunters; the healers, Cole and Maxx; and Lask's own IES clanmates—the men Lask knew, who'd joined the clan well before the influx of helmet soldiers under Krakken's command. Captain Ranger caught Lask's eye and strode over to him.

"I could have prevented all this," said Ranger, shaking his head, "but instead I sat back while my shop turned into a breeding ground for murderers."

Ranger was a good guy and a great captain, and the detective felt shitty that Ranger felt shitty. "You were just following commands," replied Lask.

"I know, but still... Krakken came on the scene out of nowhere, and my best detective told me to keep an eye on him."

Lask wasn't sure what to say; everything his boss said was true. "The people behind this are cunning and manipulative. They knew if they worked fast enough and played off Pan's murder, you would give them the go-ahead to open the floodgates. They used you just like they used Hal Adams. Harding pressured him to get the helmet finished without even knowing what it would be used for, ultimately creating the most dangerous weapon Isotopia

178

has ever seen."

Ranger paled.

"Are you okay, sir?"

The captain whirled around and vomited into the bushes behind him. Still clutching his stomach, Ranger turned around to meet Lask's gaze. "I'm just glad *you're* in charge now." Ranger patted Lask on the shoulder and sauntered away.

Lask picked Patch's voice out of the crowd as the hunter talked up his troops. Maris took a back seat, beaming at his star pupil. Patch *had* come a long way— even Lask could see that in the short time he knew him.

The smell of an unfamiliar rette blend met Lask's nose, and he followed the scent to its origin—Maxx and Cole. Lask rolled his eyes. It would be a miracle if those two didn't get themselves shot. Lucky for them, prosecuting drug use wasn't high on Lask's priority list while he was staring down the end of the world. Speaking of which, it was time to address the motley crew.

"Okay guys, let's get started." The chatter died down; all eyes were on Lask. "I assume everyone knows why we're here. If not, here's the short version: Isotopia is under attack from the inside, and it's up to us to save her!"

The message was received with enthusiastic grunts and shouts that Lask quickly tamped down. He lifted his Isodex to his mouth. "Len, you there?"

"I'm here, Detective."

"Great." Lask looked back up at his army. "Captain Ranger should've given each of you an earpiece. Does everyone have one?"

Collective nod.

"Okay, good. Put those in now, and meet my friend Len, one of the only scientists on our side. He'll have eyes in the sky for us."

"Dr. Adams is here with me," said Len through the earpieces. "Don't worry, guys—we've got your backs."

Lask thanked Len and Hal, then addressed his ragtag

crew again. "All right, here's the plan. Patch and the hunters will lead us to the spot where we believe the headquarters are located. We quickly and quietly move in, following Len and Hal's instructions."

"Uh, I'm sorry," interrupted one of the hunters. "Did you say you *believe* the headquarters is there?"

"Shut up, Jay," snapped Patch. Two of the other hunters smirked until Patch gave them a sinister eye.

"We know the helmet soldiers train in the woods," said Lask. "We heard them reference their 'headquarters' earlier tonight. Len's drone was able to confirm there is, in fact, a large structure out there." The crowd exchanged a variety of looks—some convinced and amped up, some skeptical, and a few downright terrified. Unfortunately, what Lask had to share next would not be comforting.

"We have many reasons to stay extra cautious tonight. First, we have no idea who's inside, if anyone. Len has a second drone trained on the building, and we haven't seen anyone enter or exit in the hour we've been watching. Worst case scenario, there are thirty soldiers inside, all wearing helmets."

"Actually, I'd make that twenty-five now," replied Patch with a cocky grin.

"Second, for those of you who don't know, the helmets worn by the enemy were specially designed to make this army uniquely dangerous. The soldiers communicate telepathically, so they can perform synchronized attacks with no lead time. To be quite frank, we still don't know the full potential of those helmets. The inventor, Cam Dimlan, juiced up his own helmet, giving him the ability to control the minds of the other soldiers, which makes him *by far* the most powerful. Ideally, we'll get to Cam and break the hold he has on his army, then work on locating Krakken, the mastermind of this revolution."

The silence in the air was chilling, but Lask pushed through it.

"Now, I do have one piece of good news to inject.

Along with your earpieces, our healer friends, Maxx and Cole, have provided each of you with crimson leaves, which contain properties that will allow you to hear the soldiers' helmet communications; don't ask how we figured that out. If you're not familiar with ingesting"— Lask paused to clear his throat—"*medicinal* roots, simply tear off a piece and grind it between your teeth until you achieve the desired result." If anyone had told Lask when he took his sacred oath of office that he'd be standing here today, instructing a crowd of citizens of Isotopia in the particulars of consuming mind-altering herbals, he'd have told him he was losing his mind. Now, Lask was fairly certain he was the one going crazy.

"The helmet soldiers have been careful to keep their communications to an absolute minimum, but it's possible that catching them by surprise might induce panicked thoughts, which just might provide us with more information about our enemy." That seemed to reassure the crowd, which made Lask feel like an asshole, because he suspected the army was beyond those types of rookie mistakes.

"And now, back to the bad news," continued Lask. "We eliminated five helmet soldiers tonight."

"That sounds like good news to me!" joked a voice toward the back of the crowd.

Lask waited for the titters to die down. A little release of nerves wasn't the worst thing for this group. "Yes, well, we managed to cover our tracks, *for now*, but they will figure out the truth very soon. So, it's very unlikely our attack will be a surprise."

Jay chimed in again. "We're walking into a slaughter?"

"You're right to be anxious," replied Lask over the growing chorus of worries. "This is an extremely dangerous operation. Unfortunately, we've run out of time and our best option to catch them off guard is to strike now. We have to take it."

Silence.

Words usually didn't escape Lask, but what could he possibly say to this group now? The detective was lost.

"It's okay to be scared," shouted Patch. "Hell, *I'd* even admit to being afraid if I weren't so damn stubborn." The crowd laughed and eased up, including Lask. The hunter pushed his way to the front of the group and stood beside the detective.

"Now listen up, bitches. Yes, it's dangerous. Yes, some of us might not make it through. But look around. Our own Detective Lask and his captain. Look at Bowman and Maris. Finally, look at *me*. You've got Isotopia's best at your side, and not a single one of you would be here unless we believed you were capable of this fight. So, let's go in there, and with the help of our nerdy friends and their flying cameras, take out some motherfucking bad guys!" The crowd roared, and Lask shot Patch a look of gratitude.

The hunter patted Lask's back. "We've got this!"

MAXX SPIKE

Maxx was delighted to learn that this march to headquarters wouldn't be a brutal sprint like last time. Nevertheless, he took a spot at the back of the crowd, where he could absorb all the emotional energy continuously flowing toward him as the group moved forward. Thanks to the empathogenic effects of his current cocktail, Maxx couldn't help but be consumed.

A dull roar of, "Lemme at 'em!" came at him from the front lines of the charge. Not surprisingly, Maxx also picked up on a highly contagious thread of barely-contained panic, a resounding, "We're all gonna die." And then there were the completely mute, stony-faced marchers, not giving life to any emotion at all. It was all Maxx could do to avoid spiraling into a full-blown panic of his own. Of course, he had some help from the healthy dose of xeta leaf he'd pre-toked for the occasion.

Like most healers, Maxx carried an array of mixtures with him at all times. It felt comforting to walk through the forest with a handpicked collection of natural remedies and psychoactives. You had your stims for the morning rush, your slows for the evening roll, and a whole world of wonky mixes in between. While bliss was a smooth, straightforward buzz Maxx always thought of as a "soul massage," replace just one of its active herbs (which Maxx had done quite by accident one day), and you've stumbled upon a wildly different animal in xeta—unpredictable, and because of that, dangerous. Also Maxx's favorite.

The onset of the leaf was marked by an unmistakable

hypnotic pull, which served more as a guideline than a set of rules. The limbs grew heavy, but the trunk and soul lightened, creating a state of relaxation unlike any other. After that, anything could happen; it was up to the user's imagination and willingness to be consumed by the experience. Maxx let it take hold, hoping it would lead him and his friends safely through the night. *Speaking of getting through the night.*

Maxx rechecked his Isodex. He still hadn't heard back from his old friend Sands since filling him in about Krakken's army. The Chief Advisor wouldn't have just sat on that information, and Maxx feared any action on Sands' part might just have gotten him killed.

If not for the xetaleaf pulsing through Maxx's veins, he might have been overcome by dread.

PATCH

Zap, Jay and Arlo were talking shit about Maxx and his current mental state. Enough was enough.

"Shut the fuck up!" Patch yelled over his shoulder. He smirked to himself as they immediately abided by his command. *Good boys.*

"Thanks, man," said Cole, who kept Patch company at the front of the group. "No matter how much you prepare yourself for the ridicule, it's still a pain in the ass. The funny thing is us healers are the most peaceful clan in Isotopia, yet we get *by far* the most animosity jammed down our throats."

"Yeah, I can see that. But look on the bright side—at least there are no scientists here to give you shit."

Cole chuckled. "Just the ones we're about to ambush."

"True fact," Patch said with a grin. "The perfect opportunity for you to finally kick their teeth in."

"I like the way you think."

As Patch shot the breeze with Cole, he eavesdropped on the IES members chatting behind him. Unfamiliar voices but nothing from Lask. When Lask went quiet, there was most likely a problem. Patch slowed enough for the detective to catch up.

"Lask, you okay, man?"

"I've gotta be honest. I've been involved in my share of gunfire exchanges, but none of them compares to what we're about to encounter."

"Hey, hey. Listen, man. It's one thing you froze up during your speech back there, but you've gotta snap out of it and get your head into this. Even if you're not feeling it, you better damn well act like you do." Defending Maxx. Keeping his dumb-ass young squadmates in line. Making sure the best detective in Isotopia wasn't going to shit his pants. *Am I everyone's fucking mommy now?*

"Yeah, I got it. Don't worry, kid." Patch took Lask's patronizing tone as a return to his normal state.

"Are you sure? 'Cuz I can rile people up, but I can't coordinate a synchronized gun strike for shit. That's what you're here for."

"I *said* I got it!"

"Good." Somewhat reassured, Patch caught up to Cole again.

"What was all that about?" asked Cole.

"Just talking strategy. Gimme a hit of that stim leaf." Cole registered no emotion as he handed over the burning rette—no surprise, no smug pleasure, no disappointment. Patch inhaled deeply, and soon, that oh-so-familiar rush of kickass ran through his body.

"You think Lask wants some?" asked Cole. Patch couldn't tell if he was joking.

"I'm pretty sure Lask would *never* ingest an illegal mixture in front of me, no matter the circumstances. Plus, Lask already has enough on his mind. Making it work faster would probably make the dude's brains explode."

"Sounds like he needs some bliss leaf to calm the nerves. Should I ask him?"

"You're not getting it, man. Lask doesn't need anything."

"*What* don't I need?" asked Lask, barging in between Patch and Cole.

"Nothing," said Patch.

"Bliss leaf," said Cole. Patch leaned behind Lask's back to shoot Cole a death glare, but the healer-drug dealer couldn't help himself. "I'm not saying get recked. I'm just saying, put a little wad under your tongue. You'll feel better, trust me."

"Better than *what?*" asked Lask, who had taken over shooting dagger-eyes at Cole.

"I'm just saying, you're the head of this operation. You want to be able to think clearly, right?"

"That's exactly why I don't want any of your damn drugs," responded the detective. "This whole situation is preposterous, you know. If this were any other day, I would be arresting *both* your asses."

"Whoa, man. They're medicinal blends," retorted Cole. Patch almost admired the guy for pressing on in the face of complete rejection. "All I'm trying to say is it'll clear your head of any anxiety about the situation so you can lead us without fear."

"Do you think that's a good quality in a leader, Cole?" responded Lask. "In a situation like this? Do you think I should be carefree? Head into this with the mentality that whatever happens, happens, and that's all there is to it?"

"Well no, but—"

"No buts. That's it. I don't want to hear about your stim leaf, or bliss leaf, or any of your other shit ever again. Bad enough half this crowd is using right now. And don't you dare worry about my ability to lead this group because I will lead the shit out of this group!" Lask retreated to his clanmates, leaving Patch and Cole staring at the ground.

"Well, that was awkward," said Cole.

"Yeah, nice going," said Patch. "Way to problem-solve. Staying clean is part of the lifestyle that's hammered into every IES from the moment they take their clan exams. He's not going to suddenly change just because he's stressed."

"Well, fuck, I'm *so* sorry that I felt I should at least *offer* the man something. Like he said, we've never encountered a situation like this before."

"At least it's over with," said Patch. "Now gimme another puff of that sweet, sweet stim leaf while the detective isn't looking."

Cole lit up. "With pleasure, my friend."

DETECTIVE LASK

Lask tamped down the queasy feeling that rose from the pit of his stomach. They'd reached the clearing where the helmet soldiers had dragged him earlier—the spot where Lask would have taken his last breath if his new friends hadn't shown up when they did.

Patch spun around and shushed the buzzing crowd. When he had everyone's attention, he pointed to a low-hanging branch and indicated that the hideout was just on the other side.

As the crowd bunched up against the tree to peer through the turquoise leaves, Lask took a long look at the hut. The rectangular, wooden cabin seemed enormous, way larger than it had appeared through Len's drone earlier in the evening. Lask had to admit, it was a damn sturdy-looking hut. The detective's admiration was cut short by a firm pat on the back from Patch.

"You're up, soldier."

Lask pushed his way to the front of the group, addressing them with a confident tone. "Okay, warriors—this is it. Prepare yourselves for anything." The detective spoke into his Isodex. "Len, you still with us?"

Len's face emerged through the static on Lask's Isodex. "All set. I've got one drone stationed on each end, and I'll be watching your every move."

"Copy," said Lask, shifting his gaze back up at the crowd. "Okay, here's the deal. We're going to fan out around the building and slowly move in under Len's guidance. Any sign of danger and we retreat."

Unanimous nod.

"Captain Ranger and Hunter Clan Head Maris will be handing out guns and rifles to those who know how to use them. Those who can't shoot will be provided a combat blade. Weapons are mandatory." Lask paused while the murmur of the crowd rose and fell. "We will literally be fighting for our lives, and that means *no one* goes in unarmed. Understood?"

Unanimous nod. Lask took a second to glance in Cole's direction to make sure the kid wouldn't be trying his luck with another firearm.

"Everyone should also have ingested a healthy dose of crimson leaf so we can all hear the helmet soldiers' communication. Just to remind you, the army we're about to encounter is likely to be wearing some sort of armor along with their helmets, so if you can, aim for the neck. If that's too specific a target, try for a hard knock at the chest or head. Most importantly, you'll be providing cover fire so our shooters can advance and close in on our target. Remember, the helmet soldiers are capable of things you've never seen before, and Cam Dimlan will likely be controlling the entire army through his customized rig. If you spot Cam, signal to as many of us as you can, and do everything in your power to take him down.

"Now, we have a pretty diverse group here in terms of skill set and combat experience. What we want to do is arrange ourselves to best exploit everyone's strengths while protecting those who may be more vulnerable. Healers, your job is to stay near the back and signal to the rest of us whenever you see something." Lask focused in on Cole. "You guys got it?"

"C'mon, Lask," said Cole. "I know I fucked up before, but give me a second chance on the front lines."

"Listen, I get that some of you may not like your roles, or even feel insulted by them, but no job is unimportant. We are about to engage in war, people. There's no time to stand here and debate. It's critical that you trust me and follow orders. Everyone got that?"

Cole nodded, and the nod spread throughout the rest of the crowd.

"Great, thank you. Okay, so healers are in back, scouting and signaling. IES soldiers will be up front to infiltrate the building. Everyone else will stay close to us and follow our every instruction, whether it be to reload, cover fire, or move across the room. Once we're inside, we'll have more of an idea of what we're dealing with in terms of numbers. Also, we'll hopefully be able to spot who is leading their army. Hunters—that's where you come in. You're assassins. Patch and Maris, you lead. Get in there and bring down the enemy." Patch beamed at Lask, clearly impressed Lask had snapped back to his old self just in time.

"Are there any questions?"

The entire crowd shook their heads.

"Does everyone have a weapon now?"

Unanimous nod.

"Has everyone taken some crimson leaf?"

Unanimous nod.

"Are you guys ready?"

Some nods, some blank stares.

"All right, then. Let's take 'em." The detective glanced back at his Isodex. "Len, we're going in."

LEN

This is it, for real. Len was glad no one could see his legs shaking behind his desk. The lives of all these people lay in his hands. *Not helping.*

Len hunched forward on his chair, not allowing his gaze to deviate from the two computer monitors showing the drone images. *Don't even blink, bitch. Not now. You can blink all you want after we kill all the bad guys.*

At Lask's command, Len raised the drones positioned above the front and back doors of the cabin. Hovering just below the treetops, the drones provided Len with a view of the entire army, arrayed in an ellipse around the building perimeter with Lask at the front door and Captain Ranger at the back. Both men waited with a laser pen lock-picker poised and ready to go.

"Okay, guys," whispered Len. *"Go!"* The two men unlocked the doors and motioned for the others to follow them inside. Lask was flanked by Sergeant Kane and Patch; Captain Ranger had Detective Paller on his left and Allix Maris on his right. The top IES soldiers teamed up with the best hunters, led by technology created by the scientists. The noblest of Isotopia working together for the common good. This was how it was meant to be.

With Len's drones leading the way, the army filed cautiously into the building, The drones switched to night-vision mode once inside. Nap had been working on building infrared sight into these drones before his mysterious disappearance. *Poor fucking kid.*

Len's skin crawled with every step the two teams took

191

as they snaked their way further into the depths of the building. The drones sent back images of tables arrayed with the full arsenal of weapons and grenades Isotopia had to offer, but so far, no people.

After an eternity that might have been ten seconds or five minutes, the drones met in the heart of the building, stopped, and stared at each other. *Where the hell is everyone?* Lask and Ranger shrugged in confusion.

Something caused Lask to spin around suddenly, a look of horror crossing his face. Len rotated his drones to quickly assess the situation. Lask was heard shouting, *"EVERYONE GET OUT—"*

The explosion was so loud and startling, it threw Len from his chair onto the hard, tiled floor. *Oh. Fuck!* Fighting through the shooting pain in his ass, Len scrambled back to his monitors, terrified of the carnage he was likely to see but damned if he was gonna sit on his ass if there was anything at all he could do to help. The logs on the cabin exploded in an outward ring, rocketing out into the forest. Len's drones were as close to unkillable as modern-day machines came, but one of them was knocked back by the blast and impaled by a flying log, which rendered it mortal after all. The remaining drone was alive but barely.

Len pressed forward toward the live monitor, frantically searching for signs of life. He couldn't imagine how the IES vests could handle a blast of such force, but he prayed the "Invincible" lived up to its name. Through the smoke and fire, Len picked out shattered helmets, torn suits, and blood—so much blood—but there was movement too. Bodies moving across the floor, huddled masses lifting each other to their feet, conversation, activity… *life*.

As the smoke cleared, Len observed the most terrifying part of all: a horde of perfectly synched helmet soldiers descending from the trees, rifles aimed at the wounded rebels. *Fuck*, they were all sitting ducks!

"Ambush! EVERYONE SHOOT!" Len yelled.

Complete chaos followed. The helmet soldiers fired, and the rebels fired back. Bullets and pellets flew in all directions, some finding targets and others darting out into the forest to ricochet off faraway trees. The helmet soldiers, so precise with a stable target, proved to be sloppier against the dodging victims. Bullets flew wide past the middle of the circle, spraying lethal fire at their own troops opposite them. Len forced himself to watch, but it was the most horrible job he'd ever had to do.

Patch and Lask dove toward their mortal enemies, snapping necks and slitting throats faster than Len thought humanly possible. Maris traveled around the outside of the helmet soldier circle, knocking them out two and three at a time. Others, too, had made their way to the outer ring and bravely grasped at the enemies' weapons, but the helmet soldiers were stronger and meaner than the untrained rebels, who were thrown across the ground or knocked out with a single blow to the chest. Blood spilled on both sides, and Len watched with an open jaw and tears in his eyes, shaking on the cold lab floor until the gunfire mercifully ceased.

Len guided the drone from one end of the room to the other, watching his one live feed like a hawk. Each of the rebel bodies lying on the ground sent a dagger to his heart, but Len was a scientist with a job to do.

"Lask! Come in!" yelled Len.

Coughing. "Yeah, it's me."

"Are you okay?"

"I'm alive, so that's something."

"By my count, fifteen helmet soldiers are unaccounted for."

"We have to get back to the city and warn the people. *NOW!*"

"Yes, please get back here while there's still a city to save! Meanwhile, I'll send out the emergency code."

A split-second later, the city sky filled with shrieking sirens: "Stay inside! Do not panic!"

LASK

The shooting stopped, but the screaming and the pandemonium continued. It all had to be a nightmare. Somewhere deep down, Lask knew he had to drag himself back into reality, but he was frozen by the horror and suffering of the friends around him—friends he had led right into this trap.

"Lask? *Lask*!" The detective continued to stare wide-eyed at the wreckage. "LASK!" On his knees, helpless, Patch shouted across the pile of their own fallen men until Lask finally recognized his own name and snapped back to life.

"What the fuck do we do now?"

"We have to get back to the city," Patch answered. "The rest of the soldiers are going to slaughter all the clan heads, all the opposing Panel reps, and any innocent civilians who get in their way."

"*Fuck*!" Lask followed the voice back to a wounded Cole, who was kneeling over Maxx's bloody body, performing every type of life-saving technique he'd ever learned. Lask scrambled across the floor to do what he could, but it was no use.

"He's gone." Lask's voice cracked as he confirmed what they all knew. First Pan Linner, now Maxx Spike. Isotopia was losing their gentlest souls so fast, it made Lask's head spin. Lask's gaze slipped away from the dead healer-guru and came to rest on his own leader, Captain Ranger, his forehead pierced by three lethal pellets.

"No! No, no, no, no, *NO*!" Patch dropped to the floor

beside the corpse of his Panel Rep Trey Bowman. If not for Trey's bravery, Maris and Patch never would have received the warning about the attacks. If they didn't stop the helmet army now, all of these deaths would be for nothing.

"Those monsters got Jay as well," said Maris gently, pointing with a trembling hand at the kid who'd challenged the wisdom of this raid from the very beginning. *Guess you were right, kid.*

"Arlo and others are severely injured," Maris said. From the expression on Patch's face, Lask guessed he'd never seen Maris shed a tear before today.

"We have to take care of our wounded and dead," Patch said.

"I promise you," Maris said, setting his arm around Patch's shoulders, "we will mourn each and every one of these brave men, but we can't do it right now, or we'll have an entire city to mourn."

"So, what are you saying? We just leave these people here? Fuck no!"

Cole pulled his head away from his dead mentor's chest. "Someone should stay." Cole paused and bit his lip. "It makes sense for a healer to do it. I'll take care of giving our dead a proper burial while doing my best to heal the injured."

"Are you sure?" asked Lask.

"It's what I do," replied Cole, still unable to take his eyes off his beloved mentor. "Besides, as you have pointed out more than once, Detective Lask, I'm useless at combat. You guys go, and I'll catch up when I can."

Lask gave his Captain a final nod of respect, then stood to address the healer. "Thank you for your service, Cole. A medic is just as much of a hero as any fighter on the battlefield."

Cole rose and shook Lask's outstretched hand. "Thank you for saying so, Detective." They held each other's gaze for a beat before Cole turned to tend to his injured.

Lask picked his way between the fallen bodies until he reached Patch's side. He spoke softly, cautious of setting off the volatile hunter. "Look, Patch, it's up to us to lead these people back to the city gates before it's too late."

Patch answered with a "Fuck you" glare and took his sweet old time getting off the floor. "Someone needs to stay behind with Cole," announced Patch to the group.

"I'll do it," replied Zap as he positioned himself between Bowman and Jay.

"Thanks, man," said Patch solemnly, patting his squadmate on the back. When he turned to face Lask and Maris, Patch had fire in his eyes. "We are going to slaughter every last one of those motherfuckers and display their damned heads on stakes in the middle of the city for all to see."

Lask said nothing; now wasn't the time to argue. *Let Patch blow off some steam.* The detective assumed the silence from Maris reflected similar thinking.

"Everyone but Cole and Zap, follow me," ordered Patch as he faced the traumatized crowd. "Our night is far from over. Now listen up; here's the plan."

KOOP

Roused by the warning siren, Koop leapt out of bed faster than he knew his old body could move. *It's happening! The end of days.*

The merchant heard the announcement to remain indoors, but there was no way ol' Koop was gonna sit around and twiddle his thumbs while his city crumbled around him. He swiftly moved to the back of his closet, drew in a deep breath, and pulled out a dust-covered box. He lifted the cover, and his heart sank as he knew it would. Resting inside the box, untouched since the days of Forgotten riots in his younger years, was Koop's equally dusty hand cannon. During the worst of the riots, one led by Krakken now that he thought about it, Koop had learned how to use the weapon—but thankfully never had to. He had hoped with all his heart he would never have to see the wretched killing machine again, but he'd lived long enough to know that tonight was the night to dust it off.

The brave merchant slid out into the night, his gun raised and cocked. The last he'd heard from Maxx was just before the attack, so Koop knew who was out in the forest and who, in the city, was in the most danger. What he didn't know was what had happened out at the secret HQ or who triggered the siren since the only switches were well within the city gates. Lask's army must've had some sort of inside help.

Koop remembered back to the night when Hobb mentioned a friend, a young scientist who could help identify the "mind-reading" herb. *What was that kid's name… Benny? Lenny?* Koop had to get over to the science lab and find out what had happened to his friends and what he could do to help.

Despite the chilling silence outside Koop's hut, he knew danger very likely lurked within the city gates. As he crept toward his destination, Koop traveled the perimeter of the city's center, the heartbeat of Isotopia when the sun was up. He wondered if there would ever be a day like that again: the rush of customers, the carefree Youth, the visits from his regulars—*what if it was all gone?*

Koop's wandering thoughts were interrupted when he felt something squish beneath his feet. Having a horrid suspicion of what he had just stepped on, Koop reluctantly lowered his gaze, only to find the corpse of his dear clanmate Sharon. He fell to his knees, took her cold hands in his own, and gave his friend a kiss goodbye on the forehead as his tear splashed onto her face.

What a sweet lady. Always encouraging Hobb with his studies, encouraging me to take him on when she felt it was the kid's best chance to recover from Pan's death.

Koop looked away to stem the wave of nausea that washed over him. As much as it broke his heart, he had to keep moving. He released Sharon's hands and silently apologized for leaving her. As Koop resumed his trek to the lab, he picked up on the scurrying sounds of fellow Isotopians ignoring the warning signals. *Or they could be gun-toting hooligans like the one who killed Sharon.* Koop picked up the pace as much as his old body could, gripping his pistol so hard it could've shattered in his hand.

Grateful to have arrived at the Science Lab in one piece, Koop whipped open the door and found a traumatized young man lying in front of two large surveillance screens. The scientist clan did have a reputation for working around the clock, but they weren't renowned for their fortitude, and the warning siren would have been enough to put an end to late-night studies. No, this had to be Hobb's friend. As Koop studied the young scientist's face, he saw pure terror.

"Put your hands up," ordered a strange, deep voice.

Koop recognized the modulated voice from that eerie night when the lone helmet soldier crossed the city, and it had taken Lask to contain him. *Shit.*

Koop stuck his hands in the air. "You've got nothing to worry about from me. I'm just an old man who apparently ended up in the wrong place at the wrong time—"

"He was here for Dr. Adams," said the scientist. *Len, that was his name.* Len pointed with a quivering finger toward an office at the back of the room. Koop turned to see three bullet holes in the glass windows and tracked them to yet another casualty, lying dead in a pool of his own blood.

"Quiet!" said the soldier. He took a step toward Len.

"They're gonna kill all of them," Len said quickly. "And probably us, too, just for the fun of it."

"That's *enough*!" ordered the soldier as he forcefully kicked Len and knocked the wind out of him. "Although that's certainly not a bad idea." The soldier moved his rifle toward the young scientist's head.

"Please don't," begged Koop. "He's just a kid. He's not who you're after."

The soldier cackled, which sounded particularly chilling filtered through the voice modulator. "You think you decide who I'm after? Maybe you should go first instead. It doesn't matter much either way."

If asked, Koop would have agreed with the assassin. Nothing mattered anymore with death closing in all around him.

"Say goodnight old ma—"

Glass shards flew across the tiled lab floor, and the soldier collapsed before making good on his threat, a fountain of blood spouting from his neck. Through his dazed vision, Koop saw the door bang open and an IES soldier rush inside.

"Who the hell are you?" Koop asked, unsure if he was about to be killed by the man who'd just saved him.

"Don't worry; you're safe now. I'm Sergeant Kane, and I was sent by a friend."

"Lask!" shouted Koop and Len simultaneously.

Kane nodded. "They already got to your Head Scientist?"

Len jerked his chin toward the office. "Yeah, you're too late for Dr. Adams."

"Dammit! They're going after all the clan heads and any Panel reps who haven't joined their cause."

Head Merchant Katt and Rep Ivy Tikki. Koop's world stopped spinning as he imagined both of his leaders dead. The merchant lifestyle that was the beating heart of the city would be shattered beyond repair.

"What's the point?" asked Len. "Why are they doing this? What are they trying to accomplish?"

"Who knows?" responded Koop. "Apparently, some of our supposed 'leaders' don't approve of the current system. Why else would they be taking out everyone in charge of it?"

"We'll all be dead within weeks even if we don't end up with a pellet in our head tonight," said Len.

"If enough of us manage to survive this… this revolution, we can still save Isotopia."

Koop thought about Chief Advisor Graper, the living symbol of clan society, and prayed he was safe. Isotopia would need a man like Graper.

COLE

Cole alternated between stifling tears and taking puffs of his bliss leaf herbarette as he rammed his jumbo-root shovel into the dirt. *I'd like to see that anti-herbal stiff Lask bury his own friends without a fat dose of nature's medicine.* A rustling in the nearby bushes halted Cole's shovel and his sour thoughts. If the rest of the pack had made it back to the city, this could not be a welcome intrusion.

Zap snatched his blaster from its holster and poked his head out of the grave he'd nearly finished digging, bracing himself for unexpected company.

"Cole? Cole, put your gun down. It's me."

Cole tilted his head. "*Hobb?* The fuck are *you* doing all the way out here at a time like this?"

"I'm training," said the beaming new hunter between charged, rapid breaths. "Patch says sleep is for pussies and that you have to train like a man if you want to be able to shoot like one. I'm actually looking for Patch; we were supposed to have a training session. Have you seen him? And what was that warning signal about—"

And then Hobb saw the bodies. Maxx. Captain Ranger. His friend, Jay. Hobb lifted his face to the sky and screamed Jay's name, then collapsed next to him on the ground. "What happened here?" His gaze was so intense, his eyes practically burned holes into Zap's.

Zap climbed out of the grave and tossed the shovel aside. "Look, Hobb—"

Hobb rose suddenly and grabbed Zap with both hands, slamming him against a nearby tree. "Why didn't you tell me about this?" The hunter gave no response.

Cole, watching the scene unfold and trying desperately to come up with something helpful to say, took a deep breath. He knew Patch felt guilty for keeping everything from Hobb, but the kid really needed to know.

"Hobb," Cole started, placing a hand on the kid's shoulder. "Let me fill in the blanks for you." Cole had his attention now.

Hobb released his grip on Zap, who shot Cole a look of gratitude. The healer told Hobb about the rebellion, about the battle that had taken place, and about his friend Jay, who had fought bravely for the cause. He explained that the remaining rebels had fled to the city to hunt down the enemy and that Lask and Patch had joined forces to lead the rebellion.

Hobb's ears pricked up when he heard Patch's name. "*What* did you just say?"

"I'm sorry, Hobb. Patch was worried it was too dangerous, so he ordered us not to 'dex you."

"Let me get this straight: Patch was worried about me, so he kept me completely in the dark about these attacks? He thought I'd be 'protected' by sitting on my ass without at least *warning* me that Isotopia as we know it could end tonight? Or, at the very least, give me the courtesy to let me say goodbye to my friends before they..." Hobb glanced at Jay's lifeless corpse again and trembled violently, as if his body couldn't decide whether he was more furious or devastated.

The three men sat quietly for several seconds without meeting each other's gaze. Cole knew no words could pull this poor kid out of the utter tragedy he had just stumbled upon in the deep forest and that even looking into his eyes could trigger another outburst of rage or grief. Instead, Cole shifted his gaze to Zap; after all, it was the hunter clan who'd left Hobb out to dry. It only seemed fair *they* should be the targets of Hobb's erratic behavior, not the poor, innocent Healer Drug Dealer.

To Cole's relief, Hobb managed to stop shaking and draw a deep breath. The young hunter lifted his chin from his chest, revealing a burning intensity in his eyes. "I am going to *kill that asshole*! Fuck it—why stop at Patch? Maris is just as guilty for going along with that cocky backstabbing piece of shit."

Hobb seized the rette out of Cole's trembling hands and, as he was about to storm off, glared at Zap. "And what about you, *pal*? You were here the whole time and never spoke up for me? Some 'family' this clan is. In fact, maybe you should watch your back too, Zap. Something tells me my appetite for revenge won't be quenched when I'm done with the first two."

The burial ground fell silent as Hobb disappeared into the forest, taking Cole's rette along with him. *Good god, what have I started?*

GRAPER

Party crashers had always been a pet peeve of Graper's, but the enormous hulk who kicked Nat's door clean off its hinges could've at least had the courtesy to knock first. Nat leapt off the living room couch and screamed, but Graper didn't flinch. He remained seated, right where Nat had rested her head on his shoulders seconds earlier. *Sands Graper, you fool! Why did I come here and put her in danger?*

Of course, it wouldn't have taken much imagination for Bogue Issler and her lackey to find Graper here after he and Nat had been caught breaking into Bogue's office together. What Graper hadn't counted on was Bogue's recklessness in coming to Nat's hut. There was a reason Bogue had spared them up to this point. Something or someone must have had made her desperate.

Bogue strutted up to Graper, and he stood to meet her eye—not that he ever found it easy to ignore the hideous scars covering half her face. "You're *done*," she said.

"Tell me, Bogue, what's your big plan after all this?" he asked, still close enough to Bogue that the bodyguard stood nearby with his rifle cocked. "Kill everyone who opposes you and your friends, then sit back and watch while the city crumbles?"

"I'd like to believe it's a little more elegant than that," replied Issler, "but you're not too far off. One thing you didn't account for was the magnitude of your role."

"My role? Why would I want any part of this?"

"Now, now, Sands. No need to thank me for including you. I like to reward my fellow Panel members, especially my beloved advisor."

Graper didn't even want to try to guess what she meant. "Natalya has nothing to do with this," said Graper, jutting his chin toward Nat, playing down his feelings.

"Oh, Miss Corper?" Bogue's icy smile sent a shiver down Graper's spine. "Don't you worry—I haven't forgotten about her. Levol?" She motioned for the giant to come closer. "Kill that bitch."

Before Graper could process the words, Levol blasted Nat in the heart with his oversized rifle, launching her into the wall and splattering the room with her blood. As Graper rocked back on his heels, he caught the look of wonder on Levol's face as he marveled at his work.

"Grab him, and let's go!" ordered Bogue.

Levol hoisted Graper over his shoulders. Everything went black.

ARLO

Arlo wasn't used to hunting alone; that's not how things worked in the forest. The clan watched each other's backs, and the usual perils of the forest were nothing compared to this madness ailing Isotopia, people hunting other people. But Arlo had no choice. He had his orders: sprint straight to Healer Rep Natalya's Corper's home and secure the premises.

Arlo had taken a couple of rough hits during the shootout—a pellet to his right arm and another in his lower abdomen. Cole had removed the bullets, patched him up, and dosed him with "just enough bliss leaf to run through the pain." *Poggshit.* Arlo should've known by now that "just enough" for someone like Cole meant "way too much" for any normal human. Arlo was grateful to be able to stay on his feet and do his job, but he could've done without the brain fog.

Corper's hut came into view. Arlo lifted his rifle to eye level and peered through the window. *Blood splatter.* The hair rose on the back of Arlo's neck—he was too late. He crept closer and swept the rifle scope across the room. Corper's dead body lay on the floor in a pool of blood. *Fuck, fuck, fuck!*

His senses were a bit dulled by the bliss leaf, but Patch and Maris had taught Arlo well, and he wasn't giving up now. He could still track down the bastard who killed Corper.

Arlo scrambled around to the gaping hole that used to be the front door and frantically searched for clues. Faint

206

patches of dirt dispersed around the wooden floor indicated there were at least three intruders. Three soldiers to kill one healer? It didn't add up, especially since the helmet soldiers' numbers were dwindling.

Arlo checked the ground outside and scratched his head. *Only two sets of footprints now?* Either Arlo's initial assumption was wrong, or one of the intruders had disappeared. *Or wasn't creating footprints anymore.* The hunter picked up his gun and started running.

Arlo sprinted to the outskirts of the city, keeping his eyes peeled for subtle bends in the grass that would lead him to his prey. As he tracked, he fought with all his might to ward off thoughts of his fallen friends. He and Jay had only hunted together for a year, but it didn't take much time to get to know a squadmate chasing boars side by side in the forest. Jay was a goof; always good for a laugh. Like Pan, Jay had an aura of light that spread to those around him. That light was needed now more than ever, and Jay's would never shine again.

Arlo had never been personally close to Rep Bowman either, but the man had led their squad for two years alongside Maris and Patch—quite the powerhouse combination. According to Patch, Bowman taught Maris everything he knew.

A familiar voice called out Arlo's name up ahead. Ignoring the dull ache in his belly, Arlo raced forward to meet Patch.

PATCH

"Arlo!" shouted Patch through cupped hands. "Over here!"

"Hey, watch the volume," warned Lask. "Arlo's not the only one out here."

Arlo punched through the thick branches and jogged up to Patch. "Damn, dude! You can't even keep your voice down when we're surrounded by heavily armed assassins?"

Lask shot Patch a know-it-all smirk.

Patch rolled his eyes. "Where's Corper?"

Arlo shook his head. "I was too late."

"Dammit!" Lask yelled.

Arlo jumped in again. "I think someone was with her when she was ambushed. I've been tracking two sets of footprints from her hut that led me—"

A live Isodex broadcast cut short Arlo's report. Koop's face emerged from the blurred pixels on Patch's wristband.

"Hey, guys," whispered Koop. "Len and Lask filled me in. We've lost some great men. Poor old Maxx." Koop paused to choke back tears. "And I found my dear friend Sharon dead in the street."

Sergeant Kane's face edged out Koop's. "I was unable to save Dr. Adams, but as you can see, I was at least quick enough to save this old troublemaker here along with our scientist friend, Len. What's the word on your end?"

"We lost one, too," replied Patch sadly, struggling to get the words out. "Koop, I'm really sorry. We tried to save Katt, but he was already gone."

"I know this doesn't make the loss any easier," added

Lask, "but we beat the soldier who murdered him to a damn bloody pulp with our bare hands."

Patch nodded. "We did fuck that guy up."

Koop looked sad but not surprised. Or maybe his lack of expression reflected a state of shock from losing so many people he cared about. "What about Ivy?"

"We're not sure yet," replied Patch. "but Maris is on her, and that's the man you want." Koop's grimace loosened up a little.

"They've been three steps ahead of us at every turn," Lask said. "We need to catch up to them and fast. Did you have anything else for us, Koop?"

"Do you have Graper? He wasn't at his hut, and we don't know where else to look."

"We're searching for him," Lask said.

"Hey, Patch—come check this out!"

Patch followed Arlo's gaze to the boot treads he'd tracked to the edge of the clearing, then caught Lask's attention as well.

"Okay, Koop," Lask said, "we're about to head into the Panel HQ; we have reason to believe Graper may be there. We'll keep you updated. Meanwhile, go back to your damn hut. Len set off the warning siren for a reason. I don't want any more of my friends dying tonight!"

"Hell no!" shouted Koop. "If the world is gonna end tonight, then I want to be there to witness it—especially if we might still have a chance to stop it." Kane and Len could be heard agreeing in the background. "We'll see you there," Koop announced firmly.

Koop's face blurred, then the Isodex went blank. Patch sighed heavily. The old man was going to get himself killed.

A soft swoosh near the city gates caught Patch's attention. He turned to see Hobb, decked out in full hunting gear, clearing the top of a chain-link fence. Patch's heart jumped into his throat. *What the hell was he doing here?*

Maybe the kid had been out training when the sirens

sounded, and he was just now returning home. It was possible he didn't know anything. *He certainly would soon*, Patch reasoned. All he had to do was ask one question to the group, and Hobb would learn everything Patch had been trying to shield him from. And he was gonna be pissed.

Correction—he was already pissed! Hobb charged straight for Patch, his expression twisted with anger and determination.

"Listen, Hobb. Everything happened so fast, and I felt responsible for your safety. I couldn't let you—" Hobb's fist met Patch's jaw with such force, it threw Patch onto his back. Hand-to-hand combat wasn't exactly part of the hunter clan training.

"I ran into Cole in the woods," snapped Hobb as his glare shifted from Patch to Lask to Arlo, implying their shared guilt. "I saw the bodies." Hobb's voice cracked. "I saw Jay."

Patch pushed off the forest floor and sat up, rubbing his jaw as he spoke softly. "We did all we could."

"No, you did *not!*" Hobb's face turned a scary shade of purple. "You could have called me. You too, Arlo. *Both* of you betrayed me. We're clan! Squadmates! We're supposed to be brothers!"

"They were trying to save your life," said Lask.

"This is none of your business, Detective." Hobb started to shake; tears rolled down his cheeks. He turned back to the hunters. "Truth is, I was never one of you— not when I failed all your exams, and not now, despite what Patch keeps telling me. I just feel like a damn fool for thinking I could *ever* be a hunter."

"You're not a fool," said Patch, "and I wouldn't have taken you on if I didn't think you could be one of us."

Hobb cackled, growing increasingly hysterical. "*Bullshit!*"

"Look, kid, I'm really sorry we didn't bring you with us. I felt horrible when I made the choice, but I thought you just weren't ready yet. I didn't want your death on my hands."

"Oh, don't worry Patch. I believe you. I believe that you considered bringing along your personal trainee but decided that covering your ass and keeping your conscience clear were considerably more appealing. Well, guess what? Your conscience should be *far* from clear. I know I wouldn't have been your most valuable soldier, but who knows—maybe things could have turned out just a bit differently if you'd've had one more hunter at your side. Maybe Jay or Bowman or any one of the other poor dead souls might still be alive. Oh, and let's not forget how you tried to get me hooked on Nectar."

Patch blinked up at Hobb, who scoffed. "Yeah, Patch, I knew. Cole confirmed my suspicions, but it was obvious from the moment I joined your squad. I just didn't care because I was so happy to call the hunter clan my family. You really fucked me over, Patch, and I hope the guilt eats away at your soul. Maybe then *you'll* be the one drowning in Nectar—we'll see who the stuff kills first. Shit, I'll race you there. After all, as Koop likes to say, *'Once an addict, always an addict.'"*

Patch said nothing, just stared with defeated eyes at the kid who'd once looked up to him.

"Fuck you, Patch, the great hunter." Hobb shifted his accusatory glare to Arlo, then Lask. "Fuck you all."

The kid sauntered away from the group before anyone could respond, disappearing into the blackness of the night.

BOGUE ISSLER, CHAIRPERSON

Bogue hated elevators, especially small elevators. A cramped space where everyone could see everyone else's face up close was not her idea of fun. The Chairperson traced her left index finger along her scar line as the group ascended in the dread-box to the top of the Panel Headquarters, but her usual self-soothing strategy didn't stop her stomach from churning like a carousel.

There was no one in the world who could truly look into Bogue's eyes without being sickened to some extent, and it made her so, so lonely. Sometimes, when Bogue was safely locked away in her home, she would succumb to the dark urges. Her occasional outbursts took various forms, ranging from crying herself to sleep to tearing apart her hut.

Fortunately for Bogue, she had the will and self-discipline to never, ever show another human being her vulnerable side. In fact, her ability to disguise herself and slither into a different personality for every situation allowed her to dazzle everyone she met. It also made her a manipulative bitch here and there, but hey—if you know you have a talent, it's a tragic waste not to take advantage of it.

I hate elevators. It wasn't that the HQ elevator was out of date, but the building was just so damn tall.

Suck it up, Issler. Scrunched against the back wall between her faithful minions, Bogue was already trying to forget the sight of her long-time, faithful advisor on his knees with Levol's gun pressed against the back of his head as if Graper were a beast dragged from the forest. She couldn't avoid the peripheral glimpse of Graper's pitiful, desperate eyes staring up at her. Despite the atrocities, the only emotions Graper's gaze held were disappointment and pure, naked sadness. Bogue would've preferred him kicking, yelling, and cursing her for betraying him every step of the way; that's certainly what she would've done in his position.

Normally such trivial details didn't burden her—why should she care about Graper's *feelings?*—but Bogue was uncharacteristically conflicted. Sands had always advised her honestly and full-heartedly, even when they'd disagreed.

It's so close. I'm so close. Ever since discovering her knack for leadership as a young girl, Bogue had snatched up every opportunity to work her way up the chain, no matter whose back she had to stab. After her long, hard battle to achieve the highest rank in Isotopia, after hammering out all the logistics with Harding and Krakken and outfitting her glorious new army with their state-of-the-art mind helmets, Bogue was a mere five, no *four*, floors away from achieving her childhood dreams.

Thirteen-year-old Bogue Issler knew she was born to lead. She transcended her peers in every dimension: beauty, intelligence, ambition, talent. Her conceit was not unfounded; she was *that* good. What truly set her apart, though, was her ability to manipulate people's feeble minds into doing her bidding without the slightest suspicion of her true intent. Bogue was a spicy, young woman who already had all of Isotopia's attention on her—and she basked in its warmth like a flower soaking up the sun's rays.

Other girls made wishes; Bogue set goals. She had a head for science and the charisma to do or be anything she wanted, but no matter how many accolades Bogue received, she always felt like an outsider. She could meld with society—*hell*, she planned to *lead* it someday—yet no amount of validation from her so-called peers would ever satisfy her. After all, respect from someone not worth respecting wasn't worth a damn, and the only person in Isotopia bright enough for Bogue to respect was the one person she truly loved, her twin sister Ruby. Deep down, Bogue always knew she could never have considered dreaming so large without Ruby's unwavering support.

Ruby was as sweet as Bogue was tough, but they shared that relentless, competitive edge. At thirteen, Ruby became the youngest healer ever actively recruited. Her soul belonged to the clan's peaceful and embracing community, but she became a star of the clan the instant she joined, and you can't break records at that age unless you have a warrior streak in your blood. Bogue was the only person observant enough to see the fire in her sister, and Ruby was the only one in Isotopia who could keep up with her twin's massive intellect. It was the Issler sisters against the world, and they were going to win.

First, they would take their respective clans by storm, climbing the ranks straight to the top. Bogue would make a discovery that would revolutionize scientific research, and Ruby would mix up an assortment of original remedies and save countless lives. From there, Head Scientist Bogue Issler and Head Healer Ruby Issler would be elected by their clans to serve in Isotopia's most prestigious role—Panel Representative.

Finally, when the entire city knew and respected the Issler duo, Bogue would take the throne of Isotopia Chairperson with the only person in the world she trusted by her side as Chief Advisor. Together, the twins would lead Isotopia into a golden age of progress and high spirits, and the names *Bogue and Ruby Issler* would never be forgotten.

As childhood fantasies often do, Bogue's hit a snag. The scientist-healer rivalry, as old as the clan system itself, reached its peak during the Isslers' thirteenth year. It was no secret the scientists were cruel to anyone they perceived as less intelligent, the healers being their favorite targets. The current Head Healer had less tolerance for ridicule than his predecessors and more of a capacity for violence—a combination that contributed to a climate of increasing hostility. Any clan member on either side who didn't exhibit unquestionable loyalty was shunned. Bogue and Ruby agreed that this clan rivalry bullshit would be the first thing they abolished once they were in a position to do so, but meanwhile, the twins had no choice but to appear to drift apart in the eyes of their peers. In secret, they remained as loyal to each other as ever.

The more time the Isslers spent in their respective clans, the more they came to appreciate how vastly they'd underestimated the depth of the all-encompassing, mutual science-healer hatred. Panel meetings, meant to be discussions among leaders and role models, often deteriorated into childish shouting matches between the Scientist and Healer representatives with the fights unfolding in the same, predictable pattern: the Science Rep would openly undermine the role of the healing clan, referring to their work as "hocus-pocus" or "an excuse to get recked all day, every day." The indignant Healing Rep would fire back that their mixtures saved lives better than any "synthetic bullshit made in a lab." The arguments often gained so much momentum, not even the Chairperson could break them up, resulting in wasted meetings that were intended to ensure the highest quality of life possible for the citizens of Isotopia.

These Panel feuds trickled down the chain of command to the clan heads and members. In fact, one of the first things a new scientist or healer learned from their veteran clanmates was that the opposite clan was the sworn enemy—with zero exceptions. If a healer were to treat a scientist with any modicum of respect, or vice versa, that person would be a traitor to the clan.

Bogue and Ruby learned these rules but weren't about

to let some ancient lore come between them. The sisters reunited as often as they could, always picking a different meet-up spot deep in the forest so they couldn't be traced. One day during work hours, Ruby's clan head caught her sending an Isotext to Bogue, asking where and when to meet. In an instant, Ruby tumbled from superstar to traitor and was permanently exiled from her clan.

Once news spread of what Ruby had done, the citizens of Isotopia demanded to know whether Bogue, too, lacked the strength to stand on her own two feet. Defending Ruby would only lead her to the same fate as her exiled sister and would have done Ruby no good. Bogue would have died before watching both Isslers go up in flames.

Bogue was on the cusp of becoming something great; she simply couldn't afford to risk her career. Bogue sold out her sister, told the inquiry board that Ruby had never been anything more than another low-life healer to her; her sister's attempt to communicate with her had been a one-sided display of affection. As Bogue's commitment to her lie grew, she began to believe it herself, and the thoughts that kept her up for countless nights gradually subsided.

The drama of the Issler twins became a scandal Bogue brilliantly leveraged to prove her loyalty to her own clan, vaulting her own career further up and her beloved sister further down. As much as it tore up her soul, Bogue continued to suppress her love, guilt, and self-hatred as the spotlight shifted from Ruby's betrayal to Bogue's loyalty. Bogue ascended to Head Scientist as Ruby fell out of the clan system and eventually faded from the minds of Isotopia until most citizens only knew of one Issler.

A month or so later, Bogue awoke in the middle of the night to a knock. Curious and confused, Bogue rose from her bed, half asleep, and opened the door. At first, she didn't recognize the filthy, unkempt woman standing before her, but the instant she met the stranger's piercing blue eyes, Bogue's heart shattered, and she wept for the first time since she could remember. *Ruby.*

In that instant, the truth Bogue had buried deeper and deeper in her mind leapt out of its grave. She resisted the urge to fall to her knees and beg for forgiveness and stood in her doorway as tears rolled down her cheeks. "Ruby... I don't even know where to begin. Words can't express how awful I feel for what I did to you."

Ruby replied in a soft, defeated tone as foreign as her disastrous physical appearance. "You did what you had to do." Ruby was not upset or angry as Bogue had feared; even worse, she had become no more than a talking corpse. "Nothing good would have come out of your doing anything different. Not for me, not for you... not for anyone." Bogue's trickle of tears turned into streams. It had never occurred to her that the worst form of punishment from her sister was none at all.

"How can you say that, Ruby? You're my twin sister, the only person I care about in the entire world, and I abandoned you when you needed me most!"

Ruby said nothing; her dead eyes stared in the direction of Bogue's, but the spark was gone. It was too late. Bogue trembled with terror at what she had done. She had to get her Ruby back.

"No," said Bogue. "I won't accept that." She grabbed her ghost of a sister by the shoulders and shook her, breaking out into hysteria. *To hell with self-control. Fuck anyone who frowns upon me for loving my Ruby.* "YELL AT ME! TELL ME YOU'LL NEVER FORGIVE ME!" Bogue's choppy breaths almost made her faint. "Let me know you're still in there! *Please*, Ruby!"

"I came here to say goodbye," replied Ruby. "We can't see each other again—you know that. I love you, Bogue, but don't come looking for me because you won't find me." Bogue's sister turned and walked off into the night, leaving Bogue completely, utterly alone.

In the space of three short years, Bogue ascended to Head Scientist and then Scientist Panel Rep faster than the rest of Isotopia could blink. The only divergence from her plan was that her sister wasn't sitting at the table—Bogue was on her own.

To the outside observer, Bogue was the superstar she knew she would be, but on the inside, she died a little each day. Despite her wallowing guilt, Bogue had made her decision: she'd traded her soul for her seat at the Panel table, and quitting now would make it all for nothing. Ruby was right—it would have only sabotaged them both had Bogue intervened with her sister's fall from grace.

One late afternoon, Bogue set out to interview a potential new Healer Rep for the Panel. The candidate, Natalya Corper, supposedly had talent and backbone unlike the healing clan had seen for a long time. She could never fill the role like Ruby could have, but given the circumstances, she would have to do. The journey to Corper's house involved a stroll through South City Park, also known as Forgotten Island. Bogue had heard all the chilling tales of the less-than-human occupants of the park. Rumor had it, the wastes of life who resided in the park were zombies that sat still for days on end, smoked themselves into reck leaf-induced psychosis, and occasionally ate one of their own for sustenance. Even as a Youth, Bogue knew these rumors were nothing more than fictitious horror stories, yet she had always avoided South City Park whenever possible.

Bogue felt a wobble in her gait as she ventured into this new territory, so foreign from anything she had ever known. Each step sent another shiver down her spine and another bead of sweat to her eyebrows. It certainly wasn't some psycho-zombie-cannibal breeding ground, but the park had an unnerving darkness about it. In fact, she could certainly understand how those rumors had come about. A stale, subtle yet pervasive stench of death mixed with alive-but-rotting flesh permeated the air, and Bogue tasted the smell after pinching her nostrils closed. The atmosphere had a distinct lethargic energy to it that sucked the life out of Bogue as she looked down at her pale, shaking palms.

It wouldn't have been such a haunting experience had Bogue not stuck out like a sore thumb among the clumps of Forgotten—most half asleep, slouched with their backs against a tree, others cackling as they passed around a needle, exposing the few putrid teeth that hadn't yet fallen out. Bogue gagged as she spotted a small group of these monsters feasting on a raw, freshly-killed pogg. Some appeared to be purposefully clustered together, but all in all, it seemed as if each of these Forgotten lived in complete ignorance of everyone and everything around them. She supposed it was the only way they could bear living in such filth.

Bogue fixed her eyes on the ground as she passed these rancid excuses for humans, but she couldn't escape the ghastly, hungry, aggressive eyes burning holes in her body. She could practically see their grime and sickness oozing into her own system. For the first time in her life, Bogue was spooked.

She picked up the pace. *Eyes on the prize.*

Just before the finish line at the eastern gate, Bogue broke into a jog. *Almost there.* She tripped over something—some*one*, she realized—and caught herself just before falling. Bogue's heart pounded hard and fast against her chest, and she let out an involuntary shout.

"I'm so sorry—" but Bogue realized to her horror that the body she had trampled was already dead. She placed her hand to her chest to slow her breathing.

This body was worse than dead. Bone-deep scars covered the body from head to toe, and the wounds were filled with feasting flutterpoggs and maggants. The implement of the mutilation appeared to be a sharpened, blood-smeared jumbo-root resting in the corpse's open hand. The rumors were true—this place was a living hell.

Bogue choked down another gag, but morbid curiosity took control, pulling her closer to study the monster at close range. A wave of nausea hit Bogue so hard she fell to her knees next to the body, erupting into tears. She had only experienced such emotion one other time in her entire life.

With a trembling hand, Bogue swept the hair away to peer into the face beneath the scars and blood. So, Ruby was wrong—Bogue had seen her again, after all.

Bogue fell across her beloved sister's rotting body and wept. Crying became screaming. She was attracting more attention from the zombies surrounding her, but that was nothing compared to this twisted horror. *This is what I did. This is all my fault.*

As sobs wracked Bogue's body, she snatched the stick from her sister's cold hand and stabbed the bloody tip into her own forehead, drove it down her left temple and cheek. Her sister's blood mixed with her own and ran down the fancy pogg-hide suit she'd worn for her meeting with Corper. She stabbed again, this time down the right side. Once she started, she couldn't stop. Each cut and scream offered some sick relief; she cut deeper and screamed louder as a crowd of Forgotten surrounded her to watch the show. Some stared; some laughed and cheered her on; others backed away in fear. Out of all the fucked-up activities that went on in this park, Bogue had managed to steal the show. Finally, when her arms grew too heavy to raise and her voice blew out, Bogue dropped the root and slumped onto Ruby, spilling fresh blood onto her sister's corpse.

After a while, there were no more tears to cry. Bogue wiped the blood from her face and lifted her eyes. Only one audience member remained—an old man with jaded eyes and ragged clothes—and she gratefully grasped the hand he extended to pull her up. Without a word, the man threw Bogue's arm over his shoulder and walked her limp body all the way back to the western gate, where he steadied her, then released her.

Alone, Bogue dragged herself home and cried dry tears until her body slept while her mind tortured her with an endless loop through the horrific spectacles she had witnessed.

The elevator doors slid open. Bogue glared down at Sands Graper, the man who unknowingly occupied the Panel position that was never meant for him, the man whose gentle optimism brainwashed all of Isotopia into believing the so-called "freedom" of the clan system was worth the suffering of those who fell through the cracks. Tonight, Graper would finally pay. It would be the Forgottens' turn to be free. How fitting Levol would be the one to drag Graper out onto the roof to his death.

"Oh, wait. Close the doors, Krakken." Graper glanced up hopefully at Bogue. "Nice try, Sands," she said, laughing cruelly in his face. "No, we have another piece of trash we need to dispose of."

Before anyone could blink, Bogue whipped out her blade and sliced through the helmet strap at Cam's throat. Blood spurted out, splattering everyone in the cramped space as the life drained out of him. Cam's head slumped, the added weight of the external battery pack lurching his body forward onto Harding's legs. Harding jumped back with a squeak.

"For Pete's sake, Mason, be a man and a scientist. It's just a dead body," Bogue admonished him. "And Krakken, way to let that cocky little shit think he could control us."

Bogue twisted the helmet off Cam and pulled it onto her head. *Nothing.* "Am I supposed to feel different? Is this thing working?"

No answer from the scientist.

"Harding! Get a damn grip!" The shouting snapped Harding out of his daze.

"Uh, Cam was a smart kid," responded Harding, unable to tear his gaze from the body of his brightest protégé. "We know he customized his helmet. I'd be willing to bet he made damn sure no one else would ever be able to use that thing."

"Dammit! Useless, cocky, *and* greedy. Is this how you breed your scientists, Harding?"

Harding lifted his eyes and stared dully at Bogue.

"Oh, never mind," said Bogue, growing impatient. "Just tell me what he did and how to get past it."

"If it were me, I'd have put an ID scanner into the motherboard."

"Annnnd?"

"And," Harding continued, flinching as if preparing to be the next bastard sliced open, "there's no override I'm aware of."

Bogue tugged the helmet off and flung it on top of Cam's crumpled body.

"What are you all waiting for? Open the goddamn doors, and let's get out there!"

LASK

"You think we should try to stop Hobb?" asked Lask, his eyes glued to the Panel building.

"Good luck with that. He's like me—fiery and stubborn," said Patch. "There's nothing we can do or say to stop him now. We just have to wait for him to cool off."

"Um, it didn't seem like he will be cooling off any time soon," replied Arlo.

Hobb's identity crisis wasn't at the top of Lask's worries at the moment—not with the entirety of Isotopian life on the line. "My guess is he's gone off to make sure Len's safe," Lask said. "Hobb should be fine with Len, Koop, and Kane; that is, *if* he finds them and is smart enough to stay with them." *Although he'll probably be just as pissed at Len as he was at Patch.*

Maris emerged from the quiet night, catching them all by surprise. His clothes glistened with blood in the scant light from the moon.

"What *happened* to you, Maris?" asked Patch.

"I didn't get to Ivy in time, but I caught up to the soldier who killed her. These guys leave tracks so obvious, a healer could hunt them down." Maris produced a severed head from behind his back, helmet still securely fastened, and dropped it onto the ground with an audible *splat* and a puddle of blood and brains.

"Fuck's sake, Maris!" yelled Patch as he bent to wipe the mess from his hunting boots.

"Never known you to be squeamish, Patch," Maris

said, a slight note of teasing in his voice.

"Animal blood is one thing," Patch grumbled. "Human innards are another story entirely—one I'd prefer to not get used to, thank you very much."

Maris shrugged. "Anyway, these helmet soldiers are strong, but they can be caught off guard. We have to all keep that in mind as we proceed."

The four men stood in uncomfortable silence, sizing each other up to see who would call their next move. Lask's skin crawled as he felt eyes rolling toward him from all directions. He'd always felt underestimated and underutilized within his clan, but his past bitterness was featherlight compared to the weight of his sudden responsibility.

Lask spoke with the authority and confidence his army of amateurs needed, even if he had to fake it. "All eyes on the headquarters. If you see anything suspicious, call it out quickly and identify its position."

"You mean, like those three who just appeared on the roof?" Arlo said.

Lask raised his binoculars and zoomed in on the top of the HQ. "Good *and* bad news, guys—we've located our missing Chief Advisor, and he's with Issler and that behemoth bodyguard."

"What the hell are they doing up there?" Patch asked, taking the binoculars from Lask.

"And where are the rest of them?" Maris added. "Cam, Harding, Krakken..."

A rustling in the bushes caught Lask's attention. He turned to see his sergeant emerge with Koop and Len trailing closely behind.

"What'd we miss?" Koop asked.

No one said a word, but Patch nodded toward the roof, and the old merchant clutched his chest.

"No, no, no." Koop's eyes darted toward Lask. "Tell me you have a plan for getting Graper down from there in one piece."

"We're working on it," replied Lask. "Hobb isn't with you?"

"We stopped by his place, and he wasn't there," said Len. "Why? Did you see him?"

"He stopped by for a friendly hello," said Patch bleakly.

Lask scoffed. "The kid wasn't too happy when he realized his buddies didn't keep him in the loop about our operation tonight."

Koop frowned. "Oh, shit."

"Exactly," Lask said. "He stormed off; we were hoping he would try to contact you."

"Nope. We haven't heard a peep," replied Len. "His Isodex must be off. I couldn't reach him. Ugh… I hope he doesn't think I betrayed him."

"Yeah, it wasn't pretty," Patch said, pointing to his swollen nose. "Watch your back."

"Damn! *Hobb* did that… to *you*?" Len rubbed his own nose as if feeling the blow.

"The kid may not be the most skilled hunter in Isotopia, but he packs a damn good punch when he wants to," said Arlo.

"Last time I saw him, we left on okay terms," replied Len. "Maybe I can talk him down."

"Yeah, good luck with that," retorted Patch. "Something tells me he won't be so easy to find."

Lask was growing tired of hearing about this basket case of a kid. "Can you all shut up for a second?" he snapped. "Something is going on up there."

The group fell silent and directed their eyes toward the top of the tower, where Bogue stepped forward to face the crowd of confused citizens that had formed at the base of the building. Word of mouth beat out a warning siren every time, and the commotion on the roof of the city's tallest and most important building had people more than curious.

"Good evening, my fellow Isotopians." The Chairperson's voice boomed through the citywide speakers, and the gathered crowd hushed, eager to hear what their leader had in store for them. "Ladies and gentlemen of this great city," started Bogue, "tonight is a night I have been waiting for ever since I became your Chairperson. Tonight is a night of drastic change. You see"—the Chairperson's voice rose above the frantic chatter that ensued—"some of us have had ideas for a long time about how to make our Isotopia a better place, and it is only now that we are able to start implementing them."

Despite the concern among his band of rebels, Lask stood tall, clenched his teeth, and listened.

"Well, what do you say, Isotopia? Are you ready for change? Are you ready for a better city? For complete freedom?"

Issler's remarks were met with a smattering of applause and a low hum of confusion.

"I *said*, ARE YOU READY FOR A BETTER ISOTOPIA?"

Pockets of applause gained momentum, but these people had no idea what they were clapping for.

"That's what I like to hear!" responded Bogue. "On that note, let us begin with a word from your Chief Advisor and my trusted friend, Sands Graper!"

Lask focused his binoculars on Graper. Even blurred, it was clear that was no smile on Graper's face. The detective turned to exchange a look of horror with Patch, only to find the hunter was nowhere to be seen.

Lask whirled around desperately. "Where's Patch?" *Where the fuck did that kid go when we need him most?*

Lask charged toward the building, elbowing his way through the crowd, tracking down the hunter he was going to rip to shreds.

PATCH

Oh, hell no.

There was no way Patch was letting Bogue or her minions take this shit any further. Lask meant well, but the detective had no workable plan, and he was only going to slow Patch down. There was no other way; Patch had to do this himself—and now.

After a quick assessment, the hunter ruled out accessing the roof by elevator. Surely, the Chairperson had blanketed the interior with guards. Besides, Graper would be dead before the elevator reached the roof again. *There has to be another way.*

Patch pushed through the dense crowd, then sprinted around to the rear of the building. Grateful for the climbing gear he always kept stuffed inside his jacket pockets, he quickly pulled on his suction gloves and foot treads. *Just like any other day in the woods.* But tonight, Patch wasn't after poggs or tissilisks—he was after the most dangerous and powerful minds in Isotopia.

Checking to make sure he wasn't being watched, he took a short hop, extended his hands against the building, and latched on with the treads. *Left hand, right foot, left foot, right hand. Left hand, right foot, left foot, right hand.* About halfway up, Patch lost momentum when he gave into his urge to look around. Above him lay an impossibly high obstacle that touched the clouds, and below was a fall that would break every bone in his body.

"My dear Isotopians..." A very forced-sounding speech by an even more defeated-sounding Sands Graper snapped

Patch from his distractions. "Some of you know that I, more than anyone, love and believe in the clan system."

The crowd roared with applause. The hunter focused his eyes forward and resumed climbing with fresh determination.

"Many of you share my sentiments because you see the efficiency and freedom we can achieve as a team of teams. You feel the warmth of the families each of you belongs to as you all do your part to make Isotopia great."

More applause. These poor people had no clue that their leaders, mentors, and many of their friends had just been murdered by these monsters. A wave of nausea washed over Patch as he anticipated how Graper's speech would end.

Hang on, man. I'm coming for you.

Graper sighed and continued in a choked, monotone voice. Patch picked up the pace.

"Despite these advantages of the clan system, there is also a severe consequence I often neglect to mention, a consequence nearly all of us are aware of but conveniently sweep under the rug. Many of us, myself included, go on about our fulfilling lives without ever considering the suffering that happens in the city's dark corners we citizens fear and avoid. The misery of the Forgotten is the price for our flourishing. I won't speak for you, but I believe this fear we share stems from guilt."

The applause died down as the Chief Advisor continued. "Almost all of you here tonight are part of a clan—a family, a home. But in those cold corners of the city and the unforgiving streets, there is no family. There is no civility, no love, and no happiness—all the liberties that every inhabitant of Isotopia deserves. Instead, our society's castoffs are left to fend on their own for food, safety, and good health. My fellow Isotopians, we cannot fool ourselves any longer. We cannot sacrifice the lives of others to improve our own, and I have been wrong in supporting the idea that we could. I was appointed many years ago to help Chairperson Issler make Isotopia a better place for *everyone*, and in the case of the Forgotten, I have failed spectacularly. *We* have failed spectacularly. Tonight, we put an end to the suffering of those who have fallen through the cracks of our society. Tonight, the Forgotten will claim the rightful freedoms we all enjoy and maybe even take for granted. I apologize for allowing this suffering to continue, and I also apologize for portraying the clan system in only a positive light while conveniently ignoring the negative."

Bullshit, bullshit, bullshit.

Patch had scaled all but the last floor. As he reached the peak of his massive, daunting climb, he resettled his weight, then peered cautiously over the edge of the roof. Two sets of combat boots stood too close for comfort. The soldiers likely had their weapons trained on Graper— and a third was probably positioned right behind Graper with a loaded hand cannon aimed straight up his ass. Bogue would do whatever it took to make Graper say the right words to the Isotopians below.

Searching for any available cover, Patch located a small structure several yards away—housing for some kind of equipment—and traversed the wall until he was lined up behind it. He hitched his upper body over the roofline, swung his legs, and landed quietly on the black slate. Crouched behind the air duct, Patch reached down with both hands to retrieve the small hunting blades strapped to the side of each boot.

He peeked around the equipment. The soldiers stood an arm's length apart, facing away from him. Patch lifted his blades and moved toward his targets. A gloved hand appeared over the edge of the roof, halting Patch in his tracks and sending him back to cover. Patch watched from his hiding spot as Maris swung himself upward and landed gracefully on his feet. The Head Hunter made eye contact with Patch and padded to his side.

"Where the hell did you come from?" whispered Patch.

"Same place as you," whispered Maris. "The ground. I admire your bravery but can't condone your stupidity. What the hell were you thinking, coming up here alone?"

"I don't know," said Patch. "I just had this... feeling inside me. It was like the world was going to fall apart if I didn't get up here. It all happened so fast I didn't even think to tell anyone."

Maris beamed. "I never thought I'd say this to you, Patch, but you remind me of myself twenty years ago. I knew you had exceptional talent from your first pogg hunt, but to be honest, I never thought you'd have the drive to match it."

"Yeah? And what drive is that?"

"The drive to protect and provide for others, to save the day without needing to be called the hero. You're a born leader, Patch. Whatever happens tonight, don't you ever forget that."

Against all his might, Patch allowed a single tear to dribble down his cheek. "You won't take that stuff back now that I'm about to cry like a little bitch, right?"

Maris beamed again and pulled out his own hunting blades. "Ready to save the world?"

"Hell, yes," whispered Patch. "After you, boss." Patch stood again, and with his mentor at his back, proceeded toward the soldiers.

KRAKKEN

Krakken waited anxiously for his turn to address the crowd once Graper finished, yet the Chief Advisor droned on.

"...and finally, I just wanted to say again that I'm sorry." Graper looked at Krakken, then Bogue, before wrapping up his speech.

Levol shoved the rifle into Graper's back to coax out the last few words.

"I'm sorry. I'm sorry I couldn't do more to save you. And lastly, I'm sorry that everything I just said was a lie."

Krakken exchanged a puzzled look with Bogue, and the Chairperson smiled down at her people as she threatened Graper through gritted teeth. "Say one more word I don't like, and you'll have a bullet up your ass."

Graper nodded and took a deep breath. "Bogue and Krakken are traitors and murderers! They've killed your leaders and won't stop until our clans fall apart and armed Forgotten control the streets. RUN!" The crowd erupted into confusion and chaos.

"You stupid piece of shit!" Bogue held her tone so only those on the roof could hear. "I hope you enjoyed that speech, because it's your last. Kill him, Levol."

A sharp crack drew the group's attention to the two lookouts, face-down on the ground at the feet of two knife-wielding men in hunting clan colors.

"Kill them!" ordered Bogue without hesitation. The hunters split up as they dashed toward their enemies; the older one leapt at Levol and kicked his rifle to the ground.

Before Krakken could sort out what was happening, the younger hunter had kicked his firearm off the edge of the building.

Bogue snapped up Levol's rifle and pointed it at Graper. Everyone on the roof froze, and the crowd below let out a collective gasp. The older hunter threw a debilitating punch at Levol, knocking him to the ground, then dove between Graper and the muzzle of the rifle just as Bogue pulled the trigger.

LASK

Like everyone else in Isotopia, Lask was glued to the action on the roof. Unlike the rest of the citizenry, Lask was able to watch the scene in alarming detail through his field binoculars. Graper's dramatic speech ended with an obvious break from the script, followed by a flurry of activity at the edge of the roof.

"You have got to be shitting me!" Lask muttered out loud. So much for wondering where Patch had gotten to—and Maris, for that matter—though how the hell they'd reached the roof without getting themselves killed, Lask had no clue.

Bogue popped the trigger, lurching back from the recoil. Maris dove; the bullets intended for Graper hit the brave hunter instead. Maris' body convulsed grotesquely as he sailed through the line of fire and hurtled past the edge of the building.

Patch screamed as he watched his mentor hit the ground. Horror shook Lask, but he had no time to dwell. Caution was pointless now. These people were going to kill him and everyone he loved; he might as well go down fighting. Maris had made the ultimate sacrifice for what he believed in; Lask would do no less.

He sprinted for the front doors, hand cannon drawn and cocked. Lask fired at one of the two soldiers guarding the elevators. The other darted to the elevator. Lask dove head-first through the closing doors, tackling the soldier to the ground. The doors closed and started upward.

Lask jumped up first and kicked the guy in the gut.

While the soldier writhed on the ground, Lask snatched his helmet and tossed it away, then gave him a hard knee to the nose. The soldier scrambled to his feet and landed a solid punch that knocked Lask to the floor. A hand grasped Lask's neck; he thrust his arm out, found the soldier's neck, and squeezed as tightly as he could. They wrestled, struggling for dominance. Lask rolled on top and pinned the man's shoulders under his knees. He pointed his gun at the soldier's face; it was knocked away. The soldier flashed a dagger; Lask punched him in the cheek and the knife clattered to the floor. Lask grabbed the dagger and shoved it through the soldier's neck so deep, it came out the other side.

Lask rolled onto his back. Sprawled out on the elevator floor, he caught his breath while the elevator pressed toward the roof.

PATCH

The rush of adrenaline hit Patch hard and fast. He had to strike now or lose his chance to avenge Maris' death. Patch launched himself at Krakken, using his body as a projectile to ram the crooked IES Rep backward onto his ass. Shaking with fury, Patch turned on Bogue and found himself staring down the barrel of a rifle just as she squeezed the trigger.

Patch darted to his left and dove toward Bogue with outstretched arms as the bullet rocketed past his right ear. He slammed Bogue's shoulders to the ground, knocking her weapon out of her hands and kicking it over to Graper before she could reach for it. Bogue struggled to break free, but her shoulders were pinned beneath Patch's knees. He'd never had the occasion to come this close to her hideous face, and he was here to make sure no one ever had to again.

"Your killing days are over, Madam Chairperson!" Patch raised his knives and stabbed them through the center of Bogue's eyes with a precision Maris would have admired. "Enjoy your last two scars, you fucking psycho bitch!"

Too disgusted to watch her bleed out, Patch hopped up and drove his left boot into Bogue's side. A low grunt was the last sound she made before flying off the same corner of the roof Maris had fallen from seconds before.

The crowd below roared and raged—some shouting in victory and others loudly voicing anger at the death of their leader. Patch couldn't worry about audience approval right now; his job was making sure the bitch was dead. Patch stepped to the edge of the building and peered over the side. The body of the Chairperson was splayed on the ground below next to his dear mentor. Before Patch could even shed a tear, a *ding* alerted him to the arrival of the elevator behind him.

Patch whipped around. Two helmet soldiers stepped through the opened doors, one gun pointed at Graper, the other at Patch.

"Drop the gun," said one of them in his modulated voice.

Graper held his ground as best he could, ineptly alternating the aim of Levol's large weapon between the two soldiers. Patch doubted Graper even knew how to *fire* that rifle, let alone hit anything with it... or whether the old ex-healer had the nerve to kill anyone.

Patch raised his hands above his head and shot Graper a defeated look. "Put it down, man. It's over."

A bloody body sprawled on the elevator floor caught Patch's attention—so, the bastards had taken out Cam. *One less bad guy for me to kill.*

"*Damn*, Dr. Harding," Patch taunted the Scientist Rep. "What'd Cam do, talk without raising his hand?"

"Shut up, you reck-headed hunter," replied Harding. He reached inside his lab coat, pulled out a mini hand-blaster, and aimed it at Patch with trembling arms.

The second elevator opened, revealing another bloodied corpse. A helmet soldier marched forward. *We are truly fucked now.* Before Patch could blink, the newest soldier onto the scene blasted the other two soldiers in the back and aimed his weapon at Harding. He pulled off his helmet and tossed it onto the ground.

"Lask!" Patch shouted, jumping to his feet. "You're late."

"You forgot to invite me, you reckless sonofabitch!" replied the detective.

"Well, it doesn't matter now," Patch said, nodding

toward Levol, who was back on his feet with a handgun aimed at Lask. Harding had his gun on Patch, who was unarmed, and Graper was useless. They were beat. "Just put 'em down, guys. They got us for real this time."

"Smart guy for a low-life hunter," said Harding.

"I'd advise you two to listen to your friend," added Krakken. "Enough Isotopians have died tonight. There's no reason for any more of us to do the same."

Lask lowered his weapon.

"Well, I'm glad we could all take the high road," remarked Krakken. "Now let me tell you what's going to happen here. I'm going to say something short and sweet to calm down all those worried people down there. Then Levol, Harding, and I are taking that elevator to the ground and walking away, and you people are going to stay right here and let us."

"How do you figure that?" asked Patch. Yes, they were outnumbered up here, but once Patch got his hand on a weapon, he would hunt the fuckers down and not rest until they were all neutralized.

An angry sneer settled on Krakken's face. "I'm not sure if you've noticed, given all the chaos up here, but we've got ourselves a city full of hostages down there."

Patch followed Krakken's gaze past the crowd. Hidden in the trees was a whole new wave of helmet soldiers with weapons trained on the unknowing citizens. *Not good.*

"Did you really think that small group of beta testers you were spying on was all we had?" asked Krakken with a smug grin. "That we were dumb enough to plan a revolution with a mere handful of soldiers? See, the depressing thing about the Forgotten fortunately worked to our advantage—there's a ton of 'em. For every soldier you kill, we'll throw ten more at you."

"Not to mention we can mass produce as many helmets as we need," added Harding.

Patch felt dizzy and weak; he couldn't fight anymore, and he didn't have to look to know Lask felt the same.

"If you have us beat, then why not just kill us all?" Lask asked.

"As you said, we've already won; more murders would serve no purpose," responded Krakken. "Plus, I'd rather let you live. Who better to convert to poster children for my new Isotopia than two who were the cream of the clan crop—our brightest superstar hunter and our most talented IES detective? And then, of course," Krakken said, indicating Graper with his chin, "we have the ultimate worshipper of the traditional clan system. You may not appreciate our new ways at first, but I'm sure you'll come around eventually and see this is how it has to be. And when you do, when you feel it in your old bones, you'll be able to convince the very last doubter as only Sands Graper could."

"You're a monster, Krakken," responded Graper. "I understand you went through a tough time on the streets as a kid but—"

"Oh, you *understand*? You get what it's like to be a Forgotten?" Krakken cackled. "Arguing that point would just be a waste of breath. Levol, Harding: do me a favor and keep your weapon on these pathetic fools while I address our people."

"Yessir," replied both men with their own vile smirks.

Graper beat Krakken to the edge of the roof. "This is all my fault," croaked the former Chief Advisor, peering down at the sea of misery below. The people quieted down as they waited to hear the fate of their city.

"Whoa, whoa, whoa! Get away from there!" shouted Patch as he watched Graper inch toward the edge, but the hunter's hands were tied; there were too many guns pointed at him and his friends to intervene.

Graper looked back and gave Patch a sad shake of his head. With a trembling voice, he said, "I'm sorry I let you down, son." Graper turned and faced the citizens of Isotopia one last time, repeated, "I'm so sorry," and disappeared over the ledge.

COLE

Cole and Zap sprinted through the forest to the rendezvous point. As promised, they'd buried their fallen friends before leaving. Cole prayed the graves they'd dug tonight would be their last. They had nearly reached the city gates when the healer spotted multiple rifle barrels, poking out from the branches of the tall trees in front of them. A closer look revealed clusters of camouflaged helmet soldiers with weapons trained on a seemingly oblivious crowd at the base of the Panel HQ.

Cole grabbed Zap by the arm to stop him in his tracks. "Yo," he whispered, pointing toward the treetops. "Look."

Zap followed Cole's finger. "What the hell is going on here?"

"Whatever it is doesn't look good," Cole said. "What do we do now?"

"I'm not sure," Zap answered. "Let's post up behind those bushes and see if we can figure it out."

Crouched behind leafy cover, Cole followed the gaze of the crowd to the top of the Panel HQ, where several people were standing. "What are all those people doing up there?" asked Cole.

"Beats me," Zap answered, focusing his hunting binocs on the action on the roof. "Patch and Lask are up there, and Krakken is about to speak."

The two fell quiet as a voice boomed through the speakers. "My fellow Isotopians, you have all just been through a lot, and are surely confused, scared, sad, and tired. Please, allow me to explain."

"This oughtta be interesting," Zap said.

"What is it?" Cole snatched the binocs. Patch and Lask did not appear to be saving the day. The healer's heart leapt into his throat. "We have to save them!"

Zap hushed Cole. "There's nothing we can do but wait," responded the hunter. "If we make any significant movement or sound, we'll have all those guns in the trees aimed at *us*. Can't help 'em if we're dead."

As much as Cole hated to admit defeat, Zap was right.

"I want you all to think about what Graper said. Before senility struck him there at the end of his speech, your former Chief Advisor addressed a fatal systemic flaw in the way our clan society functions." The din of the crowd grew into a loud buzz.

Cole turned to Zap. "*Former* Chief Advisor? What the hell's that mean?"

Zap shrugged without moving his eyes from Krakken. The chaotic noise from the crowd subsided as Krakken started speaking again.

"The Forgotten came by their name for a reason; they suffer while the rest of Isotopians go on about their lives, either blissfully unaware of their great sacrifice or actively suppressing your guilt. Graper fell into the latter category, as I'm sure many of you do as well. Personally, I fall into neither of these groups." Low murmurs spread through the crowd like bees buzzing in a hive. "I'm sure you're all wondering how that could even be possible. This is where I have to let you all in on a little secret."

The crowd fell silent, every ear hanging on to Krakken's next words.

"I am one of the Forgotten. Chairperson Issler knew this when she nominated me for IES Representative. She wanted the same thing I do: equality for everyone—the only way to *true* freedom. Together with Dr. Harding, we devised a solution to this 'Forgotten epidemic.'"

"Why is he talking about Bogue in past tense?" whispered Cole.

"I don't know, man. Shut up!" snapped Zap through gritted teeth. "I'm trying to listen here."

Krakken continued. "I am confident you are all smart enough to understand that a change so radical and great would require sacrifices. This is an issue we grappled with as we tried to figure out how to give everyone what they needed while minimizing collateral damage. It simply wasn't possible. In order to make Isotopia a safe and prosperous society for *all*, it was necessary to eliminate the root of the problem: the clan system. As a symbolic gesture to mark this significant turning point in Isotopian history, we had to get some blood on our hands. For those of you who still don't know, all of your clan leaders are dead."

The crowd exploded into a furious rage of shouting, cursing, and wailing.

"Did he say *all of them*?" asked Zap. "What about Maris? Did those bastards get him too?"

The collective pain of the raging crowd and the hunter flipping out next to him hit Cole with an intensity more powerful than any drug he'd ever taken. The angry crowd swelled and advanced toward the HQ entrance.

"Ah, ah, ah," said Krakken. "Not so fast. Take a look behind you. Up there in the treetops."

There was a frenetic scramble as people spun in place, shouted and pointed at the weapons, then sank to their knees and covered their heads.

"That's better," said Krakken. "See all those soldiers? Nearly all of them were alone, starving to death on the streets when we found them. They were forsaken by their own city and sentenced to meaningless lives, but they are Forgotten no more. Now, they are my soldiers and your police. There is no reason to be afraid; embrace this brave new Isotopia, and no one else has to get hurt. With Bogue dead, I officially accept the responsibility of being your new leader. You may refer to me as King Krakken—I just love the ring of that—and I see you're all on your knees already." An insane cackle rained down on the citizens of the new Isotopia.

Cole shook with fury. "I cannot just sit here any longer. We have to do something!" He shot to his feet, only to be dragged back down by Zap.

"*Damn*, are you stubborn," said the hunter. "Now is not the time to be a hero, so shut the hell up, or I swear I will kill you myself."

Krakken was taking obvious pleasure in his horrifying speech. Cole considered cutting off his ears with his hunting knife so he wouldn't have to hear more.

"Now, I'm sure that despite your excitement to jump into this newer, safer Isotopia, you're a little confused about how this is all going to work, so let me explain. You are all still citizens who will continue to contribute whatever you can to this society. Those who can hunt, hunt. Merchants who own a shop, keep it running; I think you all get the idea. No more bullshit entrance exams, no more exclusive clubs; you're all free to do whatever your heart desires as long as you contribute something to society. My new IES army is in place to keep everyone safe and productive. Consider this the end of the Forgotten and the beginning of an era of equality and freedom for all!"

No one dared speak as Krakken paused to survey his subjects, most still on their knees.

"If you'll excuse me, it's been a long night, and I need some sleep. I'm going to return to my hut now, and I strongly recommend all of you do the same. Tomorrow, you will all wake up and do what you do as if none of this ever happened. Just remember to address me as 'King Krakken' if you have the pleasure of running into me. Goodnight, Isotopia, and sleep tight."

Krakken disappeared from view as he walked away from the edge of the roof, accompanied by his mad scientist Harding and muscle monster Levol, leaving Patch and Lask behind.

LEVOL

That fateful day Krakken's men recruited Levol, his staggering reversal of fortune began. No longer was he the nameless rat, scurrying through the gutters of South City Park, fighting for every scrap of food. Just three short months after the revolution, Levol the formerly Forgotten had fashioned himself into nothing short of Isotopian royalty.

In his early years, when clans rejected him left and right—not "psychologically fit" (IES), lacks grace (hunters), lacks patience (scientists), and lacks compassion (healers)—Levol told himself, *Fuck wealth and power.* He'd wanted no part of the slimy elites preaching equal opportunity for all as countless failures slipped through the cracks of the clan system and rotted away without so much as a notice. Now that Levol had tasted the delicious nectar of power—the thrill of absolute control no herbal rush could rival—all he wanted was more.

Gone were Levol's threadbare, piss-stained rags; in their place, a long, slender black overcoat that made Levol look and feel ten feet tall, complete with spiky, red epaulets to signify his status. And a particular source of pride for Levol—the golden pyramid emblazoned on the chest, the symbol of Isotopia's new structure. The Head of Security's new quarters, a serious upgrade from Levol's most recent cardboard box—the room next door to King Krakken's sleek steel throne on the top floor of the retrofitted HQ building, now known as "the barracks" due to its impenetrability.

And possibly the best improvement, though it wasn't Levol's alone but belonged to the entirety of Isotopia: the glorious lack of bullshit politics. No more boardrooms filled with clan reps clamoring for equal rights, stretching any semblance of fairness so far, it could no longer snap back to pretend. With Krakken calling the shots, any individual who wanted work could get it; no one need be left in the dust. Basic ration packages were allotted to anyone willing to earn them, with extra incentives for those who exhibited expertise.

Basic-skilled laborers, such as the construction teams building living quarters for Krakken's soldiers, were overseen by roaming clusters of the helmet army. Specialized tasks, such as hunting and healing, remained fully operational with the vast improvement that anyone who wanted to contribute to a group could do so. Anyone willing to put in the work to properly wield a bow and learn elementary tracking skills could join a squad in the forest. No more rigged exams or ego clashes to prevent ambitious men and women from pitching in where they desired. No more wasted potential getting flushed out onto the streets. In the new Isotopia, the only people who received nothing were those who produced nothing. Pro-clan visionaries could preach all they wanted about the balance of responsibility provided by the old system, but even the late Sands Graper would've acknowledged that nothing was as fair as the present—royalty excluded, naturally.

Levol had to admire Krakken's foresight. It was unclear exactly how long he'd been plotting the revolution, but surely the king's vision for Isotopia resulted from a multi-year collaboration with the late Bogue Issler. At the very least, major elements had been set into motion well before Krakken slithered onto the Panel as the Representative of Isotopia Enforcement. Despite his longstanding disdain for authority, Levol had developed a surprising level of respect for the man in charge. He didn't necessarily agree with every decision Krakken made, but it was refreshing to share his rage with someone who mattered.

Their biggest point of dissension was Krakken's blind spot about labor supervision. Krakken held the very strong, very radical opinion that in order for society to advance, there must be a degree of "wiggle room" granted to Isotopia's most talented contributors. Unencumbered "thinking time" was essential for the scientists, for example, or how could they have ever conceptualized mind-helmet mechanics?

"You do realize that 'wiggle room' is not a concept that coexists with security," Levol had argued to Krakken.

"Ah, Levol." Krakken would sigh and launch into one of his high-minded, political theory lectures. "Potential is a liquid; it fills the shape of its container."

These ideas of Krakken's translated into all kinds of practices that would have made any Head of Security bristly, and Levol didn't tolerate bristle. Krakken's latest scheme allowed intervals of unsupervised forest time for master hunters, so long as these extended sessions produced results—the high-value targets. Levol held more than a sneaking suspicion that his boss was less motivated by advancing society than by satisfying his own belly. Krakken was known to be a glutton when it came to Isotopia's rarest forest flyer meat, but only the most expert of hunters could ensnare his favorite delicacy. For all their sophisticated technology, the helmet soldiers could not draw a bow without being detected by the sensitive ears of the winged animals Krakken favored. As Krakken was not likely to set his extravagant tastes aside, Levol took it upon himself to keep an extra eye on those most likely to take advantage of the wiggle room.

Of all Levol's many responsibilities, recruiting soldiers from the ranks of the Forgotten offered him the most satisfaction. Every person Levol plucked from old Forgotten Island was a soul saved, and this afternoon, he was going to save a soul.

Levol approached the graveyard-like field on the outskirts of town with a mixed bag of emotions. Back when he was broke and alone, this was Levol's home, and he held onto a certain... not exactly affection, but perhaps, gratitude for the place. Over the past few months, Levol had thinned out Forgotten Island considerably, but there remained enough occupants to preserve its hideous stench of sweat and blood. If only he could liberate them all... but there simply weren't enough resources within the city gates to accommodate hordes of homeless. Those who had grown too weak or too crazy had to be left behind. Hopefully, in the generations to come, Krakken's Isotopia would develop the infrastructure to obliterate the park altogether.

A peculiar pattern in the tall grass caught Levol's eye as he reached the fence surrounding the Island. Someone had cleared a new entrance to the forest. He supposed a helmet soldier could have been sent to widen the perimeter of their surveillance loops, but this dark corner of Isotopia rarely required coverage. Levol couldn't think of any special plant or animal specimen at this border that would have justified a hunter or healer coming this close to the Island. Intrigued, Levol pulled himself over the fence and tramped through the grass toward the opening.

A trail of slashed bushes guided Levol deeper into the woods where he came upon an adolescent pogg feeding on a patch of grass. The creature was so still, and its surrounding forest so vibrantly lush, the scene resembled a painting. Normally, Levol only took interest in living things if he was planning to kill them, but sometimes, the deep forest was mesmerizing in its beauty. He tiptoed closer to get a better view.

It was rare, even for hunters, to approach Isotopia's more timid beasts without scaring them off, but somehow Levol managed to creep right up to the pogg without disturbing its meal. Just as he carefully extended his hand toward the creature, an arrow of unknown origin darted through the air and pierced the pogg's eye. The startling *shoop* knocked Levol back a step. Looking down at his black overcoat, he found a splatter of blood as bright red as his epaulets.

Before Levol could gather himself, a voice demanded him to put his hands up. Whirling around, Levol saw an unkempt, slight, young man emerge from his hiding spot in the shrubs. The precision kill suggested hunter, but the shooter wore old, tattered clothing, devoid of the colors of the hunting clan or any other. Levol would have had to clear anyone permitted to hunt alone, but he had never seen this person before. Levol could have crushed him with his bare hands, but the fire in the boy's eyes and the arrow on his bow granted him the advantage—and he knew it.

"Identify yourself, or I'll put the next one through *your* eye," demanded the boy.

Levol smirked at the thought of taking orders and pointed to the emblem on his chest. "See this? It means I'm someone you don't want to fuck with."

This threat seemed to have no impact on the kid, who held his bowstring taut and ready to kill. "If you think I give a shit about your stupid rank, you're making a mistake that might cost you your life."

"*Hell*, kid, no need to be sassy about it." Levol flashed his winning smile and slowly lowered his arms to his sides. "You're treading in uncharted waters out here, as I'm sure you know."

The kid kept his weapon poised. "Yeah, well, I've been doing just fine. I have no need for whatever bullshit drama is happening on the other side of that fence."

Levol performed a visual sweep, noticing multiple entry points into the clearing. A nearby pile of charred logs suggested a series of fires. "You've been *living* out here?" Levol took the lack of response as a confirmation. "*Alone?*"

Mystery man shrugged. "You see anyone else by my

side?"

"I'm not talking about this place. I'm talking about *anywhere*. Friends… family?"

"I used to have those things," said the boy. "Not anymore."

The boy wasn't much of a talker, and his anger reminded Levol of himself in his pre-Krakken days. "Well, kid, on a normal day, I'd kill you right here just to watch the blood flow. But I gotta admit, you amuse me. How would you like to be a soldier? We may not be the warmest bunch in Isotopia, but we do watch each other's backs. And, of course, the *best* part, you get to kill any clan-loving fucker who stands in our way."

The boy huffed. "Kind of gave up taking orders a while back."

"I can respect that," Levol said with a solemn nod. Wasn't the first time he'd heard that. "Okay, look. *If* you should happen to change your mind on that account, I can offer you a place to rest your head at night and a guarantee you won't go hungry."

Mystery man shrugged. Despite his swagger, he'd definitely perked up at the idea of a bed and some food. The kid could sure as hell use a place to call home—that much was obvious. Levol could practically see the wheels turning until finally the boy lowered his bow.

"I'm listening."

Levol bit back his grin. *Let the kid have his pride.*

"All right, then. What's your name, son?"

"It's Hobb. Rayne Hobb."

LASK

Jimmy Lask awoke to yet another eerily dark morning. The light gleaming through his hut windows was tainted by a hint of melancholy and dread as if the sun had sensed the changes in Isotopia and adjusted to the somber mood. Still in a half-asleep fog, Lask extended his left arm and groped around his nightstand until he located the half-empty bottle of Nectar. He downed the remainder, shaking the bottle for every last drop, then pulled a pillow over his face and waited for his full-body tremors and throbbing headache to subside. Not for the first time, he fantasized about buying enough Nectar to kill himself three times over and chugging it down like water.

For the first month or so after Krakken's brutal takeover of the city, Lask had done his best to continue as a source of strength for his friends and fellow Isotopians. The stakes were too high to resign, no matter how useless he felt, but the constant uphill climb against Krakken's growing forces eventually wore Lask down; he'd lost his will to fight. There was no good reason to leave his bed anymore, but he had to at least wake up in the morning if he was going to continue the charade of living at all.

Lask forced himself out of bed. His feet carried him to the bathroom, his hands grabbed the toothbrush—a robot going through the motions. As he scrubbed his teeth, Lask glanced in the mirror. The man staring back at him—a degenerate with red-rimmed, pale eyes, set beneath heavy eyelids and gray, baggy jowls—had become more and more familiar to Lask with each passing day. A face that used to be filled with life and energy was now bony and malnourished, every day slightly worse than the day before. If Lask could have mustered the energy, he would have smashed that pathetic piece of shit right in the nose, but apathy and lethargy won out as they always did.

Once the water ran hot, Lask stepped inside the shower, the effects of the Nectar ramping up and bringing him closer to baseline. His body and mind were temporarily freed from the crippling symptoms of Nectar withdrawal, but Lask knew that each sip was a terrible trade: a tiny piece of his soul for the ability to survive the day without the sensation of being brutally torn apart limb by limb.

He dried himself with a moldy rag that used to be a towel and sifted through his mountain of unwashed clothes until he found an outfit he was fairly certain he had only worn once or twice. He tugged on the boxers he had fished out from somewhere in the middle of the pile and, gagging on the stench of dried ball sweat that wafted up toward his nose, he asked himself why he'd even bothered to shower.

He reached into the bottom drawer of his dresser for the unmarked box and pulled out a bag of powdered stim leaf—the final ingredient he needed to face the rest of Isotopia. Lask eyeballed an arbitrary amount of the powder and used his old IES combat blade to chop and organize the mixture into two fat lines. Next, he snatched the rolled-up half of his torn detective diploma and snorted the lines. Having completed his new morning routine, Lask peered out the window at the post-apocalyptic rubble around him. Today, just like yesterday and the days before that, was no day to be out in the world.

Maybe tomorrow.

PATCH

Patch stepped through the city gates, fresh kills strapped to his back from his morning session with Zap and Arlo. "Thanks for babysitting us, bud," Patch said to the helmet soldier who had escorted them into the forest—one of the lovely new rules Krakken had put in place to "ensure safety for everyone, both inside *and* outside the city."

The soldier said nothing in return, nor had he spoken a single word during the hunting expedition. At least the guy's helmet gave him the extra strength and stealth he needed to keep up with the hunters without scaring the prey away.

The guard took his post at the gate as the hunters made their way to the marketplace. Patch snagged some highbread rolls from his friend Lana's stand while Zap and Arlo shopped their pogg hides around the merchant stands. This time of day used to be the peak of marketplace traffic when jolly, contagious energy would spring from the crowd. Since Krakken took over Isotopia, the marketplace felt more like a ghost town. The number of citizens surging through the streets was roughly the same, but Patch may as well have been surrounded by corpses. Forgotten Island's population had shrunk, but the spirit of the place seemed to have diffused out into the world, making everyone and everything drab and dreary. Patch had thought he would, at the very least, adapt to the new Isotopia, but he had yet to walk through the city without chills shooting down his spine.

"Hey there, kiddo!" called Koop when his eyes caught

Patch's. "How'd the forest treat you today? Well enough for me to have some lunch?"

Patch wasn't in the mood to smile, but the corners of his mouth curled upward despite his sour mood. These days, the old man was one of the only sources of life remaining in Isotopia.

Patch reached into the hidden compartment of his satchel and fished for the prize. "Check out what I snuck past those helmet bozos."

Koop whispered in delight. "A silver diver!"

"Only the best for you, my friend!" Divers were a delicacy, and only a handful of hunters possessed the skills to catch them. Patch would never grow bored of the rush he felt when scoping one flying through the trees. Catching them not only reinforced his elite reputation, they also happened to be Koop's all-time favorite meal. They were Krakken's, too, which is why Patch had taken care to hide his catch from the guards. This particular diver was Patch's first in a long time; ever since that day on top of the HQ, it had been hard to hold onto ambition, even for Patch.

The hunter found his mind slipping into dark memories again, a cycle he couldn't break. Patch wasn't alone in his melancholy; in fact, it was nearly impossible to traverse the marketplace the past few weeks without succumbing to the misery festering in the streets. On top of all the crap and death he and his friends had waded through with Krakken and his Forgotten army, Patch hadn't drunk a drop of Nectar since Maris died. The fleeting wave of pride Patch felt for his own self-control was quickly washed away by the image of former-detective Lask, and Patch shuddered at the thought of his friend's dramatic downward spiral. *Be strong. There's no time for this shit.*

Patch took a deep breath, then reached into his bag again, tossed the rolls onto Koop's desk, and flipped over his *"Back in 10!"* sign. "Let's feast."

"I suppose I could take a brief break for some lunch."

"You could never turn down some fresh silver," replied Patch with a grin. "Besides, business isn't exactly booming around here."

"Ya got me there," replied Koop. "Usual spot?"

"Yep. Len's gonna join us." The hunter patted Koop on the back as they headed toward the picnic tables near center market. The lawn was one of the only spots public enough to catch some peace from the helmet soldiers. The days of privacy in Isotopia were virtually dead, and all that remained was hiding in plain sight.

"Lask coming?" inquired Koop. Patch knew it wasn't a real question. The old merchant had a talent for holding onto hope, but he wasn't stupid. A short silence wedged its way between the two men as they walked.

"Hey, there's Len," said Patch, happy to change the subject.

"Morning," greeted the scientist with a tired voice and a smile that looked forced. "Lask joining us?"

"'Fraid not," replied Patch as he shot a sideways glance at Koop.

"Just give the man some time," added Koop. "He'll bounce back. Always does."

Len rolled his eyes. "Yeah, well, he's never had to bounce back from a shitstorm like this."

Patch slammed his fists down onto the table in an attempt to snap Len out of his bitchy attitude, but the scientist didn't blink. "Can we fucking focus, please, guys? Ain't like we have all the time in the world here." Patch checked his peripheral vision to ensure their Forgotten prison guards were at a safe distance.

Len sighed, then finally found himself. "Yeah. Fine."

"Good," Patch said. "Now, where are we on that thing?"

"Nowhere," replied Len. "We were damn lucky even to stumble across that crimson leaf discovery. I seriously doubt we'll have such fortune again."

"Well, at least we have that," said Koop. "They've got to slip up eventually, and when they do, we'll hear it."

Patch shook his head. "They're not gonna fuck up, dude. The more upgrades the scientists install in those helmets, the quicker our eavesdropping leaf will become obsolete."

"He's right," Len said. "We're not going to accomplish anything with a passive approach. We need something new, something that can actively hinder them."

The hunter perked up a bit. It was refreshing to see Len so engaged in solving a problem; it restored a glimpse of the light that used to reside in him. "You got something in mind?"

Len shrugged. "Nothing real. Just ideas."

"Let's hear 'em," demanded Koop.

"What's the point? Until we find something concrete, we may as well—"

"Quit it," interrupted the old merchant. Patch was thankful to have Koop in their little gang. He had a way of batting down negative vibes before they had a chance to take hold. "We have to keep at it, or they win. Do you want that?"

Len glanced down at the table.

"Do you *want* that?" repeated Koop, this time with a sharp bite.

"Fine. No, I guess not."

Patch jumped in, hoping to reignite Len's intellect. "Look, I know we're not smart like you, but maybe bouncing something off us will shake something loose. C'mon man. All we need is a spark, and we'll make something work."

Len sighed, then finally slipped into brainstorming mode, retreating behind his wood-rimmed glasses. "One thing I *know* won't work is to keep shooting in the dark. Like I said, we got lucky once. If we want to make progress, we need to try building on what we already have."

"You mean like modifying the crimson leaf?" inquired Koop.

"I don't know. Maybe," Len said, skeptical as ever. "We don't really even know why the crimson works in the first place."

"We may not know exactly why," replied Patch, "but we do know *what* it does."

"Right. Somehow it captures and decodes information being sent between helmets. *Or...* Wait!" Len tapped his thumbs on the table.

"Wait, *what?*" demanded Patch. "Come on, man. Don't leave us in suspense. Our brains don't just magically figure this shit out like yours does."

"Oh yeah?" Len ceased his tapping and leaned closer to his friends. "What if I told you that your brains absolutely *could* figure this shit out?"

"I assure you," replied the hunter, "I have no idea what the fuck you're talking about."

"All this time," Len started, a genuine smile finally breaking across his face, "I've been overwhelmed because I was trying to figure out how a basic biological structure like crimson could perform a combination of tasks as complex as receiving and decrypting messages. But the problem becomes a lot simpler if we're only trying to explain the receiving."

"Then what's doing the decrypting? I don't understand."

"*We* are," replied Koop as he turned to the scientist for confirmation. "Isn't that right, Lenny?"

The scientist nodded. "Think about it. The only reason the helmets are able to function, even on the most basic levels, is because ninety-five percent of the work is already done. It's the human brain that's the real magic component here; our own personal super computers pluck sound waves out of the air and instantly convert them into language. All the helmet does is enhance the existing brain signals so they can exist outside the individual's mind."

"So, we don't need more crazy science shit," Patch said. "We just need an amplifier?"

Len spread his hands. "And suddenly, all of this doesn't seem quite so impossible."

Patch pounded the table with both fists. Koop threw his arm around him and flashed his famous goofball smile at Len. "One step closer to nailing those bastards, right?"

"I sure hope so. The only thing I know for sure is that I need to get back to the lab. I've got work to do."

"All right, nerd. Make us proud!" shouted Patch.

Patch's outburst caught the attention of two helmet soldiers across the green. "Shit. Be cool, guys." Patch jutted his chin to indicate the soldiers. "So much for celebrating." The group fell silent, causing the soldiers to lose interest, and they turned away.

"Well, boys, it's been fun," said Koop as he lifted himself to his feet. "I really ought to be getting back to the stand anyway."

"Yeah, all right," agreed Patch. "I told Cole I'd pay him a visit, so I'm off." He turned to Len. "Keep us updated, man. And no pressure, but work fast. Our freedom depends on it."

Len snorted. "You can't rush science, but I'll do what I can. I have some ideas on where to start. Oh, and say hey to Cole for me." Len had turned to leave when Koop grabbed his shoulder.

"Any word on Hobb?" Koop asked.

Koop's words were an ice bath poured over Patch's raw nerves, and his heart hung suspended as they awaited Len's answer. The scientist was looking a bit pale as well.

"Man, I haven't seen Hobb since that night. He's always been a sensitive one, but it's been so long since he ran off that he could be..." Len closed his eyes and took a deep breath. "I can't go there. It makes me sick to my stomach."

Len's gaze darted Patch's way before landing safely back to his feet. Len was too married to science and logic to blame Patch for Hobb's disappearing act. It would have made absolutely no sense for Hobb to have joined them that night on the battlefield while he was still learning the proper way to hold a bow. Still, Len's wandering eyes gave him away—at least a part of him did hold Patch responsible for the unraveling of his best friend. Len couldn't let him off the hook, just as Patch couldn't let himself off the hook. Everyone knew how much Hobb had looked up to him, but Patch couldn't be the mentor he needed. Now anything that might happen, or already had happened, was on Patch.

Even Koop couldn't disguise the fear in his eyes, but he never let that stop him from trying. "He'll come home."

Len nodded, still focused on his shoes while Patch desperately racked his brain for words to ease the tension. But those words never came, and the trio said their goodbyes as they returned to their own paths.

COLE

Since the death of healing guru Maxx Spike, Cole was one of the only veteran healers who continued the legacy of his clan and dear old mentor. There wasn't much left in Isotopia to grasp onto for comfort, but for the moment Cole just felt fortunate he hadn't succumbed to an epic Nectar-bender that would have certainly ended in an OD. Unfortunately, Detective Lask had beaten him to that pathetic, hopeless state. As tragic as it was that the star IES cop cashed in every ounce of his wit and confidence for buckets of juice, Lask's descent at least served as a living reminder of something Cole could never let happen to himself.

Clearing the low bar of avoiding death didn't require perfect sobriety; in fact, Cole couldn't think of a quicker route to total collapse than trying to absorb Krakken's Isotopia without taking the edge off from time to time. He was pondering the delicate nature of this balance, bliss leaf rette poised at his lips, when swiftly approaching footsteps rustled the shrubs on the opposite end of the clearing. *Fuck.* Was his babysitting soldier for the morning intruding on Cole's break? No one else knew about this spot except...

"Hey, man, there you are," whispered Patch between panting breaths as he emerged from a pair of towering bushes.

Cole rolled his eyes at his own paranoia and leaned over to grab his rette, which had slipped his grip. "Shush!" hissed Cole as he pointed across the way. "Those fuckers couldn't give a shit about personal space and especially not for the two of us to meet!"

The hunter wiped the sweat from his forehead and smirked. "You think those brutes could detect me when I'm in stealth mode? And by the way, we had agreed on the other spot today. Making me track you down so I don't get rusty?"

"Oh shit, dude—I spaced a bit out here. Forgot you were even coming out."

"Luckily, my stalking skills solved that problem, not that expertise was exactly required. I followed your path here from the old log." Patch swept his foot across the trail behind him, erasing his prints from the bent grass. "You know, it's a damn good thing those helmet fuckers still can't hunt for shit, or you'd already be toast."

"Yeah, yeah. Screw you." Cole chuckled and put his lighter to the rette, igniting the bliss leaf and unleashing a plume of gray smoke. "You want some? Or you still playing Mr. Responsible?"

Much to Cole's disappointment but not his surprise, Patch shook his head. Sorry, bud. Still being the lame guy."

The healer clicked his light again, sparked the roll's tip with a red flash, and pulled. "Fine. Be boring." He extended his open palm toward Patch. "But eventually you're gonna need to test this out." Sunlight danced around his lighter's sleek silver tank. "It'll knock your fucking socks off."

"What are you talking about? I've had bliss plenty of times, man. I've had it plenty of times with *you*!"

"No dude, not the leaf." Cole tossed the lighter into Patch's outstretched hand. "*That*."

Patch's eyes narrowed as he glanced at the silver box, then back at Cole. "A lighter?"

"Not just any lighter, man. Damn, have you been living under a jumbo-root?" Cole snatched his new toy back from Patch and pressed the rightmost button. This time when he flicked the igniter, a long blue-green flame erupted out of the tank. The spark illuminated the clearing like a lightning bolt and exploded with such power that the *pop* made Patch stumble backwards.

"Holy *shit*! What is this thing?"

Cole grinned as he pushed a different button to unleash the flame again, this time generating a blinding light show of pinks and purples. "Just the latest and greatest in reckhead technology." Cole flipped the cap back onto the tank, and the fireball retreated into its home.

"The scientists who masterminded this brilliant invention call it the Precision Laserpoint Light. It's got four different firepower settings to customize your smoking experience. Anywhere from 'lullaby-mild' to 'brain blowout-wild.' The only worthwhile thing those pretentious lab rats have ever made, besides the mind helmets, of course. They slam my clan for being no-witted voodoo practitioners, then they turn around and sculpt the most destructive tool in history."

Patch stared blankly. "Cole, what the fuck are you talking about?"

"Keep up, dude. The Laser is dope."

Patch shrugged. "I'll admit the flame color palette is pretty badass."

Cole fidgeted with the controls as he attempted to communicate the brilliance of the invention to Patch, who was clearly not getting it. "The tank's got three parallel catalyzers inside, all coiled around each other to maximize surface area. The idea is that by allowing for extreme and precise temperatures, the flame can propel herbal molecules to different categories of vibration power."

"Man, I love it when you try to talk like a scientist," joked Patch. "Do you even know what half of those words mean?"

"Very funny, smartass. I understand this stuff fine. It ain't my fault if your primal hunter ass can't wrap around it."

Patch was past trying to hide his amusement. "All right,

genius. Let my primal ass take a stab at it. Your fancy box heats shit differently so you can have a more intense..." The hunter trailed off mid-sentence, seemingly disappearing into his own mind.

"What's the matter?" asked Cole playfully. "Having trouble articulizing?"

"No, nothing to do with my quality of *articulating*," responded Patch, whose eyes were wide with discovery. "I think you and your reckhead inventor friends may have found the key to saving all our asses from Krakken and his goon squad."

LEN

The side door of Len's lab blasted open. Len lurched forward in his chair and watched Patch stride through. "Please tell me something to offset the hours I've wasted testing bogus leaf combinations."

The hunter beamed as he fished through his front pocket and pulled out a metallic box. "You seen this? You must have, considering it came from your shop."

"Looks like a second-generation Laser," Len said. "Cam was working on prototypes for these before he was re-assigned to the helmets project. I'm pretty sure he was still tweaking the design when Harding scooped him up and never had a chance to get back to it. Why?"

"Well, you must have some other ambitious, junkie clanmates because *someone* got it working," said Patch.

Len fiddled with the settings and snapped the igniter, producing a contained explosion of pink light. "*Huh.* There's definitely no shortage of junkies these days. Surely, there are some smart ones sprinkled in there." He flicked the different lights on and off, jumping around the color spectrum while he searched his memory. "Must've been one of the new guys Cam was training. There were rumors about one kid having a continuous IV drip of stim leaf just to keep his head above water in the lab. Scientists can be brutal."

Patch shrugged. "Cole says the crimson leaf is basically just a fancy amplifier. Not that he has any clue how it works, but if he's right, and we've got this new, insane lighter, does that mean what I think it means?"

Len had developed tunnel vision in his search for a weapon against the mind helmets. Attempting to recreate Cam's design would require time and resources that Isotopia simply didn't have. To Len's scientific mind, the crimson leaf breakthrough was still a lot of hocus-pocus, but he couldn't argue with success. He'd plow ahead using trial-and-error of novel herb combinations till he'd uprooted every plant in the forest if it offered a glimmer of hope. In the past, the very idea of fusing science and healing would have been taboo, if not physically impossible. The classic inter-clan rivalry shut a steel door on any such progress. For better or for worse, that aspect of their civilization was now abolished, where science wasn't confined to the hard borders separating the clans.

Propelled by the lure of this uncharted territory, Len sprang to his feet and rummaged through his lab specimens.

"What are you doing over there?" asked Patch.

"Stocking up on ammunition," Len answered. He continued riffling through his collection of herbs and stuffing his large travel pouch with all the packets of crimson leaf he could get his hands on. "We're going to light these with the Laser to boost the base effects of the crimson. The combination could allow us to actively interfere with helmet thought transmissions as opposed to just intercepting them."

"Are you saying we have an actual chance here?" Patch's voice crackled with excitement.

"Only one way to find out."

Len reached for his hide coat and swung a travel bag full of crimson over his shoulder. "Are you ready for the most important experiment in the history of civilization?"

LASK

Lask squinted at the splintered shadows on his bedroom wall. *Late Afternoon.* Could he muster the strength to turn his head on the pillow?

Fuck. The Nectar jar emptied quicker each time Lask filled it. At least he'd found the discipline to stretch the intervals between refills. Cue the nasty withdrawal. The long, full-body yawns were already beginning; cold sweats were next. He groaned each time his mind cycled back to the torture that awaited him.

His attempt to drift off to sleep was interrupted by an obnoxious knock on his hut door. Lask pulled the covers over his head. Hopefully, the intruder would lose interest if ignored. Four more bangs on the door shot that theory to hell.

"Hey man. It's Patch! I know you're in there. I'm with Cole and Len, and we need to talk to you, so get off your ass and come answer the door!"

Lask was cornered. There was no way the guys were going to leave him alone. At the very least, maybe Cole had some Nectar, and he could re-up. It was that glimmer of misplaced hope that eventually pulled him from his bed.

"All right, for fuck's sake!" croaked Lask with all the angry energy he could muster. Lask stumbled toward the front of his hut, Patch's relentless pounding exacerbating the splitting headache that slashed through his temples.

When Lask finally opened his door, light poured in and blinded him. He rubbed his eyes until the stinging subsided and cautiously blinked them open to the sight of the three concerned faces gawping back at him. "What the fuck do you guys want?"

"Look, man," said Patch, "I know where you are right now—you know I do. But we've given you your space, and now it's time to rise from the dead. We think we've got something that could put a real dent in Krakken's army, but we can't do it ourselves. We need your help."

They need my *help?* Lask would have laughed if it didn't take so goddamn much energy.

"Listen, fellas. I appreciate you checking up on me, but I promise I would be of no use to you right now. I'm still catching my breath just from walking over here to open the damn door. It's not gonna happen. Maybe tomorrow." Lask swung the hut door, but Patch extended a stiff arm that rammed the door in the opposite direction, knocking Lask backwards a few clumsy steps.

"This isn't a fucking joke, man," said Patch. "I don't care if you're puking up your intestines. We need you. *Today.*"

"Yeah? Well *I* need a swig." Lask panned to Cole. "You holding?"

Cole exchanged concerned looks with the men on either side of him before drifting back to meet Lask's icy gaze. "I don't have any Nectar on me."

"Bye, then." Lask reached for the door.

"*But*"—Cole tapped his pocket—"I *do* have some bliss leaf." Not what Lask needed, but better than nothing. "I can't promise it'll be a walk in the park, but it'll ease up the chills and the aches."

Lask wasn't too far gone to realize his best shot at making it through the day was to suck it up and listen to what his visitors had to say. "All right, guys. You win." He extended a hand toward Cole. "Let me heal up a bit. Then I'll hear you out."

Cole drew a packet from his jacket, but Patch swatted it down before Lask could snatch it.

"Get your ass out here," demanded Patch. "Then you

can get your shit."

Lask narrowed his eyes at Patch as if attempting to crush him with his lids, but Patch didn't budge. The detective shifted his glare to Len, who stood with his hands in his pockets and his gaze on the floor.

"You've been awful quiet, kid. You got a lecture for me as well?"

Len lifted his head and puffed out his chest, but the crack in his voice betrayed him. "N-no, *um*, Detective, but Patch is telling the truth. And as much as you're craving your next fix right now, I'm willing to bet you'd like to see Krakken get his ass beat even more." Len picked up confidence once he got rolling and saw that Lask was paying attention. "He's the one responsible for your current state, not us—remember? We're supposed to be on the same side, and if we aren't, our slim chances of survival drop right to zero. So please. I am begging you; find the man inside you who led us fearlessly through battle just a few months ago and wake him the fuck up!"

"I thought you said you *didn't* have a lecture for me," replied Lask flatly. Len's eyes crinkled at the edges while his whole face relaxed into a relieved smile.

Lask sighed heavily and bent to put on his boots while the three stood by silently. Patch stepped out of Lask's way as he pushed through the door of his hut for the first time in weeks, spun around, and snatched the bliss leaf from Cole's grasp.

"Okay, you got me up. Now, tell me how we're beating Krakken's ass."

The plan was simple, Lask's fellow rebels tried to convince him as they made their way toward the city gates. Len and Cole demonstrated the laser lighter and explained the mechanics of its interaction with the crimson, and Patch chimed in about the so-called solo hunting expeditions he'd been using as cover to isolate weaker helmet soldiers and test this new science-healer collaboration. Some combination of being surrounded by his trusted mates, the bliss leaf pumping through his veins, and this promising, new development in the war against Krakken was working to lift Lask's spirits. He allowed himself a tiny ray of optimism for the first time in months.

"So, Len, tell me what we're dealing with here in terms of potential."

"My guess is as good as yours, detective," Len answered. "You ever heard the saying that future technology is indistinguishable from magic?" If Lask had ever heard the saying, he didn't remember.

Patch cut into their conversation, exhibiting an admirable mastery of his impatience simmering just below the surface. "Come on, Len. Help us out a *little* here. You think we'll have the accuracy to isolate the source of each intercepted message? Can we alter those messages on an individual soldier level? And how much can we get away with before they notice someone is fucking with them?"

"All key questions we hope to answer in today's testing session," replied Len, "without arousing suspicion from Krakken's army."

Patch held up his hand, halting the group. He pointed down at a lone helmet soldier, resting against a tree with a bliss leaf rette. "Let's see what we can get out of this unsuspecting bastard, shall we?"

Cole sparked up a crimson roll with the accelerated enhancement setting on his Laser and took a steep puff before handing it over to Lask. "Desperate times…"

"Yeah, yeah, save me the speech—which, by the way, was *my* line of shit in the first place." Lask took a drag, and the rest of the crew followed.

Within seconds, Lask could hear the thoughts being transmitted to the soldier via his helmet. "Okay, that's cool," he said.

"Welcome to the party," Patch said with a smirk. "Dude, we could do that months ago."

"Moment of truth right here," said Len. "Let's start with something benign."

Len turned his focus onto the soldier. The others followed his intense gaze, watching with dropped jaws as the soldier suddenly pushed off the tree and hopped into the air for no apparent reason. *Holy shit!* Lask erupted into silent celebration with his friends.

"Now what?" asked Patch.

"Well, the hope is that the soldier couldn't distinguish that order from any other provided by Levol or another helmet soldier. If the source of the message remains hidden, we're in luck."

"Screw luck," said Cole. "Why don't we just persuade this guy to go assassinate Krakken right this moment?"

"Subtlety is our friend here," replied Len. "The soldiers use helmet orders to communicate and cooperate more efficiently, but that doesn't necessarily mean they will blindly follow an order that directly contradicts their core orders."

"Wait," Lask said, drawing surprised looks from the others. "Two of the soldiers shot Krakken while I watched with my own eyes."

"Yeah, that was Cam's helmet," Len answered with a sigh. "I wasn't able to break into his code or successfully recreate that battery accelerator. Gotta hand it to that deranged bastard—he was a genius. What we have is a fraction as powerful, but it should be enough to do the job—if we're careful."

"One misplaced, greedy directive could alert the soldiers to our presence, and it would be game over for us," said Patch. "We need to coordinate when and what to communicate, so we can keep that balance while maintaining the upper hand."

"Agreed," Lask said.

All eyes turned to him, and he realized they were no longer regarding him as the pitiful addict but actually looking to him for wisdom. Lask rolled his shoulders as if pulling on his old IES uniform, back when he was proud of what it stood for. "Just because we're mind readers doesn't mean we're invincible; we have to take the danger of blowing our cover very seriously."

"Right," Len said. "The further we burrow into their thoughts, the easier our intrusions will be to detect. We have to blend in."

"*Blend in* with their brains?" asked Cole. "How do you suggest we do that?"

Lask answered swiftly. "We have to figure out a way to manipulate the soldiers to our benefit by pushing thoughts they could have thought on their own."

"It's good to have you back, dude—*truly*," said Patch, patting Lask on the back. "I was getting sick of playing leader all the time."

"Well, don't worry. I'm here and ready to end these motherfuckers for good."

"I'm all for the new and improved Jimmy Lask," said Len, "but do you really think our small crew armed with souped-up lighters and psychic herbs can take down Krakken's entire army?"

Not to mention that the tremors were about to set in, but Lask's friends didn't need to hear that crap. He'd deal... somehow.

"You've all seen what we can do when we put our heads together. Yes, the night of the revolution was a bloodbath, but if not for us, a lot more Isotopians would have died. If anything can catch those soldiers off guard, it will be our newfound ability to fuse science and healing— and it doesn't hurt to have Isotopia's most talented hunter on our team," Lask added, nodding to acknowledge a beaming Patch.

"You guys really think this will work?" asked Cole, searching his friend's faces.

"Maybe," said Patch, "or maybe we'll get slaughtered before we even set foot inside Krakken's HQ again. But one thing is for sure: the fate of Isotopia is in our hands, and we're gonna fight until our last breath to rescue our home."

HOBB

Levol had made good on his promise. Hobb shared a small room with another recruit, and they were fed three squares a day. Nothing fancy, but Hobb greeted the sunrise with a decent night's sleep and a full belly to fuel his day in the forest. He wasn't complaining.

Levol had also told the truth about the soldiers not being the warmest bunch. Hobb tried not to think about those so-called friends who'd abandoned him—Koop, Cole, Len, and especially Patch. He'd always be a joke to them. Nah, he'd take loyalty and a full belly over friendship any day of the week. And he'd take a bullet for Levol or King Krakken or even Dr. Harding without hesitation.

"*Ah*, Brother Rayne! Just the man I was looking for." Levol's voice was that sickening crunch when you accidentally step on a metal trap in the forest—you know it's gonna snap shut, and you know it's gonna hurt like hell—and it was ten times worse when Levol was trying to sound nice.

Hobb straightened his back and hoped he looked worthy of whatever task he was about to be assigned. "What can I do for you, sir?"

Levol slapped his arm around Hobb's shoulders and squeezed tight. "Not for me, brother. For Isotopia."

"Of course."

"The king has a taste for some diver tonight. Can I count on you to make that happen?"

Hobb hadn't seen a single diver for weeks in the forest, but disappointing Levol was never an option. "Absolutely.

I was just about to head out."

"Good man." Levol flashed a line of yellowed teeth—a joyless, decaying smile. He squeezed Hobb's shoulder, then gave him a hearty pat that nearly sent him flying across the room. "I knew you wouldn't let us down."

LEN

Neutralizing the helmet soldiers proved to be less of a challenge than Len had expected. Just before sunrise, Len and Cole snuck into the bushes outside the Barracks and flared up their crimson roll. They'd all agreed it made sense for Len to send the messages today, his mind being the clearer and—Cole wouldn't have had a problem admitting it—the smarter of the two. The first command would be critical; if Len couldn't direct the soldiers away from the Barracks, their uprising would be over before it even started.

Len checked his watch, then issued his first thought command: "Assemble the citizens in Krakken Plaza." The task was familiar to the soldiers; they'd rounded up the population of Isotopia more than once to listen to Krakken's manic speeches.

Over the course of eight weeks, Len and Cole had experimented cautiously with their Laser, sending thought messages ranging from "At ease" to "Empty your weapons." The soldiers had followed the orders without incident, and as far as Len could tell, nobody was the wiser—until now.

"Who sent this order?"

"Ah, Commander Harding, good morning to you, too," whispered Cole, listening in with a satisfied grin, "and good night."

Len watched anxiously until the first squad of helmet soldiers filed out the side door of the Barracks. He tapped his Isodex, sending the message to Lask: *GREEN LIGHT.*

The explosion on the top floor went off exactly as planned at 0600. Smoke billowed out the windows of the penthouse. Harding's urgent helmet messages ceased.

Len's Isodex lit up with Lask's message: *Harding down. King secured.*

Cole punched his fist into the air and let out a whispered scream. Len knew better than to join his premature celebration.

"Where the hell's Levol?"

HOBB

A loud explosion shook the Barracks and sent Hobb stumbling to catch his balance.

"Code red!" Levol shouted into his wrist piece. His eyes were wild with shock and glee—as if his whole life had been lived to bring him to this very moment. "Come, Hobb! Your king needs you."

My king needs me!

"Stick close and cover your mouth and nose," shouted Levol over the evacuation siren.

Hobb's heart pounded so hard, he feared it might burst right out of his chest. He followed Levol's broad back into the smoke-filled hallway. Nobody was treating Hobb like a baby now, telling him to sit on the sidelines.

They trained for an invasion at least twice a week. The drills always varied slightly, but the overarching command remained the same: follow the instructions broadcast through your helmet. Hobb didn't have time to grab his helmet, which was disconcerting, but his heat rifle was strapped to his back, and who needed a helmet when you had Levol? The man was immortal.

Levol led him into the stairwell and slammed the door closed behind them to keep out the smoke. Two, three, six flights... Levol wasn't even breathing hard. For a big man, his stamina was impressive. Hobb struggled to keep up; he was more stealth than endurance.

Levol yanked open the door onto the penthouse floor. Smoke engulfed them again.

"What the fuck!" Levol yelled. "Where are the damn

274

soldiers?" He shouted into his Isodex as he barreled down the hallway toward the king's residence. "Harding, report! Fuck, fuck, fuck!"

Hobb's blood ran cold. He couldn't remember ever seeing Levol worried, and right now, the man oozed panic. Levol fiddled with his Isodex and managed a more normal vocal range. "King Krakken, come in! Sir, are you all right? *Come in, Krakken! Fuuuuck!*"

The eighteen-gauge steel door of the throne room hung wide open, dangling on its hinges. Levol tore inside the room, spewing curses Hobb had never heard before. "Krakken, are you—"

"Welcome, gentlemen!"

The voice was a shock, to say the least. Hobb had heard the same rumors as the rest of Isotopia: Jimmy Lask barely left his hut anymore except to sniff out his next batch of Nectar. Could that really be the reckhead detective, standing here in Krakken's private quarters with his rifle jammed against the king's head? Hobb was less surprised to see Patch flanking Krakken on the other side, the tip of his long blade angled at the king's throat.

Patch's cocky grin was visible even through the thick fog. "Ah, Levol! We wondered when you would join the party. Too bad Commander Harding couldn't wait for all the guests to arrive."

Hobb's gaze shifted to the body splattered against the wall at the bottom of a long blood stain, Harding's head still encased in the helmet he never took off. Jolted into hunting mode, Hobb whipped the rifle off his back and aimed the muzzle at Lask.

"Lower your weapon, brother," Levol said quietly, then made one last attempt to fire off a command into his Isodex. "Code red! Assault mode—"

Patch cut him off. "Might as well save your last breaths, big guy. That's not going to do anything. Your soldiers are taking their orders from the good guys tonight."

"*Patch? Lask?*" All eyes turned toward Hobb. "What are

you doing? You're going to get yourselves killed."

"A better question is, what are *you* doing, man?" Patch fired back. "We'd heard you'd sold out. I didn't want to believe it."

"You're wrong, Patch," Hobb said. "It's not a sell-out. This is a better Isotopia. Everyone has a place here. I have a place here." Hobb raised his chin high and prayed it wouldn't start quivering.

Levol gave Hobb an encouraging nod. "That's right, kid. You're my right-hand man."

"*Pshh*, yeah, you're a big man, Hobb," Patch taunted. "About to go out and gather bog berries in the forest? Or is it diver this time? Dude, you're no hunter; you're the kitchen errand boy!"

Hobb fought the tremble in his jaw. He wouldn't let Patch get the best of him, not in front of Levol and his king.

Patch continued spewing his clan bullshit. "Did you know your good friends here have basically enslaved all the Forgotten they've supposedly liberated? That they have brainwashed an entire army and used them not only to terrorize every citizen of Isotopia but also to skim off and hoard the finest bounty of the city and forest for themselves? And that they will not hesitate to spill blood to get what they want? They've already killed—"

"Patch!" Lask said sharply. "Cut it out." Patch shot him a glare but shut his trap.

Lask turned and spoke to Hobb as if they were the only two in the room. "Rayne, I know we've made some mistakes, underestimated your talents, left you out of the loop. That's all in the past. What's important now is that you choose the right side, here and now, and we'll let bygones be bygones." Lask managed to produce a nearly believable smile. "We'll welcome you back with open arms and a clean slate."

Hobb's heart leapt into his throat. He'd waited six long months to hear those words, but in the meantime, he'd made something of himself here, earned the trust of Levol and his king.

Levol boomed out a loud, dark laugh. "That's a rich one. You think the kid is dumb enough to switch to the losing side?"

Lask addressed Levol, controlled and monotone. "Your king is about to get his head blown off, and your army is under our command. That just leaves your ugly ass. I like our chances." Turning to Hobb, he added, "What's it going to be, Rayne?"

Hobb swallowed hard. Lask's offer was tempting, but he knew better than to trust them again.

"Levol took me in and gave me a life. I'm sticking with him."

"Bad choice," Patch said. With a flick of his wrist, he sliced King Krakken's throat.

Lask leapt forward, his rifle trained on Levol. "Sorry, Hobb, but your buddy's gotta die—unless he wants to surrender, that is."

Levol cackled, his famous sneer smothering his face. "You think the terror squads and blood running through our streets stop with me? You think killing me will bring back that little healer bitch whose neck I sliced open for sport? No, the legacy of fear and pain my people bring to you will long outlast me, so do what you will, but I will never surrender."

"Pan?" Hobb asked in disbelief, staring at the man who had given him a true home and a purpose when no one else would. *"You killed Pan?"*

Levol's grin never dimmed. "Oh, I got good and hard, watching that sweet little thing spill her innards into the streets."

Hobb raised his rifle and blasted a round of heat pellets into Levol's side. The arrogant smirk formed into a shocked O as Hobb tackled Levol to the ground.

"Who... the *fuck*... do you think you are?" Levol grunted and struggled, but his shoulders were pinned beneath

Hobb's knees, and the adrenaline pumping through Hobb's system gave him more than enough strength to hold Levol down.

"I guess you don't remember me, then?" Hobb gave him a second to think, but he blinked up at Hobb with zero recognition. "No? Here's a hint: I'm that kid at the merchant stand who you threatened to kill next after slicing up the most innocent, beautiful soul Isotopia has ever seen. Take one last look before I gouge your eyes out."

Levol pushed at Hobb's knees with all his remaining strength, but the heat pellets were doing their job, emptying the brute's charbroiled guts onto the floor. Hobb snagged the hunting blade from his boot and stabbed a sloppy circle around Levol's left eyeball. While Levol screamed and clawed at the ravaged socket, Hobb carved out his other eyeball and threw it across the room.

"Don't feel bad," Hobb said to the writhing giant. "I didn't remember you either until just now. It was dark that night. You were wearing a hood—and I was watching the girl I loved get murdered. But I know exactly who you are now, and it's time to say goodbye, you deranged monster."

Hobb grasped Levol's head between his hands and snapped his neck like a dry twig.

KOOP

Perched in his favorite spying tree, Koop's binocs were trained on the throne room. When the smoke cleared, Levol's back filled one entire window. Koop's breath caught. All was going as planned. Lask and Patch had drawn the assassin into their trap; Harding was dead; Krakken was neutralized, and... *wait*! Who was that standing next to Levol?

Hobb?

Hobb was alive! Koop had feared the worst. All these months and nobody hearing a word about his former protégé's whereabouts, but here he was, in the flesh! Koop zoomed in closer on Hobb, nearly falling off his branch when he realized the kid's rifle was trained on Lask. *What in the—?*

A scuffle took place. Hobb turned his rifle on Levol. What was he thinking, going after the monster? Koop didn't breathe again until he saw Hobb stand up, smeared with Levol's blood but very much alive. Patch embraced Hobb, and Lask threw his arms around both of them.

Hope surged through Koop for the first time in almost a year. He lifted his wrist to his mouth and spoke the words Len and Cole had been waiting for. "They did it!"

THE NEW ISOTOPIANS

Lask's boots thudded to the ground behind the Barracks. He unclipped from his ropes and raced over to untangle Patch and Hobb, who'd landed in a messy heap of limbs, clips, and cables.

"I told you the extra weight would pull you down faster," Lask chided Patch. "Do you even understand the concept of brakes?"

Patch wriggled and kicked like a beetle stuck on its back until he was able to get his feet beneath him. He reached a hand to help Hobb up.

"Thanks for the sweet ride," Hobb said.

"Anytime, man. It's great to have you on the team again!" Patch swatted Hobb on the back. "Hey, you okay? Was that your first...?"

Hobb cast his eyes to the ground and nodded.

"You did real good, kid," Patch said.

"You two mind saving this for later?" Lask said. "We've got a few people waiting for us out front."

"Lead the way," Patch said.

They rounded the building to find all of Isotopia arrayed before them—a huddled mass of defeated zombies, roused from their beds and herded by the rows of helmet soldiers lining the plaza. Expecting yet more rantings from their self-appointed king, the crowd emitted a low hum of confusion as Lask, Patch, and Hobb lined up in front of the Barracks.

Lask located Len at the edge of the crowd and gave him a nod. In perfect unison, the soldiers set their rifles onto the ground and removed their helmets. The crowd grew louder; individual voices rose above the buzz, demanding to know what the hell was going on.

Lask held up the battered helmet he'd taken off Harding's head. "Citizens of Isotopia!" he shouted. The people hushed. "William Krakken is dead! The reign of terror is over! The soldiers no longer need be feared!"

The crowd went wild. The soldiers mostly stood quietly, looking around at each other and the people assembled before them. Lask gave them a few minutes to celebrate, then lowered his arm to his side.

"My name is Detective James Lask of the IES. I know many of you do not know me, and I also know you've heard promises before. William Krakken promised you the freedom to operate outside the clan system, the choice to be exactly who you want. But under Krakken's regime, we were far from free. Sure, we could pick up a bow and hunt if we wanted, but not without a soldier hovering over us to ensure we carried out our duties." Lask raised the helmet again, a symbol of the police state that had become the new reality. "For the last nine months, the best of everything—the finest work of our hands, the bounty of the fields, the rarest delicacy caught by our most skilled hunters—went straight to the top floor of this building behind me"—Lask paused to turn toward the smoke still billowing from the windows—"while the rest of us made do with basic rations. That's not good enough!"

The crowd roared their agreement.

"As for the soldiers, you traded a horrifying fate on Forgotten Island for a different kind of living death. The mind helmets enslaved you by controlling your thoughts, just as surely as they enslaved the rest of us by restricting our movements. You're free now to think for yourselves. If you decide to rejoin the IES, I welcome you. If you choose another trade, I applaud your courage, and you will be supported." One of the helmets flew into the air, and soon, the sky was a green cloud amid a rising chorus of whoops and hollers.

"To each and every one of you here today, there is something better for you in the New Isotopia! This world will not be a police state like Krakken's, nor will it be the archaic clan system where the skilled join clans and the unlucky are abandoned to Forgotten Island."

Inquisitive looks occupied the faces of the audience, but Lask continued.

"Yes, the clan system will return to Isotopia, but not one fueled by hatred and rivalries. If there is one lesson we can take from Krakken, it's that exclusivity inhibits innovation and growth. If not for the rebellion, we never would have fused science with healing to create the technology that allowed us to take back our city today! The Scientists and Healers will set aside their differences and work together, and we will all progress as one unified world." Lask snuck a peek at Len and Cole, who both wore ear-to-ear grins.

"*And*," continued Lask, "our clan system will no longer turn eager workers away to rot in the streets. In this new world, nobody will slip through the cracks. There will be no more Forgotten."

A voice penetrated the din. *"How you gonna manage that?"* and was soon joined by grunts and others yelling, *"Yeah!"*

"This helmet was a weapon to Krakken," Lask explained. "Thanks to our Head of Science, Len Krossling, the helmets have been reprogrammed and can now be used to link the minds of a novice with an expert in his chosen field; all of the thoughts and skills obtained by the trainer will transfer to the trainee until that person can stand alone as a productive member in the clan of his choosing. No more failing exams and being told what you can't do. Each of you has the ability to become whatever you dream to be."

Lask located a young boy, maybe ten years of age, in the audience and motioned him to the front of the crowd. "Come, boy. There is nothing to be afraid of. Now tell me, what do you want to be when you grow up?"

The child pointed at Patch. "I want to be a star hunter like him! I just got my own bow, see?" The kid beamed as he pulled the bow off his back.

"Mr. Hobb!" yelled Lask, snapping Hobb out of his daze. "Shall we demonstrate for these fine people how we turn a dreamer into a warrior?"

Rayne Hobb, the boy who had turned to Levol and Krakken when the old clan system failed him, flashed a smile as he took the helmet from Lask's hand. He looked at the Youth standing before him, whose face spelled determination to be a hunter as Hobb's had long ago, before the system failed him.

"Good," Lask said. "Now someone pass one of those helmets up here!" A helmet was tossed into the crowd and floated forward on the fingertips of the mystified observers. "Excellent. Here you go, buddy," Lask said to the Youth, who threw it on with great haste. "And now, if we could borrow a bow and arrow...?"

"Zap!" Patch yelled through cupped hands.

"Done!" a voice shouted back, and soon Zap's bow and arrow rode the crowd to the front as well.

"Okay, boys," Lask said. "Strap up those helmets and press the big blue button on the side." Lask positioned himself between Hobb and the Youth, put one hand on each of their shoulders, then pointed to a thin tree trunk at the edge of the human visual range. "Okay, kid," said Lask, kneeling next to the Youth, "I want you to raise your bow and aim your arrow at that mark below the bottom branch."

The Youth hung his head. "I can barely hold the bow, let alone shoot that distance."

"Maybe in the old world that was true," responded Lask, "but now there is a new truth, and my friend Hobb here is going to show you, aren't you, Rayne?"

Hobb nodded and set his sights on the mark. He grasped Zap's bow, turning toward the target that felt worlds away. As he drew back the bow, the string stretched taut and a stream of memories lit up his mind: *His first time failing the hunter clan exams. The savage death of Pan. His first dose of Nectar from Cole. Stealing isocoins from Koop's stand. The horrible night he came across Jay's corpse in the deep forest and cursed Patch for excluding him. The day Levol found him all alone hunting in the forest. And just a short while ago, getting his sweet revenge for what that beast had done to Pan.*

Hobb watched the Youth absorb those terrible memories. *Damn,* he was supposed to be sharing his wisdom, not scaring the kid to death. With a deep breath, Hobb became one with the arrow and focused on the distant tree. He envisioned his own strength as a tangible force he could trust, and he pushed doubt from his mind.

Hobb closed his eyes; the world faded away. The barrage of memories leading him to this moment turned to empty, white light—all he knew was his bow and that tree. He opened his eyes and released his arrow, sending it soaring over the city gates with grace unmatched by any of Isotopia's masterful flying creatures. The audience applauded as the arrow split the bark of the faraway tree.

Hobb bent to the Youth. "You know me now. You know what I can do and how I do it. So, go on, kid. Your turn now. Show everyone out there you're just as much of a hunter as I am."

The Youth trembled as he scanned the crowd and took in their encouraging shouts. He drew back his bow and closed his eyes. He let the arrow fly.

The people cheered. Hopeful and proud, the Youth opened his eyes, only to find a single arrow wedged below the lower branch. He was hit by a wave of disappointment. "I missed."

"Look closer, kid," Hobb said. "You shot your arrow right through the center of mine! You didn't just hit your mark, you *shattered* it."

Quivering in awe of his own potential, the boy turned to Hobb and thanked him. A tear rolled down his cheek in gratitude for the intimate training session they had shared.

"Well done, son," Lask said, his voice settling the cheering crowd. "Come stand next to me, young man. That's it. Now, what you've all just witnessed is a small sample of the potential of our New Isotopia! I want you all to take a good, hard look at us, the rainbow of Isotopia: IES, Youth, scientist, healer, hunter, and"—Lask gestured at Hobb—"even a Forgotten. And let's not forget the old merchant in the tree. Wave to everyone, Koop!" Ripples of laughter floated up to the branches where Koop sat waving and grinning like an old fool. "We stand together as the clan of Isotopia!" Wild cheers, then the crowd hushed to soak in more of Lask's inspiring words.

"And who's to say these are the only choices? Where are the artists? Raise your hands." Lask waited while a few brave hands poked up from the masses. "Okay, good! How about the teachers? And where are the builders? The musicians and dancers? Storytellers?" Laughter and light conversation flitted through the crowd. A new energy pulsated through the plaza, a hope for a brighter tomorrow.

"We need all of your voices, all of your skills. A clan of clans where no one will be Forgotten. This is *our* Isotopia of the future!"

ACKNOWLEDGMENTS

On Jeffrey's behalf and my own, there is much gratitude to dole out.

I'm sure Jeffrey would thank his dad first and most vigorously. Larry wins the award for reading *Isotopia* the most times through and engaging in the most hours of conversation about plot, characters, and structure. I'm sure Jeffrey would thank me, too, knowing full well I enjoyed almost nothing more than talking to him about his writing. Jeffrey would undoubtedly acknowledge his sister, Lindsay, for sparking his interest in psychology and for always being a great listener and loyal friend. Because it will always be relevant, here's a passage I lifted straight out of Jeffrey's Master's Thesis: "I also dedicate this work to Michael Kahana, Ph.D. not only because he inspired me to study Cognitive Psychology despite my complete lack of experience in the beginning but also played the role of an incredible mentor during my undergraduate years and continues to do everything he can to support me and further my career."

Sadly, Jeffrey never had the pleasure of meeting several of my beautiful "writer friends" who generously donated their time and expertise to this project. To my astute beta-reader, Shelley Gibson, I offer my sincere gratitude for your eagle eye with continuity and clarity and for helping me nudge the final draft in the right direction while respectfully preserving Jeffrey's voice. To my editor extraordinaire, Susan Atlas, whose insightful observations extend well beyond language and always enrich the revision process, I thank you for sharing your warm heart in addition to your wisdom. To Betti Gefecht, a talented artist on so many levels, thank you for managing to craft the gorgeous cover, which so perfectly captures the essence of this story. A special thank you to Di Brown for your patient assistance with the sorcery of formatting files for print and electronic distribution.

To each of Jeffrey's friends, colleagues, and family members who supported his writing or listened to his theories, thank you for encouraging his creativity and helping him discover he had his own story to tell.

ABOUT THE AUTHOR

From his earliest years in the quiet town of Weston, Massachusetts, Jeff (Jeffrey Alexander to his parents) Greenberg exhibited a creative streak and a flair for fantasy. He held a deep affection for the Road Runner, Roger Rabbit, and Darkwing Duck, and could happily entertain himself for hours drawing his favorite characters while composing long, detailed stories about their adventures. "A happy little person living a happy little life," as he described himself in fourth grade, Jeff lived with his parents, his little sister, Lindsay, and their yellow Lab, Boomer, filling his free time with tennis, basketball, skiing, swimming, and Nintendo.

Jeff's passion for storytelling matured with his fascination for TV shows with complex characters and intricate storylines: *House, Breaking Bad, The Wire, The Leftovers, Game of Thrones*. At the same time, his academic curiosity led him to study cognitive psychology at the University of Pennsylvania with his mentor, Dr. Michael Kahana. "I was mesmerized by the brain's ability to translate our complicated world into an environment humans can understand through memory, perception, and attention," Jeff wrote in his application to graduate school.

Jeff began working on *Isotopia* in July of 2013 and was diagnosed with leukemia one year later. Despite the challenges of his disease, Jeff earned his master's degree in Cognitive Psychology from Ohio State in 2015. He returned to the Boston area and worked as an outcomes analyst for the Boys & Girls Clubs of Boston. He lived to the age of 26 and is dearly missed by all who knew him.

Made in the USA
Columbia, SC
12 May 2018